THE SINGING FOREST

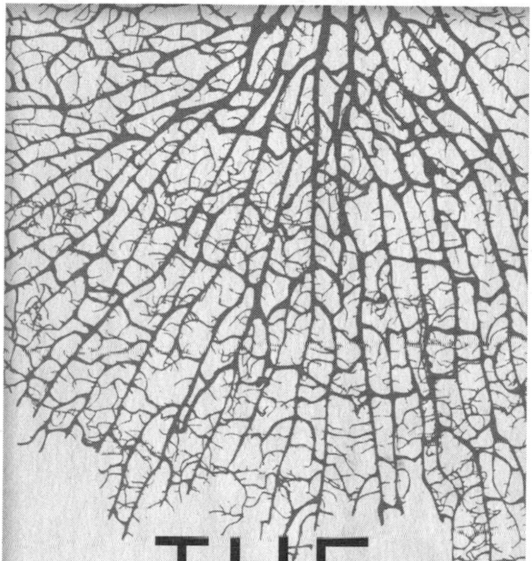

THE SINGING FOREST

JUDITH McCORMACK

A JOHN METCALF BOOK

BIBLIOASIS
WINDSOR, ONTARIO

FIRST EDITION

10 9 8 7 6 5 4 3 2 1

Library and Archives Canada Cataloguing in Publication

Title: The singing forest / Judith McCormack.
Names: McCormack, J. A. (Judith A.), author.
Identifiers: Canadiana (print) 20210213299 | Canadiana (ebook) 20210213345 | ISBN 9781771964319 (softcover) | ISBN 9781771964326 (ebook)
Classification: LCC PS8575.C668 S56 2021 | DDC C813/.6—dc23

Edited by John Metcalf
Copyedited by John Sweet
Text and cover designed by Ingrid Paulson

Canada Council for the Arts
Conseil des Arts du Canada

ONTARIO ARTS COUNCIL
CONSEIL DES ARTS DE L'ONTARIO
an Ontario government agency
un organisme du gouvernement de l'Ontario

Canada

ONTARIO CREATES | ONTARIO CRÉATIF

Published with the generous assistance of the Canada Council for the Arts, which last year invested $153 million to bring the arts to Canadians throughout the country, and the financial support of the Government of Canada. Biblioasis also acknowledges the support of the Ontario Arts Council (OAC), an agency of the Government of Ontario, which last year funded 1,709 individual artists and 1,078 organizations in 204 communities across Ontario, for a total of $52.1 million, and the contribution of the Government of Ontario through the Ontario Book Publishing Tax Credit and Ontario Creates.

PRINTED AND BOUND IN CANADA

For Peter—wise, yet inexplicably hopeful

ONE

A man should stay alive, if only out of curiosity.
JEWISH PROVERB

Children found the bones more than once. This was one of those times.

They should have known something, of course. They did know. They didn't know. They had no idea it was as bad as that.

It was a soft, deadly secret that had settled into the small forest, blanketing the ground, wrapping itself around the rough skin of the trees. The people nearby tended it silently, patting its edges, smoothing it, the metallic taste of it always in their mouths. As soon as they thought they knew it, though, as soon as they believed they could run their hands along its contours in their sleep, they would remember something else, hear about something else, something they had forgotten or perhaps never knew. Then the secret would assume a different shape, a new form, still soft and baleful.

The black vans. The barking dogs. The shooting in the night. They closed their eyes, their ears, they stuffed their fists in their mouths, desperate to escape the clammy terror. They knew instinctively that secrecy was the only possibility for these things, that this was the only way to survive, even after so many years. They knew it without a word to each other, a mute understanding that bound them—reluctantly—together. But even after these things were gone—and who would know when they were gone forever?—the fear remained, settling in along their spines, so much a part of them that eventually they began using it to place themselves, to find their bearings.

This secrecy, this silence had an existence of its own, though, its own offshoots. Other things sprouted in it, unbidden, unexpected.

Two boys. Suddenly there, scuffling through the layers of dead leaves, needles, surrounded by the smell of sweet decay. Shafts of autumn sun glinted off their hair, their arms as they wandered through the copse, kicking at fallen branches. From a *kalhas* nearby, their family was part of the collective dairy farm—herds of coarse-haired cows, vats of buttermilk and soured cream. The older one, Efim: stubborn, wearing a faded red shirt, a mole on his hand. His brother, Makar: pudgier, round-faced. The dog: a dirty white hound, pushing his nose into piles of leaves, digging with his front feet, and then loping on to the next pile, the next rotting branch.

They were curious, recklessly curious—the eleven-year-old cocky with it, the nine-year-old his loyal follower. Something so hidden, so lied about must be worth knowing, and they wanted to know.

They had slipped off after the first milking, dodging around the cows in the sheds, slapping their flanks, the grassy breath of the animals rising in the cool air. Naturally, they had been warned over and over to stay away from the forest, to stay away from these very trees, the spiny larches, the spruces with their drooping boughs. But they had been warned so often that exploring the place was irresistible, and all the evasions had made the older one itchy.

They wandered through the trees now, kicking at clusters of red chokecherries in the undergrowth. The air was old, undisturbed, as if no one had been there for years, something that was almost true. A place of shadows, lost in an uneasy sleep.

The older one picked up a stick and swiped at a tree trunk, marked with the wormy tracks of bark beetles. The stick cracked in the silence and the dog bounded off, lost in a geography of smells. The younger boy stopped to kick at a log beside a buckthorn, the sides fallen in, the wood shredded with decay. A current of wind rustled through the branches of the trees, a hint of the cold weather to come.

Then, suddenly, the dog was back, leaping with young dog joy. He dropped a white knob in front of the older boy, and stood, panting. The boy picked it up, rolled it around in his fingers.

What is it? said his brother.

They followed the dog, watching him pounce and whirl through the undergrowth, attacking bushes, a brown puffball. Then a hollow, a broad depression in the ground, a stretch of sandy earth. The dog was digging into the sand, and poking out of it were odd-shaped branches, blunt ends, an old boot half-buried on one side. He picked up something large, globe-shaped and began shaking it, and they saw the sockets in the front, the gaping mouth, a broken tooth.

Recognition. A hair-trigger shock. The younger boy grabbed his brother in fear, and they began to run, tearing through the scrub, twigs scratching their bare legs. They ran panting, out of the forest, into the secret.

Shush, shush, shush, said their mother comfortingly, as they gabbled away, the smaller boy shivering. It was nothing. Deer bones. Bear bones. Badgers. It was nothing. Nothing at all. No more talking about it.

A few days later, the older boy woke up in the middle of the night, in the middle of a bone dream, and thought:

But what about the boot?

. . .

This is Belarus, a country of shifting boundaries, a map reshaped so many times that its edges are frayed. Home to godwit birds, red deer, and a collection of wary people, people given to fits of yearning, bouts of knifelike courage. No accident that their folk tales are filled with mischief, with sudden twists of fate.

A landlocked country, bounded on all sides, not an ocean to be found. Someone looking for salt water would have to travel south down the Dnepr River, through Ukraine, and all the way to the Black Sea. Or go west across the Dvina River, through Latvia, and into the Gulf of Riga to arrive at the algae blooms of the Baltic Sea. Or—less likely—travel west again along the looping Nyoman River, through Lithuania, to the Curonian Lagoon and into the Baltic by that route. Ukraine, Latvia, Lithuania—together with Russia and Poland, the five countries that surround Belarus, that fence it in.

A restless group of neighbours, something of a misfortune at least, if not an actual curse. Some of them are on the peevish side, quick to give offence, even quicker to take it. Or they attempt to lay claims to pieces of the country from time to time, to use it for their own ends. The result? A nation invaded, divided, annexed, given away, retaken. A place of turbulent beauty, forced into constant rebirth.

But it was in the late eighties, the tail end of the last century, when a hawk-eyed archaeologist began asking questions. He had heard whispers about the bones, and he had his suspicions. *Tell me,* he said to the people who lived around the forest, *tell me what you know.* And because he sounded as if he knew already, that it was only a matter of filling in a few facts, they did. They told him stories that had been building inside them for years, the details spilling out. *It was my nephew, my cousin, the school-teacher. My son. It was the vans rumbling by in the dark, the crack of the guns, the dogs, always the dogs. It was the blood in the earth, the blood that made the garlic head mushrooms grow in pink.* The archaeologist took it all down in notebooks and saved it, waiting until the time was right, waiting until he thought someone else might listen.

A flickering, a loosening of the climate, and he was ready. Finally, the Procurator's Office was forced to do something. A flock of people—criminologists, doctors, more archaeologists—descended on the sunken earth in the forest. They measured and dug intersecting trenches, they drank hot tea, they made drawings and took photographs. When they had excavated down to the first layer, they drew maps, noted depths, the smoke from their pungent cigarettes curling around their heads. Then they began—methodically, gingerly—exhuming what they had found: bones, skulls, rotten clothing, combs, buttons.

Bullet holes, said the medical experts, turning over the skulls.

Russian guns, said the ballistic experts, holding cartridge cases up to the light.

A grim job, said a young criminologist later, studying his glass of vodka as if there might be some additional findings there, a finger bone or a vertebra.

Grim, but fascinating, he said reverently after two more glasses. In a terrible way, he added quickly.

A report was submitted to the Procurator's Office, full of treacherous facts. Among them, though, this one stood out, this one was the starkest:

Thirty thousand bodies.

Thirty thousand? The official number. Unofficially: two hundred thousand.

Consternation, alarm. How could they make these facts smaller, fainter, how could they blame them on someone else, how could they make them disappear?

But it was too late. Around the forest, a long, quiet sound began to spread, something that was part sigh, part whisper. The sound of relief that this place of hidden graves was no longer deniable. Relief that the exhaustion of keeping this secret was over. Relief that this distant piece of time, these bodies would in some prickly, solemn way be finally given their due.

They were wrong, of course.

. . .

2019, a new century, already leaking away. And Leah Jarvis is in the thick of it, called to the bar a year ago, her head still full of radiant law. She is surrounded by doctrines, tenets, precedents, all waiting for the right case, the right time. They rattle around in her brain at odd moments, like scraps of songs impossible to dislodge.

Full of random truths, these doctrines, but high-handed as well. The fruit of the poisonous tree. The doctrine of odious debt. The spider in the web rule. A collection of fables, rumours, hopes, lies. Not only perfect, but so far almost perfectly useless.

She is sitting at a counsel table now, a quizzical face, smooth skin, a flood of dark curls down her back. *Ashkenazi hair,* says her aunt. Strands of DNA sliding down an ancestral ladder. Although genes can hardly be blamed for a headful of disorderly thoughts, a rueful laugh.

She is almost startled to be in this courtroom today, even though she should know better—she does know better. But sometimes she thinks of herself as a small mutiny against the world of law, a stone in its shoe. *You flatter yourself,* says law. Still, the idea means that she is often slightly puzzled to find herself performing legal acts, as if these things had climbed out of her law books and taken on lives of their own.

Soon this will all become second nature, though, these hearings and motions and trials. She knows this because other lawyers tell her so, sometimes slapping her on the back a little too heartily. Before long, in spite of herself, she will have acquired the elements of practice, its customs, its quirks in the same way that they have—less of a profession, she thinks, than an unfortunate habit.

She is not much of a mutineer, in any event—she admits this. Too undecided about law, one day a heretic, another day a believer, always hoping for the best. And her face is too transparent, expressions flit across it too easily—serious, mocking, a trace of hilarity. She is working on this, working on developing a more impassive manner, but for now her face, her voice sometimes betray her, her gestures often give her away.

Beside her, the senior lawyer stirs restlessly. Louis Rappoport, in his fifties, bear-bodied, thick-fingered, not a comfortable man.

That morning:

Come with me today, he says. A motion to stay, an interesting case. A war criminal.

He says this casually, gathering papers into his briefcase, as if it had only just occurred to him that a junior might be useful.

Now? she says pointedly. Right now? This very moment?

This very moment, he says. Lucky you, he adds.

A man who falls for nothing else, he falls in love with his cases as swiftly and easily as a cat rolling over. Seduced in a minute by a story with a manila folder around it. Perhaps this is what has sustained him over the years, has kept him from becoming jaded. Even now, after two decades, he is still able to pick shiny pieces out of some wreck of a file.

She is more dubious, a survivor of these enthusiasms, often finding herself stranded in a legal blind alley, cursing his sudden passions. But a war criminal sounds intriguing.

And this is not really an invitation.

Hurry, he says impatiently, and she hurries—running for her legal robes, stuffing them into their blue velvet bag.

Outside, on the street, he walks more deliberately, no sign of a rush. This walk—from his office to the court—is how he girds himself, the peppery city air around him, the rhythm of his strides settling him. A ritual that allows him to arrive at the courtroom door in a particular state of mind. Marshalled. Honed.

In front of them, a man in a reflective safety vest is hosing down the sidewalk, a stream of clay-coloured water running into the gutter. He lifts the hose and for a second—less than a second—the water spray in the sun turns into a prism, colours clinging to the droplets.

Then he lowers the hose again, and they skirt around the small lagoon on the road.

The case? she says.

A deportation. Revoking a citizenship for fraud, for lies and omissions on entry. We're on the government side for once, asking for the deportation.

A deportation. She almost sighs, but catches herself between the inhale and the exhale. Part of their bread and butter, part of the waves of humanity in motion that make up immigration law. The flow of people coming in, the ebb of people going out, the tide pools of people in limbo. But usually they are acting for the deportee. What happened to the government's lawyers? Why are they sending this out?

I know what you're thinking, he says.

Does he? Very likely. A man adept at reading people, when he takes the time, when he takes the trouble. Not something obvious from his appearance—that heavy head, that fleshy nose. Or the offhand arrogance of his manner, an arrogance he wears naturally. He looks like someone more absorbed in himself than anyone else—true more often than not. And his greying hair also gives him a certain unearned distinction, something he finds amusing.

Counsel, says the judge abruptly, startling her out of her thoughts, back into the courtroom.

Louis shifts again beside her. But this is not meant for him, the judge is speaking to the lawyer on the other side, a man making long-winded submissions—all the more endless because the courtroom is hot, the sun pouring in one of the arched courtroom windows.

A trickle of perspiration is starting under her hair. Louis is wearing his summer robes—the sleeveless waistcoat, the lighter gown—but she has only the winter version, yards of black wool, a long-sleeved vest. This spring has been so fickle, so strange, though, that dressing for the weather has become something of a game of chance anyway. Spring? No, this is an imposter of a season. Racing back and forth from winter to summer, one day wet snow coming down in clumps, the next day unsettling heat, staying long enough to fool people into thinking summer has come. *This is it,* they say with conviction, as if they had some way of knowing, some inside connection to a moody weather god. Or they say it proudly, as if it were all their doing. Then the weather changes again, back into a chilly half-season—and they shake their heads, forgetting their declarations immediately.

Today—the heat, an old air conditioner buzzing uselessly in the corner. She lifts her heavy hair off her neck, twists it up for a moment, and then lets it fall. If the perspiration begins dripping down her face, she has nothing to mop it with except the wide sleeve of her robe. And even a junior should look composed, unruffled. Or at least not visibly sweating.

But they are all sweating, the spectators as well, pushing their hair back from damp foreheads, fanning themselves with statements of claim, statements of defence, anything else they can find. A crowd of applicants, respondents, their lawyers, waiting for their time to speak, to make their cases. All moving now, flapping and fluttering like a cloud of giant moths.

Is there a way to make the perspiration retreat into her pores? Think of something cold.

She thinks hard.

Ice. Ice water. Water. Rain. A storm.

She thinks harder.

The moaning starts in the distance, she can hear the heavy winds rising, filling with water. The sound starts out low, then the pitch begins climbing up to a howl. A storm? No, a hurricane. A few more minutes and there it is, gusts pounding at the courthouse, rattling the windows. The downpour starts, rain whipping across the roof. Then the glass windowpanes begin to shiver and fracture, shards flying across the room, the bailiff ducking, throwing his arms up to shield his head and face. The howling is deafening now, blotting out all other sound, and the pressure, the tension in the air, is impossibly tight. Suddenly, a piece of the roof lifts off, and wind and water come roaring through the room. A torrent catches the opposing lawyer—spindly-legged, sallow-cheeked, a paunch—tossing him into the air, slamming him against a wall. A piece of debris strikes his client on the side of the head, and he is carried off by the water, eyes blank, body spinning around.

Extreme? Probably. Justified? Certainly.

Although she is still hot.

Look, there goes the judge now, caught up in the flood, clutching for a handhold as his dais is swept away. And the spectators? All these anxious people, angry people, the leg-jitterers, the yawners, even the coughers. Thrown against their seats, motionless for a few seconds, their mouths gaping, before they are engulfed, clinging to the balustrades.

Isn't this satisfying? Isn't it exhilarating?

No? Perhaps she should try to avoid injuring people, then. Perhaps her storm needs a few alterations. The lawyer on the other side is expendable, more than expendable—he is droning on at the moment—but his client should be kept safe, if only to be deported, to get the reckoning he deserves.

And then there are the spectators again, what should happen to them? Do they deserve to be carried away in a rush of dirty water? Probably not. And the judge? They need him, he is crucial, there is no one here more crucial than him. It would be difficult to say that the court clerk and the bailiff had done anything wrong either. The clerk is mean-silly, but the bailiff is amiable enough—neither one really deserves a watery end.

She sighs, and her storm begins to fade away. In a minute, the courtroom is dry again.

Inordinate delay, repeats the lawyer on the other side, standing at the rostrum. Excessive delay. Extreme delay.

This is the basis for his motion, his attempt to halt the deportation proceedings.

A man with flabby lips, a protuberant face. He looks like a camel, she thinks.

He grimaces at his notes.

A camel with a toothache.

Delay, delay, delay, he says, as if this were needed to express the sheer slowness of it all.

A fact, Louis had said. Nothing we can do about it.

Not a few weeks, not a few months, but decades before the government woke up from its postwar slumber, decided to find these men, to pursue them. Several years after they had identified this man in particular. A good argument, then, but the other lawyer is making it badly. Instead of speaking with any emphasis, any expression at all, he is reading his notes in a monotone.

Of course, this is a common problem, this reading of notes out loud. She has seen other lawyers do it, as if making the notes alone had drained them, as if they had no more to give to putting these thoughts forward, nothing to convey by the sound of their voices. Perhaps this is true, but she is sometimes seized with the urge to go up to them during a break, to whisper to them: *At least try. Take a stab at it. Be bold.*

Although she is not in a position to give this advice, or really any advice for that matter. She has done only a few cases on her own so far, small cases where the stakes were low, and in the last one she rose to her feet for the final argument, only to find herself inexplicably frozen. Suddenly, bafflingly, her tongue had thickened, her lungs emptied, her heart was banging in her chest. An isolated problem, she hopes desperately. No doubt only a passing difficulty. A brief stumbling block on the road to the republic of law. Something that will be solved by experience. Who knows why these things happen?

She glances at the man across from them now. What does a war criminal look like? An alleged war criminal, that is. Stefan Drozd, a man in his nineties, his face cross-hatched with lines, the skin on his hands like cracked varnish. Sitting stoically as his lawyer makes his submissions, the whites of his eyes yellowed, his neck pouched out. The man the government—their client—wants to deport. Why now? A deterrent to others, to refugees who lie their way in. Or to keep him from benefiting from his crimes. By a remarkable coincidence, says Louis, also a way for the government to rid itself of a moral dilemma, a black eye.

Not so fast, says the man's lawyer now, shifting from one leg to the other. Look at the delay.

Louis snorts.

Too much time has gone by, says the man's lawyer, pulling at the end of his nose, tapping his fingers on his paunch. How can he defend himself? Witnesses are dead or lost, documents have been destroyed, memories have faded. And the man has built a new life in this country—an industrial glassblower until he retired. A maker of bottles, vials, flasks.

How is the nature of his job relevant? says the judge impatiently.

He must be hot too, this judge, sitting up there in his sash and robes. A man who spends his days with every flicker, every blink, every expression under scrutiny. The lawyers watching him intently for clues as to how he is leaning, looking for signs that might help them increase their chances, silently amending their arguments on the fly. Was that a nod? A sigh? Which points are reaching him, which ones are falling flat? What should they play up, what should they play down?

The applicants, the respondents are also watching, besieging their lawyers at the breaks in their cases. Why did he write that down? What did that mean? Did he raise his eyebrows? Did he seem agreeable? they say anxiously, their lawyers turned into interpreters, oracles. The lawyers are noncommittal, though, they know too much about the twists and turns of cases, the unexpected reversals and successes. Hard to tell, they say. Difficult to predict. We have to wait and see. But despite their words, they say this in a manner that manages to suggest that the case is going well in some indefinable way.

The judge looks meaningfully at the clock and back to the rostrum. This is a man who was a lawyer himself once, and not so long ago. A sea change, or at least a lake change—first a life of talking, an unnaturally vocal life, rolling out phrases, endlessly turning thoughts into words. Then a sudden switch to a life of listening, at least during the long hours in the courtroom. Do the judges who challenge the lawyers—who get into debates with them—simply miss their own voices, the use of their former skills? Perhaps their mouths become too dry, she thinks, and they begin to panic in some inner part of their beings.

Well? says the judge. Relevance?

The harm, the prejudice suffered by my client, says the lawyer hastily. The life he has built here.

He knows there is little point in saying: *How could a man who works with glass—a substance so transparent, so delicate—how could he have possibly committed these acts, these crimes?*

Two grandchildren, he continues, a girl and a boy. *How could a man who has grandchildren—so genial, so family-like—have done these things?*

Only one ear is required for this baggy argument, only half an ear, she thinks. She studies the courtroom instead—one of the older ones, a certain weary elegance. The oak balustrades, worn to a brown-gold by a thousand hands, the carved tendrils twining around the judge's dais. The floor—mosaic, the grout blackened around the once beautiful tiles, endless patterns of spirals, hexagons, diamonds. Now they are chipped in places, and in one corner the surface is patched with cement, as if the repairers had given up trying to match the tiles, and thrown up their hands instead.

The murals, though, they still have a faded dignity. Lining the top of the walls, Greek figures in white robes, giving the place a shadow life of its own. They sit under date palms, reading scrolls, gesturing to each other. The colours are bleached—pale greens, tans—and the paint has flaked off in places, leaving bald spots. This means that some of the figures are missing body parts, a hand, half a nose, an ear. Despite this, they are still studying their scrolls, their graceful heads inclined, oblivious to their injuries. Oblivious to everything, in fact, the cases in front of them as well—a majestic indifference to pleadings, dockets, arguments.

Are you hot too? she asks them silently, looking up at the walls, at their long-fingered hands, their curled beards. But they are scholars, musing on some point of law, absorbed in their own discussions—they have no time for material things.

And you? she says to the rearing lion and unicorn on the coat of arms behind the judge. They are indifferent as well, though, lost in their own ancient battle, tongues flickering, eyes on each other.

I know what you're thinking.

This is one of Louis's talents, this ability to make people believe him, believe things about him, or at least believe the story of who he is at that moment—a story that he is in the constant process of creating. He talks about himself, the happenings around him, as if he is composing a description of his life, revising as he goes along—even at the same time he is living through it. But this description is not only for the benefit of other people—he seems to be continually describing himself to himself, often with some satisfaction.

And if he doesn't know what she is thinking, then she does. Now, in this courtroom, sitting beside him, now that she has read the pleadings in this case, the facts, now that she has seen the history of the man they are trying to deport, this is what she is thinking:

Brutality. Torture. Murder.

. . .

The court clerk coughs. Thin, sharp shoulders, he has an entire vocabulary of coughs, and this one, delivered with a slight pinching around his nostrils, means *your time limit is almost up.* He manages to convey a trace of spite at the same time, something in his tone.

The other lawyer stretches his neck, first one side and then the other, and continues on with his reading.

His youth, he says. Fifteen, sixteen at the time. A mitigating factor.

I've reviewed your motion record, counsel, says the judge. No need to repeat things in the affidavits or materials. It would be more helpful if you could highlight your leading points.

This judge—so incisive, so trenchant.

Of course, Mr. Justice, says the lawyer, I'm in your hands. I'm always in your hands.

Then he begins droning on again.

If you were in my hands, Louis murmurs, I would strangle you.

. . .

Fifteen-minute recess, says the judge.

Outside the courtroom, lawyers are gathered in knots around the columns in the hall.

Over here, says a friend, waving at her.

What's new? he says as she comes up, and he means it. What does she know?

Faces turn towards her. They have a weakness for rumours, they are as inquisitive as crows. They long to pass on tidings about judges, cases, each other—an affair, a trust fund, a partnership feud. Surprising, this—the tougher they are, the more seasoned they are, the more fascinated they seem to be.

A war criminal, she says.

They look interested in spite of themselves, their robberies, their assaults forgotten.

But Louis is behind her now, and he needs strong coffee, the client as well.

Any chance of an espresso? says Owen Menzies wistfully. A government official, fiftyish, a long face, licorice-black hair, pale skin. He is their liaison, the bureaucrat with the War Crimes Section in his portfolio. A man who selects what he says coolly, carefully, something that has contributed to the longevity of his career. His views are supple, his thoughts adjustable, all apparently at the disposal of his employer.

So different from the people who usually sit beside her in court—the refugees, the immigrants. All those luckless people who have been caught up in cases, who have stumbled unwittingly into the bear trap of law. Sitting there, dressed in cheap clothing, their faces messy with hope.

If this man has hopes, she suspects he would ensure they were unknown to anyone but himself. Although there is no doubt that there are advantages to a more cool-headed client—he is not someone who requires hand holding, who needs amusing, who demands minute-by-minute assessments of the proceedings. Only an espresso.

A stop beforehand at the Lady Barristers robing room, a name from another era, a name that still makes her laugh. The room is deserted at the moment, a whiff of spicy soap at the sink. She strips off her waistcoat, the shirt and swabs herself down with water. Relief. Although the heat is not the only problem. Perhaps what she really needs is a bottle or two of distilled patience, some elixir for suffering fools gladly—at least long-winded ones.

A swift pat dry, and back into her sticky clothing, this costume. She has to admit she is attached to it, seduced by its quiet formality, the close fit of the waistcoat, the folds of the robes, even the starched collar and tabs—the sheer white and blackness of it all. Other lawyers scoff at it, but she suspects this is only a blind. Who can resist clothing that has the power to transform them, to reshape them into more solemn people? Keepers of archaic phrases, old customs. *A barrister and a solicitor.*

Perhaps she needs this wrapping more than they do. You're a *lawyer?* people sometimes say to her, as if this occupation was particularly surprising.

Yes, she says shortly.

Really? they say, as if she might be mistaken about this.

Do they see too much, the traces of jobs to pay for school still clinging to her? Ghost marks of a research assistant, a bartender, a clerk in a bookstore. Then again, perhaps they merely sense her own doubts. There are moments in which she believes in herself utterly, and moments when this fails her, when she starts to wonder if the parts of herself add up to little more than a subtle confidence trick.

Is it possible we bluff ourselves into existence? she thinks, looking into the mirror. Is that how it works? She searches her face, her eyes—yellowish brown, flecked with green and grey—for proof of something, anything.

But the person looking back at her is silent.

She shakes herself, and sets off in search of espresso.

On the way, she passes a stained glass window, the sun throwing patterns on the floor. The light stripes her, the other people walking by for a second or two—their faces, their shoulders briefly lit up in rose, gold, violet.

A burst of laughter from one of the knots of lawyers; most of them are good mimics, polishing their anecdotes. Then she has the coffee in hand, another minute, and she delivers it to Owen and Louis. A few gulps and they are back in the courtroom.

All rise, says the clerk, and they bow as the judge comes in—the lawyers deferential or ironic, the spectators awkwardly or not at all. People are still fanning themselves, the smell of hot bodies floating off them.

Louis begins his argument, his hands holding the rostrum, a pen in one. He does this because otherwise he moves his hands too much, they rise and dip, the palms turned down for emphasis, turned up in disbelief.

Distracting, he says. All that movement. So he keeps them fixed on the rostrum or holds them behind his back in an effort to ensure that the judge will be doing more listening than watching. And listening to Louis is unusually satisfying, his voice has its own liquid intelligence.

Now this, she thinks, this is an argument, something worthy of the name. How does he do it, the shades of tone, the shifting rhythms? She wonders for a moment if it could be set out in a form of musical notation, as if it were some sort of undersong, only with a smaller octave.

Usually he exudes a lazy self-possession, but the laziness drops away when he argues, leaving only the assurance. Once in a while, away from a courtroom, she sees a threadlike crack in this confidence, this presence—a hesitation, a tiredness at the back of his eyes—and she wonders if there is some cost to it, whether it has a weight of its own. But then the crack is gone and he is looking at her, amused by her inspection.

Think about it this way, he says now, setting out his points, his voice rising and falling. Or think about it that way. The value of justice, the meaning of justice. Do these things diminish with time? Surely a delayed justice, an old justice, is better than none at all.

He makes the word *justice* sound as if he had some intimate knowledge of it, as if it were a crony of his. Someone—a little testy—sitting beside him at the counsel table, looking annoyed.

Even the spectators are paying attention now as he goes on, describing the impact of the case, the implications, the consequences. Describing the bigger picture, the smaller picture, offering sharp pinpoints of clarity.

This is what the other side is really saying, this is the gist, he says, beginning to wind to a close. That however terrible the crimes, the passage of time has dehydrated them into a piece of history. But think about the dead now, the tortured, the victims. Imagine them lined up silently against that wall. Too much? Too dramatic? But they can't be here, surely they should have standing, surely they deserve faces. Delay? Delay? For them, the harm is never-ending—the lives they never led, the children they never had.

He allows a hand to escape for a moment, to make a gesture towards these phantom people.

And delay? This man himself, Drozd, is the real cause of the delay, disappearing into the chaos of Europe during the war. Disappearing, then emerging later into a new life, his history gone. Someone who hid his past thoroughly, but not forever.

Suddenly, the man himself is up on his feet, shouting, harsh-sounding syllables—Belarusian? Russian?

Probably Russian, says Owen. More common even in Belarus.

In any language, his anger crackles across the room. The indignation of an innocent man? Or the deeper outrage of a guilty one?

His lawyer puts a hand on his arm, the bailiff starts towards him. A moment, please, says his lawyer. He whispers urgently, insistently to the man, who whispers back, clearly uncowed. More whispering, and the man begins to droop slightly—reassured? Placated?

We're ready, Mr. Justice, says the lawyer, although the man's fury is still hanging in the air.

Louis takes up his argument again. They want to convince you that deporting him, sending this frail old man—harmless now—will do no good for anyone. Not so frail, he says. Not so harmless.

The outburst has been a piece of luck.

Louis. If he has his faults—many, says Nate, the other junior—he also has this gift, this ability to weave strands of words around a reluctant judge, coaxing him, luring him into one thought after another. This is something she hopes to learn from him, something she wants above all from him. Perhaps it will be contagious—rather than learning it manually, studying his techniques, perhaps she will simply catch it if she spends enough time with him.

A minute later, though, his voice starts to falter, and she looks up. He seems lost for a second, as if he had suddenly found himself somewhere unexpected, somewhere unknown. He sways slightly, steadies himself on the edge of the rostrum, and then sits down abruptly at the counsel table.

A moment, Mr. Justice.

He pushes his scribbled notes over to her.

Go on, he hisses.

What?

Go *on*.

She looks at Owen—no doubt he will want an adjournment to find someone more senior. Needless to say, he will not want her.

But he looks surprised, and then a quick assessment crosses his face, followed by his usual coolness. He hesitates, and then nods.

Not an adjournment? she says, her voice rising.

No, he says quietly. We want this over with as soon as possible, before there is much in the way of an outcry, before the various groups can muster their forces, before they start to harangue us from all sides.

But I'm not prepared, she says, alarmed.

Win or lose, either way has benefits on this one, says Owen calmly.

An orphan case.

This thought should be comforting, but instead, she feels a lurch of anxiety. A war criminal. Doesn't this matter, doesn't this count in some legal sense, even some broader sense? Is that her throat thickening?

Counsel? says the judge sharply.

Go, Louis hisses again.

She stands up, her pulse beating in her ears, her hands cold.

. . .

And? says Nate, back at the office.

A disaster, she says glumly. I ended up reading his notes.

. . .

Nate—her ally, her accomplice, her rival. A friend, too, with all the hazards this involves. Although he is a careless friend, an uncertain friend—often kind, but unreliable. Tall, wide-shouldered, he shaves his head, his scalp naked and smooth, his eyes grey-blue slits.

An egghead, says Louis dryly.

And a strand running through her work life, a daily presence. He is—they are—a rolling conversation about cases, evidence, strategies. About brief triumphs, smarting losses. About irritable judges, the plights of their clients, about opposing lawyers who attempt to bully or mislead them. Her quick-fire thoughts, his ballast, her restlessness, his calm—these are all parts of this shifting bargain.

There are only the two of them and Isabel, the office manager—Louis no longer hires articling students. They kept turning into lawyers, he said to her. Like caterpillars into butterflies, only in reverse.

Not you, of course, he added, a little late.

A small firm, a splinter of another. But Louis is well-known, even though his practice keeps merging, dividing, dissolving.

Criminal lawyers, says Nate. Unrepentant loners. Even the ones who do immigration law. And notorious for their bare bones staffing.

All of them?

Most of them. Some of them.

So how did he explain it, the sudden handover in court? he says now.

A dizzy spell.

He almost laughs.

There was certainly something wrong, anyway. He seemed to suddenly dissolve into unrelated parts.

Nate is trying not to roll his eyes. He is not trying very hard.

. . .

She is walking home—Louis's cure—hoping it will clear her head, will chase the case out of her mind even for a few minutes. The litany in her head: if only she had asked for a few minutes to prepare, if only she had been faster on her feet, if only she had paid more attention. She has replies for these things, explanations, qualifications, but her critic is wily—the more she summons up defences, the more insistent the litany becomes. She is simply no match for herself.

Is it possible they might lose the motion because of her? No, this can't be right. Presumably the case will speak for itself. She hopes. *Fumus boni juris.* The smoke of a good right. Something from international law, not applicable here—the first impression of the merits of a case, a measure of its worth. But she is tempted by the idea that rights, that rightness itself might have a scent of their own, a particular odour that can be detected.

But these thoughts are useless. If she walks home along the waterfront, perhaps they will sail away across the lake, billowing out into nothingness as they go.

Don't be such a worrier, her aunt would say.

Until her last stay in the hospital. Then she said: *Now you can worry.*

Yes, she is a worrier, but usually her worries are not like this, not things that nag at her. Often she has luxuriant worries, giddy worries, cottony worries—worries that sustain her, that rouse her, that hold out their soft arms to her. And she falls into them, knowingly, ruefully, but unable to avoid them.

The day has changed now, no longer hot, the sun stranded behind layers of clouds. The wind is fresh and raw, shuffling through the leaves of the trees along the wharf, heavy with the uncertainty of rain. Out over the water, the sky—marbled in grey and white—is shifting and changing, clouds rolling across it. For a moment, some light breaks through, casting a silvery gleam across the waves of the lake. Then it fades away again as the clouds slowly drift into each other, gradually merging, separating. She inhales deeply, filling her lungs with the cool air, attempting to blow away the sludge in her head.

Farther on, a man is sitting on a bench, his knees spread out, his shirt straining over his bulging stomach. He tosses bread crusts from a paper bag, and a flock of gulls peck at them, their white heads jerking in and out. One glides in for a landing, graceful, coasting on motionless wings for an impossible length of time.

Suddenly there is an explosion of beaks and wings, shrill cries—a fight. The birds scatter for a second or two, and then they are back, searching the ground.

As she nears them, they turn towards her and then begin waddling in her direction, expectant.

If hope is the thing with feathers, what does that make you?

They look at her with foolish faces.

Birds. Dimwits on the ground, maestros in the sky.

To one side, the lake swells and retreats, leaving strings of seaweed, ruffles of dirty foam on the beach. In the shallows, the tiny pebbles are rust-coloured, green, grey. The smell of a dead fish, half-buried, catches in her nose—she sees it in the sand, a piece of driftwood snagged around it. Behind that, the sense of space—the water and sky stretching out until they disappear in the slate-blue mist of the horizon.

Ahead, a woman in a cardigan is sitting on a rock, her posture unfinished. She watches a ferry churning towards the quay, trailing streams of white wake, the gulls circling it, dipping and soaring. Lifting her head, she wraps her arms around herself, then looks towards Leah for a moment—her eyes drifting, hungry for something.

A minute later, she is seized with an impulse. She steps off the boardwalk, kicks off her shoes, pulls off her stockings, then buries her feet in the sand, cold and soft. Now into the water—even colder—up to her ankles, her knees—a dense, blunting cold.

The breeze catches her hair, the air smells like algae. The shallows around her are dark green, and farther out, the surface of the lake wrinkles and smooths. A hawk soars overhead, climbing the wind currents.

Her feet are aching, but her head is clearer. Out of the corner of her eye, she sees small shapes flitting through the water. Fish, she thinks with surprise. No bigger than goldfish, dark bodies quivering, shooting forward.

In a minute, her feet and ankles are numb, and she wades back out of the water, onto the sand, sitting down on the remnants of a bleached log.

The wind picks up again, and a life preserver bangs on a pole.

He wants to see you. An hour after the motion, Isabel had been at her door—pale hair, dry skin. A poet from Colombia, someone who helped to put out a literary journal that had been too brash, angering the wrong people in a country prone to violence. Forced to flee, now one of the people in limbo, working in the office until her claim is decided, until she has more means, more possibilities. In spite of her ethereal appearance, she is as practical as soap, scornful in both English and Spanish.

He wants to see you, she said again, a warning in her voice.

Louis—sitting back in his chair, his barrel body turned to one side. Often he seemed to have more grain, more presence, than most people—to occupy an additional area around his physical being. All the better to keep people at a distance, something he did well. What did she know about him, after a year of working there?

She knew this: he was a reader, more than that, an urgent reader—unable to stop himself, unable to help himself. Books sustained him, fed him. Not the tiny legal library they shared with another firm—his own office shelves were filled with hardcovers, paperbacks, some leather-bound in maroon, slouching between bookends. Usually five or six open at one time, on his desk, on a chair, on the floor, many of them with torn covers, page corners folded over, coffee stains. He had an intense relationship with them, as if they were a group of papery, argumentative lovers.

Legal philosophy, legal history, even religious law, anything but the statutes or reports that might apply to cases, that might be useful. He seemed to be drugged by words, an endless inflow that soothed something in him, a craving that could only be eased in this way.

Perhaps all these words have fed his arrogance, though. Last month, a few glasses of wine into a Bar Association dinner, he began holding forth—only half-jokingly—on a taxonomy of stupidity he claimed to be compiling.

Wilful ignorance, he said. Hubris. Disastrous judgment. Extreme recklessness. Outright idiocy. And some people are more than one type, more than one genus. Include them all, and it adds up to a pile of dolts and nitwits.

What about smugness? she wanted to say. Her instincts roused, she was immediately on the side of the dolts. *A toast to folly and blunder, long may they reign.*

But he has a certain stray warmth as well, something that surfaces unexpectedly—a touch on the shoulder for a client, a rare word of praise for her or Nate. This is oddly disconcerting, particularly since he often becomes more remote afterwards, as if he regretted it. Married to an artist—Carla—often exuberant, someone who teases him gently in front of other people. A little boy as well, a later-in-life child, endearing, wild. Once, when he mentioned him, the look on his face was weak with affection.

Even when he is critical, though, pointing out her shortcomings, he often sounds eerily kind—a tone that was *more in sorrow than anger*. Not today, though. Today he was caustic.

That was quite a performance. What possessed you? You could barely get a word out of your throat. You embarrassed me, you embarrassed the firm. You embarrassed yourself. You were unprepared, not paying attention.

If there was anything he despised, it was his polar opposite—a lawyer who was stiff, awkward, at a loss for words. Her excuses rushed to mind again, but she could feel his contempt.

How could I be prepared? she protested. It was last minute.

Last minute is a fact of life in practice—better get used to it. That is, unless you want to change professions, which you might want to consider.

What about you? she wanted to say, stung. The man who was stranded mid-sentence. The man who lost his place, lost track of himself for a few minutes, who had to have someone else take over. Was he daring her to raise this? Was this an aggressive way of defending himself? But it seemed too risky to say anything about it, a small minefield.

Some of it's true, though, isn't it? said Nate later. You weren't paying attention.

Nate, not a person of cheap sympathies.

She puts her shoes back on, starts walking again. This time she turns north, across the strip of sand with its plumes of scrub grass, and suddenly—in its city-like way—the lakeshore is gone and she is walking up side streets.

If Louis was so hard on her today, she must ensure he never finds out about the case where she froze up entirely. Now this, this is a fatal problem for someone who wants to be a trial lawyer. This is a dream-strangler.

Take long, slow breaths, say the experts, the suppliers of free advice. But this is a useless idea for someone who is unable to breathe at all. *Tense and relax your muscles,* they say. But this is impossible when her muscles are already seized up. *Imagine yourself performing the desired action, and all the details of what you are seeing, hearing, and feeling. You can create your own outcome, you can produce the result you want.*

She finds this last one vaguely surreal. What if the lawyer on the other side is also imagining his desired outcome, the opposite result? Would this create duelling realities, some metaphysical game of Rock, Paper, Scissors?

No, the cure for this is practice, experience, speaking so often in court it will become almost effortless. After a while, sentences will flow out of her mouth seamlessly, long ribbons of words wrapping around cases. Even Louis must have been nervous as a young lawyer—although this is hard to imagine. But eventually the problem will disappear. Eventually it will go away. Why? Because it has to. Because it must.

A few more blocks now, and she is home.

This place. A narrow house, the bottom step to the porch sagging on one side, a stack of newspapers listing precariously on a chair by the door. The window sashes are newly painted, though, a small blow for order in their ongoing feud with decay. And it is a feud, the place is porous, the wood soft with age—water seeping into the basement, drafts hovering around the windowsills. For every advance, a setback.

The dampness gives it a spongy quality in the summer, turns it into a drunk of a house. But it dries out in the winter, dries out so thoroughly that the curtains, the pillows rustle with static electricity. This is its best moment, though, dusk, when the lines of the house emerge more clearly, some trick of shape and light, a moment of subtle coherence. Perhaps the builder designed it at dusk, not realizing that these lines would retreat in daylight, would retreat again as dark settled in.

Now she sees Gus has fixed a rain gutter—this morning sagging off the side of the roof. For every setback, an advance.

As she pushes open the door, the pruney smell of old carpets, mice, and cigarette smoke meets her. Rudy is home, fussing over his cooking, a pork stew of some kind. An uncle, one of three—almost part of the house themselves, the walls, ceilings imbued with their hoarse voices, their bristly faces.

Rudy, the oldest—beaky, a puff of grey-white hair around the edges of his skull. A dandelion seed head of a man, sour-sweet, someone with low blood pressure who faints easily. He starts to waver and then looks around frantically for a chair, or sits down on the ground abruptly so that he will not fall and crack his skull. This makes it seem as if he is fainting deliberately, as if he lies down first and then faints, but falling is dangerous, and this move is born of long experience. *Eat salt,* says his doctor, and he does—sardines, olives, pickles—with little result. He is never out for long, but she learned from an early age how to catch a sinking body, or at least break its fall.

Later, at dinner:

What's in this slop? says Malcolm, grimacing after a couple of bites.

Rudy glares at him.

You cook, then, he snaps.

Something he says often.

I don't cook, says Malcolm derisively.

Something he says often.

Then he shakes his head, a little more emphatically than required. A man who thinks of himself as good-looking—a genuine feat of self-deception. In fact, he looks as if someone had dragged a damp cloth across his features, blurring them.

But it is true that Rudy is a poor cook, his dinners are barely edible. His sense of taste is fading, and he has begun adding ingredients almost randomly—cayenne, paprika, bay leaves, celery seed. His tongue is going blind, and his dinners show a frantic longing for flavour, a yearning for something elusive that goes with it. The results are peculiar, but he is their only cook and they need him to cook, however lacking it is; Malcolm and Gus are hopeless, and she has no time and even less interest. The appeal of mixing, baking, roasting eludes her—she is puzzled when Nate exclaims over a fiery pepper, a salty cheese.

Malcolm pushes his plate away and lights a cigarette, dragging in the smoke, his body visibly relaxing. He is a devoted smoker, he loves it in a way he loves nothing else, smoking is his darling. The routines—shaking out the cigarette, the click and flash of the lighter, the first deep inhalation—have worn furrows in him. Gus smokes as well, but not like this—he smokes doggedly, as if it were a requirement, some sort of obligation. Between the two of them, she grew up in a tobacco haze, the rough smoke familiar, comforting, part of the climate of the house.

She tries the pork stew now.

Good, she says, without much conviction.

Malcolm hoots, and even Gus gulps back a laugh.

Rudy glares again and throws down his fork, tines bouncing off the table onto the floor.

Gus makes a mild sound in his throat. He is her soft spot, more than a soft spot, a dough-faced man, burly. A man who still believes T-shirts are undershirts, who leaves glasses around with the dregs of rye and ginger ale. When her six-year-old self ended up in this house, she had been almost feral with shock—her senses enlarged, her body rigid. She had sniffed out a faint trace of gentleness in Gus, something on his breath, on the surface of his skin, and had attached herself to him with an unchildlike ferocity. Rattled at first, he tried to rally—they all tried, even Malcolm went through the motions. Mortified by the man—their brother, her father—who had disappeared a few years earlier, leaving a note and three hundred dollars wrapped in a piece of cloth. *I'm sorry,* said the note. Only that. *I'm sorry.*

Then her mother gone, several years later—crushed inside a heap of twisted metal.

What else can we do? said Rudy.

Their brother. Their niece.

None of our business, said Malcolm.

It's only on weekends, said Rudy. The aunt will take her during the week.

Gus nodded.

And he'll come back. He'll hear somehow. This is only for now. He'll come back once he hears.

You have no idea where he is? said the social worker. *I don't believe it for a minute,* said her tone.

No idea, said Rudy. I'm sure he would be here if he knew.

In fact, he was not at all sure of this. The youngest brother, the father—witty and weak and self-absorbed. And a man who was afraid, desperately afraid of—what? Of being ordinary. Of leading a rye and ginger life. Chasing anything that might save him from this, like a distracted dog. A fugitive from the everyday, the commonplace, always searching for a way out.

He'll turn up soon, said Rudy.

He is far from sure of this either.

The aunt was the formal placement—the mother's half sister, nineteen years older than her, almost another generation. But a woman whose kidneys were starting to fail, scarred organs slowly breaking down.

I can't handle her full-time, she said miserably, exhausted by the disease.

The social worker knew enough—too much—about the foster home system to send the child into its labyrinths. So this arrangement would have to work—the aunt during the week, the uncles on the weekend. She did what could be done, the things that were possible. A session on child-rearing, simple advice, checklists on clothing, food, sleeping. The child was the only one who read the lists, though, or tried to—her small finger tracing out the letters she knew until the papers were stained and dog-eared. Hoping that somewhere in there were the clues she needed, the answers to what had happened, how her life had jackknifed so wildly. But she also passed along anything she understood to Gus.

A taciturn man, something that suited them both. He used words sparingly, as if he had only a limited supply, and was storing them for some future use. Instead, he preferred silence, or a range of silences: dusty silences, steep silences, warm silences.

A clam, said the social worker to her supervisor. But soon he became used to the child winding around his legs, and developed a clumsy affection for her. Not a man who was a good bet in other ways, though—someone with serial bankruptcies, an instinct for failure.

Raised by your uncles? Nate says in the same tone someone might say: *raised by wolves?* His voice is dark, slightly hoarse. He is intrigued by this odd household, intrigued as only someone with two card-carrying parents can be.

I raised her, says her aunt. They looked after her.

Anna Rubin. Puffy-faced, her skin floury, her dark eyes circled with shadows. Persistent in her own way, determined that the girl would know something of this other life, that she would have some sense of its latitudes and longitudes.

No such thing as half-Jewish. Don't let me hear you say that. If your mother is Jewish, you're Jewish. *Halacha.* Those are the rules.

Those are the rules, echoed the girl, curled under the woman's arm.

But her aunt had more to say, much more. A personal mission, built around *tzimmes* and the ten plagues.

The plague of locusts. The plague of frogs. The plague of water turning into blood.

The girl held up a hand, raising her small fingers.

Only three, she said.

She was a literal child.

A selection of the best, said her aunt.

Behind the scenes, though, her kidneys were silently abandoning their functions, the toxins in her system slowly building. Soon—too soon—it was the uncles during the week, the aunt on the weekend.

Not even a Jewish disease, said her aunt disgustedly, her skin yellow.

No need to tell that social worker, she added.

What do you do when you're there? Malcolm said once, not so much interested in the girl as the aunt, any possibilities for money.

The child hesitated.

We eat brisket, she said after a minute, the only thing that came into her mind. She had no words for this briny, tender woman, for her kitchen, her houseplants, vines running along mantels, trailing down shelves. For the moth orchids everywhere—windowsills, bookcases—leaning over pots, their grey air roots twisting around them.

Malcolm looked at her uncomprehendingly. The idea that the girl was half-Jewish, the idea of Jewishness itself was so foreign, so baffling to him—to all three of them—that they ignored it. They had an unspoken agreement to treat it as if it were an awkward genetic problem, something that was better left unmentioned. And after a while, she understood that she was not to talk to them about it, that this was something she had—she was—with her aunt.

Is it only for girls? she said to her, early on. Being Jewish?

Who told you that? Full of men. Look at Moses. Look at Einstein. Look at Marvin next door.

Marvin—thinning hair, mild, someone who yawns a lot. Ida's husband, content to drift in her slipstream. Neighbours.

She's not the brightest, but she has a good heart. And he shovels my walk in the winter.

And Moses? Einstein? Other neighbours?

Big shots, said her aunt.

That night:

Men can be Jewish, too, she said to Gus, putting her to bed.

He said nothing in an agreeable way.

Look at Moses. Look at Marvin.

More nothing.

She sighed, the world-weary sigh of a six-year-old.

Those are the rules.

. . .

Half-Jewish. This is unsound genetically as well, she discovers later in biology classes, not a matter of chromosomal halves. Instead, she has a mix of genetic variations, extending in all directions. If some of them mark her as a carrier of Tay-Sachs disease, Bloom syndrome, and an inability to drink milk, one non-Jewish parent will make no difference. This is a mess of a genome.

. . .

A week after the motion. Nate is sitting on the arm of one of her office chairs, cracking pumpkin seeds in his teeth. *Lime, chili, salt—I roasted them myself.*

You're distracting me, she says, although the truth is that she was already distracted. The stay motion has been stalking her thoughts, intruding everywhere. She is waiting for the decision, although this is a wholly pointless exercise—it could be issued tomorrow, next week, or even next month, especially if the judge decides to write extensive reasons, not at all improbable. Still, she feels suspended in the web of this case, in part because she is still possessed by the idea that if they lose, it will be her fault.

Unlikely, says Nate. Although not impossible.

Or that she will be blamed anyway, whether it is her fault or not.

Not quite so unlikely, Nate admits. Give me your hand.

She stretches out her palm, and he leans over and shakes some pumpkin seeds into it.

She studies them absently, and then puts them in her mouth.

But I thought the government didn't care about the outcome, he says.

It must be a posture of some kind, she says. She still finds it difficult to believe.

Suddenly her mouth is burning, and she grabs for a glass of water on her desk.

How much chili did you put on this? she says, coughing, sputtering, her eyes tearing. You're a lunatic. You must have a tongue like leather.

You should be hardier, he says, laughing.

She is up now, in search of water, ice, anything.

I brought in some grapefruit sorbet, he adds to her back.

In the tiny office half-kitchen, she spoons up the sorbet, holding it against her tongue, the roof of her mouth, tart, cold.

As she stands there, the case floats by again. *Old justice.* Louis's words. What do they mean, aside from a turn of phrase, a flourish? Old justice must be as murky as young justice, whatever that is, whatever it might be.

A skeptic—how could she be anything else?—but she has been at least partly hooked by law, mesmerized, tenet after tenet claiming to make sense out of some particular cluster of circumstances. *The doctrine of ripeness. The principle of attractive nuisance. The duty to rescue. The duty to retreat.*

Finally, she had thought, finally, she had found the antidote to luck. Luck, that mobster, that tyrant, doling out favours and cruelties on a whim. Now, instead of luck, there would be justice, the reordering of a thoughtless world. Now she would see these rules in action, they would provide remedies, they would rearrange tragedies and jackpots, if only she could put together cases that invoked them. But the cases are turning out to be muddy, or a series of dubious riddles, the law itself full of weak spots.

She is trying to ignore this, though, she is afraid that otherwise air will begin slowly leaking out of her convictions, that she will start to deflate in some strange, professional way. And she often finds law heady, enthralling in itself, a slow two-step of surmise and conjecture, a string of tales turned into logic. A snail in a bottle. A carbolic smoke ball. A hunted quail.

Another spoonful of sorbet, cold against her tongue, her lips.

Don't knock luck, her aunt would say. But the mobster had gotten to her anyway, her kidneys terminally failing at fifty-nine.

A restless presence, though.

So almost anything is better than luck. And her clients are such fervent believers in law—at least those seeing it for the first time—she wonders whether they might re-inject her with their hopes. All their convoluted explanations, their frantic optimism—they believe more deeply in law than any judge, any lawyer. But only until the wrong verdict comes down. Then they are astonished by this betrayal.

Not Owen, naturally. Someone with a smooth coating, unflappable. Merely trying to return a man to the country he came from.

An Act for the remitting prisoners with their indictments to the places where the crimes were committed.

Where divers felons and murtherers, upon feigned and untrue surmises, by writ and otherwise, before the King in his bench, and cannot by the order of the law be remitted sent down to the justices of gaol-delivery or of the peace or other justices or commissioners, to proceed upon them after the course of common law: Be it therefore ordained and enacted by the authority of this present parliament, that the justices of the King's bench for the time being have full authority and power, by their discretions to remand and send down the bodies of all felons and murtherers brought or removed into the counties where the same murthers or felonies have been committed and done.

. . .

Good God, says Louis, paper in hand.

Don't sound so surprised, she says, even though she is surprised herself.

You better call the client and give him the bad news.

We won? says Owen, disconcerted for once.

All three of them think: *now we have to do the case.*

. . .

She is dreaming a twitchy dream. The man Drozd in his shirt sleeves, his forearms freckled with age, veins standing out on his hands. A maker of bottles, vials, flasks. He is creating loops of molten red glass, twirling them into brilliant arcs.

What are you doing here? she says, puzzled.

Now he is adding orange glass, grey glass, sending them into the air in flowing spirals. The glass is so naked and luminous that it makes her dizzy to look at it.

How do you do that? she says.

What are you making? she says.

Doesn't it burn your hands?

Of course, says Drozd, but he keeps on turning out the arcs, twisting and folding them, rolling them out again.

She puts out her hand to touch the hot glass herself, and wakes up, the dream disintegrating.

Glass.

Soda ash, limestone, sand.

So hard, so transparent.

So beautiful. So breakable.

TWO

Life has improved, comrades. Life has become more joyous.
JOSEF STALIN

The pig is trussed, lying against the roots of a tree, squealing. Its small eyes are white-rimmed with fear, hooves scrabbling in the dirt. The early winter air is tinged with the smell of hen manure, smoke, split wood.

The man standing in front of the pig pauses, hefting the sledgehammer in his right hand, a bottle of *samahon* in the other. He is waiting, waiting for something—perhaps a sign of the right moment for death to overtake this animal. He is not squeamish—not at all, he is hard, a hardness that has accumulated layer by layer, almost everything else wasting away, leaving only a stony sediment and a strand of self-pity. This pig? This pig is meat, and only meat. If anything, he takes a certain pleasure in its misery.

He swigs from the bottle, sets it down. Suddenly he hits the pig on the forehead, and the animal sags, motionless, into the leaves. He throws the rope circling its neck over a branch of the tree, and then catches it, pulling it down with the weight of his body. He begins to hoist until the pig is in the air, suspended, and then he lashes the rope to the tree. Now the knife—thin, double-sided. He brushes his thumb across the blade, even though he honed it on an old whetstone in the barn only that morning. There can be no hesitation—the pig is only stunned at the moment, it must bleed out before it dies or the meat will be sour.

Now. He slashes the animal's throat at an upward angle, through the tough skin, the fat, across the jugular. Blood spurts out, staining its chest, stomach, and then pooling below it. The pig begins jerking convulsively, its legs trembling and twitching. Its heart struggles to keep pumping, then slows, beat by beat, as its brain begins to die from lack of oxygen. A few minutes later, the animal is still.

The man takes another swig from the bottle—he makes the *samahon* in old milk cans—and looks around as if he expects applause. But there is only his small son, dirty-faced, his hair dark, unkempt. The farmer next door who owns the pig with him will come over soon for the butchering; two of these tiny homesteads needed to buy the animal, to afford the feed. By the time the other farmer arrives, the man will be sullenly drunk, and they will quarrel over the strips of ribs, the loins, the belly, the lard.

Now he waits while the pig drains, the pool of blood staining the snow. In the meantime, the boy—five at the most—builds up the fire under an old oil drum full of hot water, feeding in sticks, then split logs, and finally one end of a whole log, pushing it farther and farther in as it turns slowly to a glowing shell of grey and white ash.

Get moving, barks the man. The child tries to go faster, trying to avoid a kick or a blow, tripping over himself in his haste. As the fire blazes up, steam begins slowly rising from the water in the oil drum, white-fingered wisps curling in the cold air.

When the pig has bled out, the man swings the carcass over the oil drum, into the boiling water. After a few minutes, he hauls it out again, pulls it onto a makeshift table, and he and the boy begin scraping off the hair and scurf.

When most of the bristles are gone, the man steps back and looks at the body, holding the sticking knife in his hand, taking another swallow of liquor.

Bucket, he growls, and the boy runs to bring it over. Then, swiftly, the man slits the animal from throat to hams, pulling out lungs, slippery intestines, the dark liver, the stomach—as fat and curled as a fetus—letting them fall out below. He throws something to a brindled dog, dancing around in anticipation, and then another gulp of the *samahon*.

Take the bucket, boy. Take out the organs. Pull off the fat.

The boy pulls the bucket over to the table and plunges his small hands into it, separating the warm guts and the organs. Clumsily, he pulls at the lacy caul fat, the connective tissue until he has most of it off.

Now rinse them.

He uses brackish water from the well, he works as quickly as he can—he knows instinctively how drunk his father is, how drunk he will be, and how brutal he is at each stage of his drunkenness. Almost another sense, one finely tuned by fear.

He lives inside the borders of this fear, fear stretches the air around him, softens the ground beneath him. Fear lives in his throat, on his scalp, in the tiny bones of his inner ears. Fear is his gauge, his understanding, his negotiation with the world. His world? A tiny farm, ignored by collectivization, a field and a half of barley, potatoes, turnips, a few squawking hens, several goats, an old horse for plowing, the whole of it bare and badly kept. A place where he was working almost as soon as he could walk, digging potatoes out of the sandy dirt. A place where, even at this age, he watches the smallest things, keeps his eyes open, something essential to survival. This watchfulness is not only a matter of detecting his father's tempers—he is always looking for anything that might be edible, the warblers' nests with their greenish eggs, the ground holes left by the field mice. Always watching, always listening, straining to understand. A scrawny, wary existence.

. . .

The woman is screaming, hoarse, ragged screams. She has been in labour now for seventeen hours, her face is white with exhaustion, her hair is damp with sweat. The pain began quickly, a hard, mad pain, but the baby is stuck now, stuck in the birth canal. The neighbour has mixed a tea from black cohosh root to move this child along. She tries to pour sips of it into the woman's mouth between the screams, but it dribbles down the side of her cheek. Stand up, she says, hoping gravity will lend a hand, but when the next contraction seizes her body, the woman doubles over and falls to her knees. On and on the pain grinds, she twists and turns on the straw-stuffed mattress, the screams turning into rasps.

The neighbour turns to the husband's mother, who is praying in a desultory way by the wood stove, and lifts up her hands in a gesture of helplessness. The husband's mother is irritated by this gesture, her uselessness. Muttering to herself, she goes over to the bed, uncovers the woman, and surveys the bloody mucus between her legs. She hesitates for a moment and then pushes her hand deep into the birth canal, grimacing. She can feel the curve of a head, a sharp shoulder, and she grabs on and yanks hard with the next contraction, and the next one and the next. One last pull and the baby slides into the light, his head smeared with the white wax of a newborn.

The neighbour wraps him in an old blanket, and puts him beside the mother. She looks at him, tries to smile, her mouth still twisted from the pain, unable to believe that this torment is over. She whispers to him, and then closes her eyes.

The infection sets in soon after, silent, lethal. First a fever, then shivering in fits and starts, her face the colour of old chalk. Later, she begins to babble, strings of incoherent words. Then she is quiet again, too quiet. At the moment of death, her hands uncurl slowly on the bed.

The child is a small bag of bones, first squalling, then mute with hunger. His grandmother dips pieces of cloth in goat milk so that he can suck on them, his eyes already dark and wide. Kindness? Affection? No, this feeding is a reluctant loan, a stake in future labour. If she had a choice, she would rather have the mother alive—someone who could work—than the child.

An endless struggle, this farm—an existence shaped by scanty crops, fields bordered by sedge, carnation grass, gooseberries. Breaking up the ground with the iron plow, seeding potato eyes, digging up the tubers, a relentless chain of work repeated over and over. If it rains, the barley is covered with mildew and the potatoes rot in the ground. If there is no rain, the rutabagas are infested with maggots, the larvae leaving small tunnels.

But these fields are also places of sparse beauty, where wild caraway grows in the thickets, feathery stems with caps of white flowers. Places where silver-blue mist gathers on rivers at dawn, wreathing trees, blurring rocks and banks. Where a black-eared hare lops across the fields at twilight. Where a lone stork wheels in the sky, white plumage, neck outstretched, wings the span of a man's height.

If only this were enough to sustain a child.

Idiot, says his father, who rides him mercilessly. Dirt. Less than dirt.

And for all the boy knows, he is right—the rot, the mildew is his fault, not the fault of the rain, or the spores drifting in from other farms. In the evening, he lies on his pallet and watches the fire in the stove, too tired to think even a child's thoughts. Every once in a while his father, maudlin, pulls him onto his lap and sings about soldiers leaving, lovers dying, his breath heavy with drink. A moment of false comfort, an arm around him, he leans against the man's body, closing his eyes. But a few minutes later, the man cuffs him off, roaring at him through drunken tears.

Now, with the pig still on the makeshift table, his grandmother comes out with a mug of tea. She wants the man to be sober enough that the farmer will not walk off with the best cuts, leaving them with the tougher pieces. She will be doing the brining, the curing, although she will get the little rat to help as much as he can. This meat will be a change from their usual fare, sorrel soup, dried fish, potatoes, always potatoes—green and sprouted towards the end of winter, too long in the root cellar. Or the pickings from under the trees, roots, the mushrooms, sometimes the bracken she collects to pound in a mortar, to stretch the rye flour.

She sits down on a log, smiles at the boy, crooking her finger, holding out a piece of bread with a smear of honey. A bee's nest—she found one in a tree trunk a few weeks ago, and has been using the straw-coloured liquid since then. The sweetest thing he has ever tasted, the sweetest thing he has ever known at all. It makes him feel dizzy, as if his head might burst, and he is astonished that such a thing exists, even in small amounts, even for a moment.

He looks longingly at the bread, although he is afraid, his fear, always present, is shouting at him. But he knows there is no way out of this. If he ignores her, it will be worse, and he is so desperate for affection, for food that it is impossible not to hope that this time—this one time—her smile, the bread will be harmless.

He sidles over to her, trying to make himself as small as possible. When he gets close, hoping, dreading, the smile disappears, and she leans over casually and slaps him on the side of his head, hard enough to make him stagger. Then she breaks the bread in two, gives him half, and eats the rest.

. . .

His father is scything the barley, the blade gleaming in the sun. The boy—older now—is following behind him, shovelling the cut seed heads into the cart. When the field is done, they will take the grain into the small barn, and beat it with a flail, separating out the chaff. Meanwhile, the day is hot, his mouth dry from the dusty stalks. He is thirsty, a thirst that nags at him, that fills his mouth and throat with longing. Every few minutes, when he has shovelled up the grain, he leads the horse and cart ahead to catch up to where his father is working.

The brindled dog is loping around, older now too, muzzle greying, no longer fast. He is watching, waiting to see whether a vole or a field mouse will be flushed out by the scythe. Each time the cart stops, he lies down under it, panting in the heat. The boy envies him this small patch of shade, this escape from the sun.

They are moving along the side of the field, the side closest to the road. A man with a horse and buggy is driving by, a dark cap pushed back on his head, his face leathery, his beard trimmed. He is in his shirt sleeves, a black vest, and behind him is a load of goods—salt, soap, thread, eyeglasses. This man, he has seen him before, showing his grandmother a tablecloth—a slow, mild talker. A man who had nodded to him, a hint of a gentle smile around his lips.

Jews, says his father, almost spitting. Filth. Animals. Pigs.

The man is too far away to hear him, but looks resolutely ahead in any event, as if he is concentrating on a spindly tree far off in the distance. Every few minutes, the boy glances over, watching him until the man has dwindled to a speck.

In the meantime, the field, still hot and dusty. Each time he leads the horse forward, the dog scrambles to his feet and dodges out the side of the wagon, then returns to the shade when the wagon stops again. He does this again and again—down and panting when the cart is stopped, up and dodging out when it moves. Over and over, too, the hacking of the scythe, forking the cuttings, the thirst, his dry tongue.

His father straightens up, stretches his back, and watches the boy lead the horse forward again. The dog darts out from under the wagon, but this time he is a few seconds too slow, a little too late. The back wheel catches his leg. He yelps, a piercing yelp, and then begins limping and whimpering, his leg at an awkward angle. The man's face twists in anger, and he starts back towards the boy, scythe in hand. The boy takes one look and is already running, but the man throws the scythe after him, and then grabs the whip from the wagon. He catches up to the boy, grabbing his shirt, shaking him, pulling him down. Then he begins lashing him across his bare legs, his arms, his head. When he stops for breath, the boy wriggles free, leaps up, and runs again, runs towards the forest, a forest where an eight-year-old can hide. Hollows, dips, brush, undergrowth. His father goes after him, but gives up after a few yards.

The boy keeps running. He runs until he can no longer hear his father cursing, until he can no longer hear the dog yelping. He runs until he is running past tree trunks, darting around brambles, until his lungs are aching. He runs until he trips over a hummock, and falls, rolling on the ground, on the dead leaves. For a moment, he lies there, listening intently.

The forest is dim, marshy, cool. Dark moss everywhere, carpeting the ground, clothing the rocks, the tree trunks, muffling the sound. The silence seems to wrap itself around the boy. A thin wind rustles through the alders and subsides. Above him, a woodpecker tocks. If only he could stay here, lie where he is, sleep in these shadowy depths, at least for now.

But his father might still be after him, might crash in here at any moment.

The woodpecker tocks again. He eyes the tree above him, a black alder, patches of pale lichen on its trunk. Safer to be higher. He gets to his feet and begins climbing up, lodging himself in the joint of a large limb. Then he waits.

. . .

Night. The forest sighs around him. A shrew squeaks and scuttles through the bracken. Bats flutter noiselessly, circling above him in the dark sky. A nightjar picks a moth out of the air. He is cold, hungry, the welts from the whip are smarting. By now, his father will be passed out, drunk, his mouth working, his hands twitching from time to time. A curt man in daylight, he is a sleep talker, sometimes even a sleep shouter, his nightmares vicious.

The boy is shivering, he clambers down the tree, back through the forest, then into the field again. The moon has risen, a pale slab, the stubble in the fields ghostly in its light. He is closer to the neighbours' house than his own, he will go there, perhaps they will have food hanging in their shed that he can steal—meat drying or milk curdling. He walks quickly between the rows, looking around every few minutes as if his father might suddenly appear, rising up in the midst of the bleached stalks.

This house is larger than his, wooden shingles instead of thatch, even a small bathhouse. They are still up, smoke is drifting out of the chimney, he can see the firelight through the small window, he can hear voices—a woman, the low voice of a man. A child wails for a few seconds and then stops, soothed by something.

He hesitates, hanging in the moment. He is fearful he will be caught, but he is hollow with hunger, and he is less afraid of this than going home. A spasm in his stomach urges him on, and he edges over to the shed, lifts the latch on the door, and slips into the musty dark. Another step, and he falls over a rake with a clatter, a bang. He tries to pull himself up, but now the door is open, and a man is there, his form outlined in the uncertain moonlight. In a second, he has the boy in his grip.

The Drozd boy, he says to the woman, bringing the struggling child in, sitting him on a bench beside the wood stove.

Stay there, she says, and you can have something to eat.

She takes a kettle of soup from the oven and spoons out a bowl—turnip, potatoes, a few small pieces of meat, floating in a greasy broth. Then she cuts off chunks of brown bread and puts them in front of him. He eats quickly, one arm around the bowl.

After he eats, the woman wipes his welts with water, then his face, his hands.

What in God's name are we going to do with you? mutters the man to himself.

Nothing tonight, says the woman. Into bed with you.

She puts him down with the two-year-old, a little warm body. The smaller child curls up reflexively against him, as blindly as a puppy. An unfamiliar sensation, this closeness, the rise and fall of another child's chest. The boy, exhausted, sinks into a leaden sleep.

He wakes suddenly in the middle of the night, hope knifing through him, so unfamiliar, so alien he barely knows what it is. Perhaps they will keep him, these people. Perhaps they need another pair of hands. Perhaps his father will let him go, *a useless mouth to feed,* he says often enough. In the faint glow from the wood stove, banked down with ashes, he spins a new life for himself, a life of warm blankets, of meat soup, of a woman saying *into bed with you.* Then he is asleep again, as abruptly as he woke up.

. . .

The day is windy, although the morning sun is still mild. The man has one arm around him, the other holding the reins. The boy has protested, he can hold on to the mane, but the man grips him tightly—to keep him from falling? To keep him from escaping? The clip-clopping of the horse's hooves on the packed dirt road echoes the words in the boy's head, the words he wants to say to the man.

I can seed, I can rake, I can dig, I can slop.

But the words are stuck in his throat.

Perhaps the man knows these things anyway, perhaps he knows how much help the boy could be. He must know.

I can fence, I can pick, I can hoe, I can muck.

His house. The man pulls up in front, slides down off the horse, taking the boy with him, still holding him tightly.

See how he is holding me, thinks the boy. As if I am already his.

I can catch, I can fetch, I can net, I can chop.

His father is there now, his arms crossed grimly, his grandmother beside him.

Good morning, says the man stiffly.

Good morning, says his father.

We have something of yours, says the man. He pushes the boy forward.

The boy stands very still, waiting for him, willing him to say more. But the man says nothing.

His father grabs the boy, jerks him back beside him, and begins cursing him. The man shakes his head, says something under his breath, but swings himself back up on the horse and rides off.

The boy is stupefied, his mind folding in on itself. Then the fear descends on him again.

His grandmother, triumphant, grabs him from his father, clouts him hard, once, twice.

A red kite soars above them, sending out its whistling, singing cry.

. . .

No, his grandmother says. That is not how it was. That is not how it was at all.

THREE

Sleep faster, we need the pillows.
JEWISH PROVERB

Lies, half-truths, stories painted on air. Deceit is an art, an accident, a condition. And the basis for these deportations, these applications to revoke citizenship, a citizenship obtained by fraud. The deportations used for refugees, originally people in flight. Torn from their homes, families, their occupations—in some cases, their sanity. Beset by tyranny, poverty, conflict—broken bodies, broken minds.

Who can blame them for changing a past, a present? Leah thinks. Their lives have suddenly become so unstable that the facts they knew—fixed, settled facts—have already been shaken loose. And who can blame them for wanting to protect themselves, their children, to find a haven? Or merely to pry open the gates of possibility. Urgent lies, offhand lies, fuelled by fear or need, they neglect to mention the existence of a relative, a deed, a political party. Or they magnify hardships or misfortunes that are grim enough as they are. People who have taken an elastic approach to their histories, desperate to improve their futures.

Difficult cases. Is there anything more final than extinguishing someone's citizenship? Depriving them of their right to be where they are, to exist where they are. Interrupting a highly specific life, filled with accumulated circumstances, incidents, experiences.

This case, though, this is a different kind of lie. About a different kind of life.

She is surrounded by paper sent over by Owen, affidavits, reports, dispatches, records, wading her way through them. This is what she has discovered so far: these innocuous-looking documents are unsafe, full of risks, hidden brutalities.

AFFIDAVIT

I, Samuel Rybak, of the City of Minsk in the Republic of Belarus make oath and say as follows:

1. In 1938, I was a sub-editor at a Yiddish newspaper published in Minsk. I lived in the Nemiga quarter with my wife, Malke, our baby son, and our two daughters.
2. At that time, there were nearly 70,000 Jews in Minsk, almost a third of the city's population. As a result, the newspaper had a wide circulation.
3. One evening in April, I was working late in the office overseeing a print run. My wife had given me a flask of borscht for dinner, and I was sitting down to eat it when three officers from Naródnyy Komissariát Vnútrennikh Del (NKVD), the Russian security police, burst into the room. They seized me, threw the borscht all over me, and began kicking me in my head, my stomach, my groin, my kidneys.
4. As they did this, they shouted "Where is the money?" over and over. I told them where we kept a few rubles in the office for daily expenses, but this small amount only enraged them

further. They searched the editorial office, throwing papers off the shelves, pulling out drawers, breaking windows, and shoving things through them.

5. Then they arrested me for propaganda and agitation against the Central Executive Committee of the Byelorussian Soviet Socialist Republic, and took me to the NKVD building for Minsk *voblast* where they ordered me to confess my crimes against the state. When I refused, they began hammering my head against the floor, and then beating me on the ribs and spine with a truncheon.
6. Over the next two weeks, two of the officers continued to order me to confess, and to name other people who had also been involved in propaganda and anti-Soviet agitation. When I refused, they took turns beating me on the face, on my body and testicles. They also forced me to squat for hours, which they referred to as *swinging the kerosene.*
7. Sometimes they beat me on the bones of my feet with a wooden club. Then they made me stand in the middle of the room and turn around and around until I passed out. After that, they poured cold water on me until I woke up, and then forced me to start turning again.
8. At other times, they shouted "Pray, Jew, pray" and hit me until I recited a *Shema* in Hebrew. Every so often, they forced me to sing Yiddish songs. Once, they ordered me to do a Jewish dance and I tried to perform a *rikudl* while they beat the calves of my legs.
9. My legs and feet swelled up, and I had sores on the soles of my feet. My body was covered in clotted bruises and lacerations, three of my teeth were knocked out, and my arm was broken, the bone sticking through the skin.
10. Often the officers brought in a clerk to help them, to cover for them for stretches of time when they would rest or have

meals. He would ensure that I was still squatting, pour water on me if I passed out, or spin me around on my painful feet.

11. After fifteen days of this treatment, I confessed to being involved in propaganda and agitation, and named two other men, one who had already been arrested, and the other who was dead.
12. The clerk wrote up a confession for me to sign, and I was sent to a penal colony in Krasnoyarsk for six years, where I worked in a quarry, loading rock. The only food was a thin soup, provided twice a day, and four pieces of bread. I almost died several times from starvation and the extreme cold at night. I am five feet ten inches and I weighed ninety-four pounds when I was released.
13. While I was at Krasnoyarsk, I met another man from Minsk, from the same *voblast*. He told me that he had been tortured by two officers with the help of a clerk as well, and that he had heard them call the clerk "Drozd."
14. I have now been shown a picture of Stefan Drozd, attached as Exhibit A to this my affidavit, and although he is much older-looking, I believe he may well have been the clerk in question.
15. Between the NKVD and the Nazis, particularly the Nazis, nearly half a million Jews were killed in Belarus. Most of the Jews in Minsk were killed. When I was released, I learned that my wife, my children, my mother, my uncle, and my brothers were among them.
16. I make this affidavit in good faith and for no improper purpose.

Sworn before me this tenth day of April, 2009, in the City of Minsk. Ivan Stasevich, a Notary Public in and for the Republic of Belarus.

The rawness of this takes her by surprise. She has been trying to develop some detachment from her clients, their harrowing lives. Second-hand disaster looms so large in this work, she knows she must find ways to stay at a distance herself, to avoid absorbing every harsh detail into her own being. But this, this is wrenching, this has ambushed her. *Pray, Jew, pray.*

What did you think a war criminal was? says Louis.

A man linked to something more impersonal, more sweeping, perhaps. Not this dirty individual torture, this personal violence. Although, strictly speaking, these are not war crimes—not committed in the course of armed conflict. What are they? Obscenities, horrors.

The NKVD humiliated people to break them down, says Owen, who has been getting briefings from the War Crimes Section. Sometimes they forced prisoners to make animal noises. Confessions were crucial, they had quotas to meet. And later on, they were so desperate to meet the quotas they began turning each other in.

No, no, no, says Drozd.

He is invading her daylight hours now, not merely her dreams, rasping in her ear.

These things did not happen, he says. People distort them, they exaggerate, he says. This is what they do—they try to justify naming other people, justify giving information. And if—*if*—there were cases where pressure was applied, a small number, I was not involved. I was not that man, the clerk. I was barely a man—young. Fifteen. Or sixteen.

Fifteen. Or sixteen. When do people become moral beings, or at least beings with moral capacity?

Twelve for girls, says her aunt. Thirteen for boys. B'nai mitzvah. The rite of moral responsibility.

There is no denying this, though: the linking of Drozd to the affidavit is hearsay, and shaky hearsay at that. They will need something stronger to deport him.

Hearsay—a tale of a tale. *You must not come to tell a story out of another man's mouth.* The rule at a time when seeing was believing, when the hearing was considered more trustworthy, when memory was believed more faithful. *A witness must speak to what hath fallen under his senses.*

But this rule is still here, sitting beside her like a stuffed frog, blinking at her, unmoving. And perhaps still better than accepting borrowed truths, still safer than second-hand realities.

She takes another affidavit out of the box.

. . .

Una bomba, says Isabel, her fine-spun hair a pale mass. Your war crimes case. Here. Or perhaps at the courthouse. The police say they suspect it is a hoax—she pronounces it *hocks*—but still, they take it seriously, they notify the parties, they search the office.

They are milling around on the sidewalk, together with other people from the building, all of them still clutching the things they had been holding when they left. From offices, studios, a gallery, people standing with a croissant, a drafting ruler, an old book in their hands. Some of them are looking at these things in a puzzled way. *Why do I have these scissors?*

We had bombs in Colombia, says Isabel reproachfully, then she looks over her shoulder as if they might have followed her here.

She tightens her grip on Leah's arm.

Why do they think it's a hoax?

They do not say exactly, although they say a hoax is not uncommon. But even so, they take steps.

A trill of fear. Who would do this? The man Drozd, an attempt to disrupt the proceedings? Or perhaps someone who supports him. Or someone who despises him.

Who are these people now, olive green hazard suits, deep-sea divers appearing suddenly on dry land? Climbing out of a truck, helmets bobbing, their faces in shadow behind their visors.

Stay back, they say calmly. Stay back.

They lumber over to the building in their suits, heavy collars up around their faces—people out to search the ocean depths of the office, looking for sea creatures with explosives. But they are brisk for all their calmness, all their bulk.

Stay back.

Nate is there now, his hands cupped around the back of his neck. Louis? she says to him.

Court, says Nate.

He looks sharply at Isabel, who is becoming more agitated. Now she is stroking Leah's arm, over and over.

Let's go for a walk, he says.

How long does it takc to find a bomb?

The trees are leafing out above them, branches arching over the pavement. A fitful sun is out, sifting through all this young greenery, newly alive. Yellow seedlings are littering the sidewalk, last year's dead leaves clogging the gutters. Now they are walking under an umbrella of crabapple blossoms, bark peeling and blistered on the branches, sun glinting though them. Looking up, far up into this light-filled vault, she feels something inside herself expanding, reaching out, spinning through the branches. A brief swell of elation fills her chest, her head.

Look up, she says to Isabel. Look up.

Isabel looks up for a second and then down again.

This city—Leah is often startled by the odd pockets of loveliness it produces out of nothing, out of dirt and cement. These moments when some tired street bursts out into foliage, when a dead-looking hedge produces cascades of white flowers for no reason—some invisible algorithm of weather and season. Why this day, and not that day, this week and not the next? Sometimes she stumbles across a river of pale blue irises where there was nothing a few days before, or a patch of garrulous tulips, an old garage dripping wisteria. They insist on themselves, these things—so simple, so heady—and then disappear as quickly as they come.

Nate has slowed down his strides so that he can talk to Isabel, talking about nothing in a careful, airy voice.

Outside, his bare head makes him look smoother, lighter, all of a piece. Egg-shaped, yes, but harder, a mineral egg, an egg made of ivory, perhaps. Something about this head, this big-boned body makes him seem unusually coherent, defined—as if he had finished becoming who he was at an early age, had completed the shape of his personhood early on.

So different, she thinks, we could belong to different species.

He is unhurried, grounded, she is restless—she twists her dark hair up and then drops it, she crosses and uncrosses her arms, she puts her hands in her pockets, stretches her legs. Sometimes she tries to hold herself still, but this only lasts for a minute. Pins and needles? She was born on them, lives on them, is propelled by them into motion. And one motion flows into the next and the next, a stream of disquiet.

They say that we should watch out for suspicious parcels as well, says Isabel abruptly, stopping and twisting her fingers together. But what does this mean, how will I know, what does this look like—a suspicious parcel?

Her face is distressed. Suddenly, the lives of other people might be in her hands. Or her hands might be blown off.

Nate reaches out to put his arm around her, and she brushes him away.

I thought this was a safe country, she says, her voice accusing, bewildered.

. . .

Safe? No such thing, says her aunt. Who's safe? Not us, anyway. A tribe of people forever gambling on existence.

. . .

More affidavits, more brutal stories, more problems of proof, of evidence.

The office has been declared bomb-free for the moment, and she is making piles of paper, making labels for the piles, changing the piles, changing the labels. She is looking for something solid, something to build a case around. None of this is working, but the stories are slipping out, creeping over the edges of the boxes. The arrested, the tortured, the dead, their accounts recorded by wives, fathers, brothers, cousins, friends. All these stoical people, all these matter-of-fact descriptions. Full of small, shimmering braveries—*If I must give in, I will not do it easily. If I must name people, I will name people who have already been arrested, already dead.*

So personal, so intimate. For the victims, of course, but even for the perpetrators—perhaps shattering bones, inflicting pain, creates not only a physical intimacy but a moral one as well. Or rather an immoral one, but at least a proximity of sorts, a permanent linkage.

The emotion is largely drained from these documents, though, little here in the way of grief or rage. But they are all the more powerful for the missing parts, the unspoken words. *This was agonizing. This was heart-rending. This was unendurable.*

How do they survive it? Are they numb, afterwards, half-paralyzed? Do they strain themselves to the utmost to avoid talking about it? Or do they talk ceaselessly, unable to stop? *Let me tell you about being beaten, about being tortured. Let me tell you about being worked and starved in a slow form of murder, about riding the edge of death for months, years. Let me tell you about losing everyone I ever loved. Everyone. Every single one.*

What does it do to them? Scarred, wary, determined to make sense of their own survival. But how do they manage to live anything resembling a normal life with these nightmares, this anguish buried inside them? How can they stand the feeling of someone else's skin against their own again, to kiss a crying child? Can they possibly have tears left for anyone else?

Tearless. A chronic condition, said Nate when they first began working together. The body begins attacking itself, its own saliva and tear glands. The mouth becomes dryer and dryer, the eyes become dryer and dryer, sometimes blurring.

I can't even cry, he said.

But he said it in a bemused way, as if he wasn't sure whether this was good or bad.

She felt a sudden impulse to touch his eyes, to run her fingers across his eyelids, his lashes.

Now, she thinks: These people. These people inhabiting the affidavits—are they living dry-eyed existences as well? Or perhaps it is the opposite, perhaps they spend hours weeping uncontrollably. Either way, they are turning into spiders in her brain, picking their way around her frontal lobes. Urging her, hectoring her.

Go away, she says to them.

No, they say in a graceful, spidery way.

I'm doing what I can, she says.

Do more, they say.

Law, sleeping in the background, turns over restlessly.

. . .

We're lawyers, says Louis. Not alchemists. We can polish up the facts, frame them differently, show them in the best light. But straw into gold? Impossible.

Lead into gold, she says. She is in his office, sitting across from him.

What?

The alchemists were trying to turn lead into gold. Spinning straw into gold was the miller's daughter in Rumpelstiltskin.

God give me patience, he says, pinching the bridge of his nose.

He means this. Despite his cynicism—or perhaps because of it—he has taken to dropping into a small synagogue from time to time. She wonders if this impulse is the result of that moment when he seemed to have misplaced himself, when he seemed adrift in a world suddenly emptied of substance, only the outlines left. Perhaps this has sent him searching for an anchor of some kind, for additional purchase.

She envies him his careless Jewishness, though—the idea of dipping into it from time to time. The thought that he has so much of it merely sitting there, that he can pick it up or drop it whenever he wants, even waste it. Her own seems much less reliable—sometimes she feels as if she has to hold on to it deliberately, or it might skitter away from her. But she also feels unexpected surges of it once in a while, surges that are almost palpable. A flood of something potent, like a wild sweetness in her veins. I am this. This is me.

Anything else? says Louis. You do have your own office.

Owen, she says. We have to speak to him, alert him to the problems. We have to tell him we need more evidence, better evidence.

No, he says, looking at her sharply. We do the case we're given. Owen is as astute as they come. He is certainly aware of any problems, and the case is enough of a hot potato as it is. Some of the associations—Hungarians, Ukrainians, Russians, Germans—are opposed to these kinds of cases proceeding, and the Jewish groups want them to go ahead. We don't want to present him with a dilemma where anything he does—even nothing—will incur political liability. He needs cover—if we ever want more work from him. And we do.

But we're likely to lose.

Lose? say the spiders, shocked.

He hesitates.

You don't know that, he says finally. Anything is possible. Very few judges will want to see someone walking away from these things. Especially when the end result is only a deportation. But we're not raising it with Owen, at least not yet. So for now, you're going to have to cobble together something that works. Look again. See what you can find. It doesn't have to be a perfect case, a watertight case—just something respectable that gives us a shot. Now get out.

He rubs his face with his hands.

. . .

She needs Nate—where is he? He is a necessity, a requirement, she needs to talk about the case.

This is what they do, and when they do it, they are good at it. When they talk about law, they are nimble, acrobatic, casting up ideas then prodding, poking them for weak spots. He has a more instinctive feel for it than she does; in school, he took to law effortlessly, as if he were rediscovering a dialect he already knew. She had to acquire hers by hand, every piece hard-won.

She had been immersed in an art history degree, engrossed in the painters of *Der Blaue Reiter*, their deep, bright colours, their sensual lines swirling around her. One day she realized—belatedly—that this would not produce a livelihood, not the one she needed, not without more degrees and time than she could afford. She had torn herself away from her courses, miserable about the loss, resentful at her own lack of foresight. Looking around for something that would provide a living, she slid sideways into law.

At first she refused to consider whether she could take any pleasure in it, as if this might be a form of infidelity, faithlessness to her first love. And the law itself irked her.

So clumsy, she had said to Nate. So inept. Blundering around in human lives like that.

He raised an eyebrow.

They had found each other the first week of classes, had detected a possible kinship, standing in line for casebooks.

Not clumsy, he said. Something else. Muscular.

You have to concede this, then—the logic is bizarre.

I concede nothing, he said.

But she found the shift from art to law unnerving. She felt as if she had been exiled from a world of hues and pigments, and sent to a place of flat words, a place from which all the colour had been leached. Banished to some arid country she had no idea even existed.

After a while, though, she began to realize that if she listened closely enough, there was something like a dry song running below the surface of these words, the rolling Latin phrases. And she was tantalized by some parts of it—by the obsession with fairness, with rightness, by the flirtations with morality.

The doctrines lured her in further, each one a piece of reality that had been carved up and tied into a bundle. Ideas exhaling the air of other centuries—the British ones in particular, their cases spreading out to the colonies, to her colony. Even their names had a dusty ring: the Lords of Appeal in Ordinary, Viscount Maugham, Lord Morris of Borth-y-Gest. Eventually she began to come around, first to the point of declaring a ceasefire, and later a partial surrender. And slowly her paintings abandoned her, although pieces of them still bobbed up from time to time—a woman in a dark dress disappearing around a corner, a blue-black fox curled in sleep. Sometimes, in dreams, she found herself inside one of the pictures, part of it—climbing up a Mediterranean hillside, or moving through a formal public garden, people in top hats strolling around her.

I concede nothing.

All of this took longer than it should have, too long. School inched forward, turtle-paced, and then she would be out of money—forced to take a job for a spring term here, a fall term there.

. . .

A thousand dollars, said Rudy.

She looked up, worried. A new debt?

They sat down beside her, around the dining room table, and Gus began fanning out bills, Malcolm looking on unhappily. Six hundred of this was his, a long odds bet on a horse. Vain, selfish, the uncle who had been married and divorced, who had returned a year later. A man with a flair for duping people, but who did it so affably, so kindly, that people almost lined up to be duped. And the horses, the racetrack—one of his haunts. All those possibilities, all those people thin-skinned with eagerness.

Not a man who would give up money easily. But Rudy and Gus had wrestled it out of him, harassing him, nagging him, rattling him until he handed it over, coming up with the other four hundred on their own.

For the school fees, Rudy announced.

She was speechless. How had they done this? They must need the cash for other things.

Yes, said Malcolm.

Never you mind, said Rudy.

These men, she thought. Looking around at them—Gus sheepish but pleased, Rudy grinning, Malcolm's face screwed up, torn between pride and resentment. These men, taught by circumstance to keep their eyes on the ground, the few skimpy prospects they had disappearing over the years—they believed in her illogically, boundlessly.

Something rare, this belief. A windfall. She felt a rush of fondness, she was almost haplessly grateful.

Then Rudy started to waver, to slip to one side in his seat, another faint rolling over him, and she and Gus leaned forward to grab his arms.

. . .

The basement, says Rudy sternly. Now.

After dinner. She had planned to work on the case, read more of the paperwork, but there is no arguing with him.

He is a discarder of things, he is constantly paring down. Left to himself, he would toss out most of the basement contents without a qualm, send bags of it sailing through the air to the curb. But she is a keeper, whenever he attempts to jettison things from the basement—a cracked butter dish, a rocking chair with a broken spoke—she reclaims them, collecting them from the sidewalk, the bin. This is not a game—the loss of these things is genuinely disturbing.

You do it, then, he says. Make some space.

Usually she agrees and then ignores him. Tonight, though, he is insistent, and she realizes the basement would be a welcome distraction from the affidavits, from fractured limbs and bodies.

The room is next to the furnace room, a weak light bulb, green-painted walls, a concrete floor. Quiet, dim, it seems almost underwater, a horde of objects floating in it. The flotsam and jetsam of various lives. Musty suitcases, a cracked butter dish, a hammer with a broken claw, a lamp that no longer works. *What should we do with this rusty birdcage, missing a door? Put it next to the chess set, missing a rook.*

You never know when you might need something, says her aunt.

Yes. You never know. How is it possible to know? Leah is convinced that the lamp can be repaired, that the butter dish can be glued, that the rook will turn up, wedged behind a cushion. That the broken hammer, the birdcage will somehow save the day, some day. And she is right, she is convinced she is right, except that she is beginning to suspect that the timeline for this is longer than she thought. Perhaps the moments when these things might turn out to be valuable are scattered over a decade or two, not this year or next year or the next. In the meantime, though, she is determined to hold on to them, to have them sit here silently in this green dimness, waiting for their hour to arrive.

They are restful, too, these things. She is standing beside the shelves where Gus keeps his tools—old coffee cans full of wrenches, clamps, boxes of finishing nails, bolts and nuts. An incurable fixer, whistling breathy non-tunes as he repairs a step, replaces a window. He has a small stock of skills, but his real virtue is patience, his willingness to keep going when—inevitably—the wood splits, the nail bends. And his tools, so unassuming, so quietly useful. Perhaps some of their restfulness will transfer to her if she stays down here for a while, keeps them company.

Rudy's dog—a golden retriever with a white muzzle, flecks of saliva on her jaws—pads downstairs, sniffs around, and then comes over to rest her old head on Leah's leg, looking mournful. She scratches the dog's ears and watches her rheumy eyes close.

She can hear Malcolm upstairs, his voice comes down clearly. He is usually buoyant after the racetrack, but today he sounds sorry for himself, today he must have lost. Three-year-olds, colts and geldings, he says, disgusted.

Another good reason to stay down here.

He does have his own peculiar form of generosity, not about things—unless they are pried out of him—but about events or circumstances. As if he were distributing possibilities to other people like some kind of modern largesse, doling out prospects. *Here, this set of chances is for you. Look, this possibility, this long shot is for you. Over there, these breaks, these prospects, these are for you and you.*

A mismatched group, these uncles. One day, eight years old, she had looked around and realized that her family was unusual, off-kilter, lacking in certain features. Determined to shape them into something more acceptable, she did her best to impose a parallel order on them, to make them more family-like. There must be two uncles at parent interviews, no more, no less, since her aunt was too exhausted to go. Two uncles at school concerts, two uncles at dance recitals, a set of contrived parents. Why did they tolerate this, her insistence on this regime of twoness? School was a foreign country for Rudy, the rules murky at the best of times, and Gus was accustomed to following her instructions. Malcolm, though, for Malcolm, these were opportunities to practise his spurious geniality, his talent for deception.

Hello there, he would say to a teacher, already flirtatious if the teacher was a woman. If the teacher was a man, he would shake his hand in what he considered a forthright, gruff way. From there, the conversation flowed down a set of known alleyways.

Do you have to do that? she said once when she was older, cross as only a ten-year-old can be. There was something suspect, something crude in these methods that even she could see.

It works, doesn't it? he said, and he was right.

Does a child want to know how easily people can be fooled? Not this child—life was slippery enough already. Parents who had vanished without warning, one after another, without her permission, without her consent. A sleight of hand, disappearing without even a puff of smoke. All too compelling, all too convincing as a lesson in the instability of events.

No more people would disappear, no more people would evaporate into air if she had anything to do with it. She herded these men together on the sidewalk when they walked to the pub for dinner, she counted them incessantly. She pulled them back from crossing against the lights, insisted they hold handrails on stairs.

Isn't that sweet? said a passerby once, but it was deadly serious for her. She knew that she had to exert whatever meagre control she had over events, over circumstances. How much was that? Something unknown, unclear, but she was determined to do what she could, what was possible. She knew one thing with a hectic certainty, one thing in an almost tangible way: fate could not be trusted for a minute.

Now, she looks around for something she can throw out, something to pacify Rudy. The dented flour sifter? The broken guitar? Something catches her eye—over there, a box. Her aunt's box, sent over after she died. Something she poured over at the time, something she hasn't opened for years.

She reaches over, pulls it out.

Inside, on top, a small portfolio. Her mother's photographs. She begins leafing through them, tiny shocks of recognition.

A sleepy baby, a crawler gumming a key chain. A skinny four-year-old drinking from a hose, a tricycle-rider, head down, intent with effort of peddling. What was her mother thinking about when she took this picture, caught this moment? What did she mean by this shot, what was she saying? But these pictures are not talking, they offer no hints to the photographer.

Then a picture of an older woman—a mesh of lines around her kind eyes, greying ginger-brown hair—looking out steadily. The colours are strong—a wine-coloured blouse, a yellow wall behind her—but her face is so alive that it dominates the picture, her expression a mixture, warm, melancholy, sardonic.

She feels her chest ache, she holds the picture close to her, trying not to bend it.

I miss you, she says.

I know, says her aunt sadly.

But for her, Rudy would be tempted to toss this picture, the first thing to go. *The aunt,* they called her with particular emphasis, this tart-tongued woman with so much to say. Enumerating their child-rearing failings, a catalogue. *A sleeping bag is not a blanket. A swimsuit is not a gym suit. A bowl of cereal is not dinner.* They would listen to her silently, without response, sometimes glancing at Leah reproachfully, as if she had betrayed them.

Too many shadows, though, living in these photographs, waiting below the surface. The small darkroom, the trays of chemicals for developing the pictures, a drying line. The sound of her mother humming under her breath as she dipped the negatives into one bath after another, the black tongs, the burnt match smell of the fixer. So absorbed, she would only come to with a start when the girl began howling or hopping up and down.

Then she would stand with the child in front of her, both of them looking at the pictures pinned up on a line. A slender, springy woman, large eyes, short dark hair, a lilt to the way she moved, the way she talked. Running her hands up over the girl's forehead, sweeping the hair back from her face, over and over. A girl who looked like her, a small edition, gawkier but still alike. *More Rubin than Jarvis,* she would say. And then she would go back to humming.

Fiddle dee dee, fiddle dee dee, the fly has married the bumblebee.

A photograph of her father holding her, a serious toddler. This father, smiling uncertainly, this figment of a person. So few traces of him, this man, greedy for unknown things, for experiences beyond his reach—just out of the picture frame. This Andrew Jarvis.

What did you find? she says to him. Was it worth it?

What did I have to lose? he says.

She studies the picture again, familiar, but not familiar. Were there any signs of a future departure in his clothes, in his hair? Was there anything about him that suggested a man about to bolt? *I'm sorry.*

More photos of the child—does she seem content, this three-year-old in overalls, standing against the front of a sofa, one arm up along the cushions? Does this naked toddler, jumping over a sprinkler in the sun, look happy? They are strangers, though, even a glimpse of their thoughts or feelings hard to see—they simply *are,* existing in these moments on paper. Small beings fixed in an instant.

And her mother—if she had lived, what kind of photographer would she be now? Someone who took bold, startling shots? Someone who created subtle images, enigmas for the viewer to unravel? Searching for the eye of the beholder.

Underneath the portfolio are other documents—school reports, a lifeguard certificate, an old library card, a full-length birth certificate. *Full name of father: Andrew Gregory Jarvis. Full name of mother: Miriam Rubin Jarvis. Female child born alive at 2:30 a.m.* And here, the motor vehicle accident report, yellowed and brittle now. How many times had she been over this spare, cryptic document, looking for clues?

Date of Accident: Unknown. Discovered October 14, 1978. Coroner's office estimates accident occurred a day earlier, based on state of driver's body.

Cause of Accident: Vehicle left the road, impact with a large tree.

Location of Accident: 4th Line and Side Road 15.

Damage to Vehicle(s), If Any: Extensive—see circled areas on chart.

Injuries to Person(s), If Any: Female driver killed on impact or died shortly after, child diagnosed with fractured femur.

Witnesses: None.

Other Notes: Reason why vehicle left the road unconfirmed. Driver's blood alcohol content over the limit, allowing for alcohol from decomposition. Child found dehydrated, strapped into back seat.

The basement around her trembles.

Loud, she thinks, the only thought she has time for.

A din of crashing, splitting, falling, disintegrating. The noise is everywhere, she is lost in it. The car begins settling in jerks, each one with its own sounds. In a few minutes, the settling stops, and there is only snapping and creaking. Eventually this subsides as well, and a soft, chilly darkness sinks in. She can smell gasoline, dead vegetation. Blood on the grass, bushes, the metal door, twisted sideways. Only a few shards of glass left in the window beside her. Her leg and side are hurting, an enormous, dull pain. The seat next to her is covered in sour vomit. After a while, a long while, the only sound is the soggy drumming of the rain.

Then the basement, the bare bulb is back, and she can feel the report in her hands.

. . .

Jews don't drink, says her aunt.

Manifestly untrue, but a grain—half a grain—of fact.

Then they drink less. Something to do with the genes, less tolerance.

Gus has an inarticulate spasm when she asks him about it.

She liked the sauce, he admits reluctantly. But she wasn't a drunk.

4th Line and Side Road 15?

The two of you were up at someone's cottage, he says. You don't remember?

No.

Was that why her father left? The sauce. Perhaps he was unable to handle it. Perhaps he was a drinker himself. Or did her mother begin drinking because her husband left? If she was a drinker.

I don't know, says Gus, appalled by all this talking.

. . .

Andrew Gregory Jarvis. This is what she knows about him—he is unfindable. He is an absence, this is his category, his fundamental trait. Missing. Not even an enigma, too insubstantial for that. Not much more than a rumour.

Gone. Untraceable. As a child, she had accepted this unquestioningly, as she had accepted the existence of gravity, of air. Later, in a new century, a century of online searches, she had plugged his name in half-heartedly, quickly deterred by the number of results. And unable to shake the rooted belief that this was futile, that he could not be found.

What would she do with him if she did find him? she thinks now. If he were no longer missing. How would this shift the sticky configurations in her life, how would it change her understanding of things, her pacts with reality?

Perhaps it would be a good thing, though, something to shake up all those moving parts. A small streak of chaos. Perhaps this is the moment for at least a glimpse of him.

Over to her desk. In a minute, there it is, unblinking on the screen—a list of Andrew Jarvises, a small paternal collection.

And now?

. . .

What kind of bomb do you think it will be? Nate says conversationally. A pipe bomb? A suitcase bomb? Simple enough to make one, to look it up. Saltpetre and charcoal.

How handy for the bomb-inclined, she says, but her stomach is twisting. She can see this bomb, this explosion far too clearly. A deafening boom, the walls staggering, the ceiling starting to collapse. Screams of terror, of pain. Clouds of grey-black dust swelling around her, filling her nose, her throat. Then silence.

Perhaps she should begin dropping into a synagogue as well.

But she is a rickety agnostic, an incurable doubter—unsure even about that. The idea of a god—the sense of a god—is tempting, even elating. A clue that opens up the possibility of some existential pattern, even a logic of sorts. But as soon as she begins to feel a longing for this, a hunger for transcendence, as soon as she feels some internal balance start to shift even slightly, she is assailed by a sense of implausibility, by an analytical twitch.

Doubt wisely, says Donne.

I'm surprised about Louis, says Nate. If ever there was a confirmed cynic.

Perhaps he grew up with it. Perhaps old habits are dying hard.

Not the habits of her childhood, though, one that featured a complete absence of creed. This was not a matter of conviction, but a lack of interest so absolute as to be dead air. Her uncles had forgotten about religion, and simply kept on forgetting.

And her aunt—quarrelling with her own God, despite her efforts to fill the girl with a certain strain of Jewishness. Her faith in this God was an irritable one—*I have my reasons, believe me.* Instead, she attempted to infuse the girl with a specific way of being, to envelop her in its stories, its smells and tastes. She taught her songs about goats or old wars, they ate grated horseradish, parsley sloshed in salt water. She showed her how to make walnut bread in round loaves, they struggled to put together a burlap hut, her aunt cursing fluently. Seders with Marvin and Ida—the neighbours—around a plate with an egg marked with black smoke and a shank bone. Dipping their fingers in syrupy wine to mark the plagues with dark red drops. (All ten—happy now?)

Baruch etah Adonai, Eloheinu melech haolam. Even the blessings she learned seemed more like chants rather than prayers. Strangely beautiful in their own way, whole things in themselves, but she was only dimly aware that they were related to some kind of deity. They had sunk into her anyway, into her ribs, her sternum—ancient ribbons of song flowing through her.

But she is godless now, now when it might be useful, even practical, to have an omnipotent guardian. Now with a bomb threat grinning at her, only a foot or two between them.

. . .

Pick a pile, she says to Nate the next day, still surrounded by the pieces of the case. He is standing in the doorway to her office, and his body seems suddenly intensely present. She has to resist the urge to touch his shoulder, run her fingers down his spine, up the back of his neck.

Not my case, he says stiffly.

What? This is not how they do it, this is not how they work. Is that resentment in his voice? Or perhaps something more complicated. Had he wanted this case?

He is a generous rival, but still a rival. He juggles these things with casual skill, and when—inevitably—they come into conflict, he simply shrugs with wry amusement. Every so often, though, she sees a glimpse of his ambition, a spike of ruthlessness.

Where does it come from? Some primeval instinct? His father? But his father is a cheese maker, he makes hard cheeses, soft cheeses, blue cheeses wrapped in chestnut leaves, sheep's milk cheeses rubbed with rosemary.

Imagine. A father. A father and a cheese maker.

Quaint, she says.

No, says Nate. A highly technical operation. The mixture of milks, the introduction of bacteria, the heating to precise temperatures. Then the curing, the aging.

Would someone immersed in this small, exact world instill such drive in his son?

But perhaps Nate had wanted the case for its own sake, lured by the history running through it, the idea of some overdue redress.

Go ahead, take it. For a moment, she is tempted to say this—the stories are so haunting, but the evidence is so full of holes. Not only shaky hearsay, but double hearsay, anonymous hearsay, vague statements, missing archival records.

The benefits of losing the motion. Too late now.

But even as the words are almost out of her mouth, she thinks: *no*. No, she won't—she can't—give this case away, disturbing as it is. No, this case has attached itself to her now, she is stuck with it. This case fits her in a way that few of her others do.

Sometimes she feels the various parts of herself are crowded into this job, packed in together. She avoids showing any trace of this to Louis, though. For him, she tries to make it clear—in the way she nods, the way she speaks, the way she holds herself—that she is remarkably suited to this position, that if she were plotted out against a diagram of its elements, she would be revealed as the answer for everything.

Unlikely, says Louis.

He will take more convincing now.

. . .

How long have you been with the Ministry? she says, hoping to distract him.

Owen is calling to find out how the case is going, for a measure of its chances. He is a client, of course she must speak to him. She is tempted for a moment to refer him to Louis, but he will be angry if she shifts this problem back to him, this exercise in tactful evasion. Perhaps even worse, it might suggest that she is unable to handle it, to engage in the footwork required. No, instead, she will be as skilful, as careful as she can be, exceptionally careful. This is only an update, nothing more, no questions on her part, no bids for more evidence, no dilemmas presented. Some small talk, then a quick discussion, circling around the danger spots.

With the government? he says. A long time, too long, but I've been in the Department of Justice four years. My last department was Fisheries.

And did you catch much there? she says, straight-faced.

Only a bout of bureaucratic flu.

She laughs.

So why did you decide to send this case out? she says. Instead of using your own lawyers.

We have excellent people, but we're short-handed. Secondments, a chronic illness, two leaves of absence. And these things can be delicate.

Is that the flu coming on again?

He laughs this time, a discreet laugh.

Perhaps. But with the Director on leave, I'm keeping an eye on things for the moment, so tell me about this case.

We may not be able to link Drozd to the NKVD through records alone, she says. He wasn't an officer, he was a clerk, hired locally.

Ah, he says.

Certainly the NKVD were involved in widespread torture and executions. It would be difficult to dispute that. The problem is that they did ordinary police work as well, so even if we could show that he was hired by them, that wouldn't prove much.

Can we connect him to the incidents in the affidavits? he says.

A man expert at omissions himself, he can spot them instantly. And *incidents*—such a sanitized word.

Much less clear, she says. We only need to prove that he lied, but this is the essence of his lying—that he concealed these things. Or failed to disclose them.

What about linking him to more widespread killing? The War Crimes Section seems convinced that there is something more to find. They suspect something even worse—that he was involved in other crimes, perhaps executions, perhaps on a larger scale.

I haven't seen anything yet, but I'll keep looking, she says. What do you think about his age?

We have only his word for it—his documents were all re-created, not unusual after the war. But no one was coercing him, he was nobody's victim. And sixteen is not so young. Especially in Belarus. Especially at that time.

Not so young, she thinks. How young is that? And is there a moral discount for age, some sliding measure?

So our chances overall? he says patiently

He is very patient, she realizes, smoothing out any irritation, any annoyance he feels. She sees him in her mind as they talk, his narrow face, the dark lines around his mouth, slight hollows under his cheekbones. The trace of humour that he extends to people, vanishing in a second if there is no hint of reciprocation, expanding slightly if there is. Everything about him is finely tuned to the next meeting, the next appointment; his muted suit, his tie loosened but not loose, his shoes polished but not new. If there is any self-importance to him—and she suspects there is—he hides it well, he hides everything well. Was this ability to obscure things acquired through his work, built up over the years? Or was he given the position because it was something he already possessed? Perhaps someone interviewing candidates looked at that calm, sealed exterior and said to himself: *perfect.*

Our chances? A complicated question, she says, so many factors involved.

What are the strengths, the weaknesses, then?

She talks as much as she can about anything other than the evidence, skipping, deflecting, sidestepping.

What about linking the specific incidents to him? he says again.

There is no putting him off.

Generally speaking, she says, almost under her breath, almost to herself—generally speaking, without the right records, we need better evidence.

Ah, he says.

He does know.

How bad is it? he says.

Difficult to say.

A pause.

We used archival evidence in the Nazi cases, he says, but the Germans were much better at documenting things, including their own crimes. The Russians are less accommodating about the NKVD records, which are far from complete, anyway. No help from Belarus—their records are still closed. And there's some diplomatic sensitivity here as well.

She says nothing.

I suspect that the appetite may be low for pouring more money into a weak case. But we have an MP who's preoccupied with the NKVD—he has a cluster of expatriate Russians in his riding. He's been harassing the Minister, so I'll take a quick reading of the temperature.

. . .

Why is the sun so hot? she said. So recently arrived, hoping to keep her aunt by the bed, to delay the moment of turning off the lights, the moment of darkness, departure.

Do I look like an encyclopedia? said her aunt.

The child was undeterred. All she had to do was find the right question. Where does the music on the radio come from? What makes cars go faster? How do birds stay up in the air?

How do you think? said her aunt.

Invisible strings?

Close enough.

The girl had been hoping for some instructions about flying, some tips. She had plans—she wanted to fly herself, to take off, weightless, to soar over the trees, to perch on electrical wires. She wanted to watch from above as drivers hopped out of delivery vans, horns honked below, bicycles swerved between cars.

Even now, even as an adult, the desire to fly sometimes nags at her, the urge to swoop and glide, to hang in the air dizzily, unhindered by machinery. She wonders whether there was a time when humans were able to fly, some long-forgotten detour or dead end in evolution. Did we lose this, she thinks, like flightless birds? Are there small, vestigial wings hidden in our bodies somewhere? Why would this yearning for flight be so strong, so widespread? Why is it so bittersweet?

. . .

This is the truth about glass, she says to Nate. It has the molecular properties of both a solid and liquid, something in between. An amorphous solid, they call it.

Why is that the truth? says Nate.

. . .

She has read most of the affidavits now and they all have weaknesses, serious problems of proof. For the moment, she is out of ideas. Perhaps if she leaves the case alone for a day or two, lets it settle, some silt will drift to the bottom, some wisdom will float to the top, something will emerge.

But the spiders are awake again, making elegant gestures with their legs.

No, no, they say. No, no, no. Don't give up.

Don't give up, says her aunt.

I'm not giving up, I'm letting it settle. A different thing, entirely different. But there is something I have to tell you, something you should know. A caution, a warning. Whatever it is that you want to happen, whatever it is you think will happen, this is the distorted universe of law. A garbled reflection of real life. The chances are that nobody finds what they want here.

But the spiders are not listening.

. . .

She rubs her sandy eyes. Up late the night before, she had allowed herself to sink into her Der Blaue Reiter painters again, to become her old self for a little while in their soothing arms. Her friends, these paintings—sunlit terraces, men rowing skiffs, people in the rain, holding umbrellas high. Now her thoughts seem to be sliding away from her, the warmth of the room making her sleepy. She puts her head down on her desk.

I did my best with Owen, she says to Nate. I did my best with him, but he's too quick, too shrewd, there was too little room to manoeuvre. At a certain point, I began sounding evasive.

But Nate is not there, he has been replaced by the judge on the case, busy unnailing a crate of doctrines and principles. See that? he says, pulling out a doctrine. See that? A robust vintage, this doctrine. A perfectly aged law.

And then he is gone as well, and there is Drozd, staring at her with hatred in his eyes.

Why are you obsessed with this case? he says. What is wrong with you that you want to persecute an innocent man? To destroy a life, a life I have created from nothing, from less than nothing.

It's not a question of persecution, she wants to say. It's a question of justice. But her tongue has folded up.

What is this justice, what does it look like? Whose justice is it? How can it be justice, if I am innocent of these things?

How can we know that you're innocent unless we hear the evidence? she says thickly. *Nemo debet esse judex in propria sua causa.* No man can be a judge in his own cause.

Because I tell you so.

But a guilty man would say the same.

Lawyers. I am sick of lawyers.

She says nothing.

You want to tear down a decent man, Drozd says. A man who survived the war as well as he could, who did what was necessary, and now you want to impose some twisted view of justice decades later. You have no idea what justice is, what it means in reality. You want to destroy a good man, on the basis of nothing. Nothing.

That's your story, she says.

. . .

Under Norman law, says Nate, if a person wrongly called someone a "manslayer," he was required to pay damages and to publicly confess that he was a liar, while he held his nose with his fingers.

No, she says in disbelief.

It's true. But if you prefer this, under ancient English law, a slanderer would have his tongue cut out.

. . .

Get in here, says Louis, dangerously calm.

Before you say anything— she begins.

You're fired, he says.

FOUR

For that which is without a beginning, a final cause need not be sought.
MAIMONIDES, *THE GUIDE FOR THE PERPLEXED*

The weather is harsh, the winter long, a dusty cold. He grows slowly, his body stunted, almost night-blind from malnutrition, although his mind is sharpened by the ever-present fear. By ten, he has learned how to avoid some of the blows, to dodge and duck and hide. Curled up inside the fear, though, something is growing, something bitter is filling his chest. And then his hard world begins expanding awkwardly, in small jolts.

Jolt. Piles of beets, eggs, garlic, radishes, pickled cabbage, handwoven shawls. He fingers the wrinkled sausages, entranced, before the seller shoos him away. The market is crowded, people pushing past him, blocking his path, their bundles knocking against him. He runs a furtive hand over the shawls as he passes by another stall. The smells—sheep hides, seed bread, bunches of dried thyme strung up on a line.

Men in rough linen shirts, girls in kerchiefs, mothers with red-faced babies, the babies wailing in the clear air. More people here than he has ever seen together before. He is overwhelmed by them, almost reaching out to feel the dark hair of a child, shining in the sun, to touch the skin of her older sister, so close to him.

While his father is haggling with another farmer over the price of barley seed, the boy wanders from stall to stall. At the end of the line of stalls, a girl—fifteen, sixteen?—has set out a collection of things on a blanket on the ground: bunches of onions, a bowl of eggs, some mismatched dishes, old lace curtains, a wool vest. She has a broad brow, dry lips, a chipped tooth, fair hair falling in a tangle across her face. A baby is crawling around her, over her in the sun, pulling at the front of her blouse.

Here, she says to the boy, gesturing towards the blanket. Bring your mother to buy. Bring your father.

The baby begins pawing at the onions, tries to put one in his mouth.

No, no, no, says the girl, laughing, pulling it out of the baby's fingers. He begins to howl, and she sighs, picks him up, and tucks him firmly in the crook of her arm. Then she brings out a small white breast, and the baby settles down to nurse. Her body relaxes, the baby relaxes, asleep in a minute.

The boy is mesmerized by this breast, by the tracing of blue veins, the fawn-pink nipple lodged in the baby's mouth. The girl catches his eye, smiles at him, showing her chipped tooth, and shrugs.

Pick something out, boy, she says.

But he has no money. He tries on a sneer, and walks away.

A fragment of music. Three people standing together, playing a ragged melody. The piping is reedy, underlined by the jangling of the timbrel. One of them gestures to the pile of kopecks on the ground in front of them, and he backs away.

A burst of laughter from a group of young men, slapping each other on the back, their shirts belted with rope. He draws closer to hear what they are saying.

We have a mouse with big ears, says one of the young men, reaching out to the boy and shaking the back of his neck. The boy is so startled he almost bites him, but jumps back instead, and they laugh again.

Jolt. A few months later, the river. Black water surging around, clear sheets of it sliding off rocks, the light reflecting across them. He wades in, barely keeping a foothold, clinging to a rock to avoid being swept away.

There, says his father. That one. And that one.

The boy struggles to lift a stone, then to wade back, fighting the drag of the chilly water. He is almost at the bank when he drops it. His father swears. Back he goes for another one, his small chest heaving. He manages to push this one onto the grass, and his father loads it into the cart. Another and then another, black rocks speckled with grey, they will use them to shore up the crumbling foundations of the barn. Stones worn smooth by the river. How long does it take for water—the softest of things—to shape stone, the hardest of things?

Half an hour later, he is exhausted. A last trip, he slips and the current seizes him, rushes him away, his legs, his body scraping against the rocks. Panicking, he splashes wildly, trying to keep his head from going under.

A rotten log, sticking out of the water a few yards downstream. He grabs at one of the branch stubs and manages to hold on. Hand over hand, stub over stub, he pulls himself over to the bank.

On the way home in the cart, he is shivering, dripping, his sides, his legs bruised. But his head is piercingly clear. For the first time, he thinks: this river goes somewhere, somewhere else. Past other farms, yes, he knows this, but somewhere else. More places. Other places. A water road.

Jolt. Sunday morning. His grandmother combs out her grey hair and rebraids it, wrapping the braids around her head. Next her blouse embroidered in red and black, a shawl, her best head scarf. She rubs her lips and surveys herself in the black-spotted mirror, satisfied.

Backward superstition, says the government. The stupefaction of the working class.

But these services are comforting, elemental—the chanting, the singing, the candles. A familiar solace.

His father usually drives her to the wooden chapel—bleary-eyed, cursing, his head aching from *samahon.* This morning, he rolls over in the iron bed and says: *the rat can do it, he's big enough to handle the horse.*

The boy is indignant, he handles the horse every day, putting on and taking off the collar, the girth strap, attaching the cart shafts, leading it out to the field to spread muck. But he is still small and skinny, and the horse is a draft horse, heavy—driving the cart requires more strength, strength and weight. Hovering in the background, too—their suspicion that if the horse doesn't take off, out of control, the boy might.

Where can he go? says his father to his grandmother today, his throbbing head wiping out everything else.

The horse is balky, but the boy understands that this is a battle he must win. He jerks the animal's head back with the reins, wrestling it for control, whipping it over the flanks and neck until it settles down to sullen obedience.

Twenty minutes later, they are at the chapel—a small building, painted white, the three-barred cross on top.

Inside, she says.

She doesn't trust him to wait, she doesn't trust him to return for her. And it will do him good.

The smell of stale incense envelops him as he steps inside. In the dim light, he can see the icons on the wall, the altar covered with brocaded cloth. His grandmother crosses herself, bows, and motions him to do the same. A quick nod to some of the other congregants, and then she waves him over to the men's side while she joins the women. They stand for the service, no pews or benches—only a man with a lame leg has a chair.

The others are singing already, a hymn, low, haunting. People drift in, light a candle, move over to stand in position. Then the singing stops—some signal given, received—and the priest emerges, inclining his head with its cylindrical hat. His voice sonorous, he starts the liturgy. Now and then, he fingers the silver cross on his chest.

The boy is mystified by the words, but he watches the others closely and mimics them as they chant, as they sing, as they cross themselves again and again. The procession starts, the painted chalice held up, some of the people kissing the hem of the priest's cassock. Not his grandmother, though, so he stays where he is. But then he follows her to line up for a piece of wine-soaked bread. Some of the others look at him questioningly, but his grandmother waves him forward.

The next Sunday, the same, and the next, and then it is every Sunday. Now he is accustomed to it—proud of mastering the horse, knowing the rituals. And soon he has learned the order of the liturgy, the hymns, the epistle, the creed, the calls and responses. *Lord have mercy. To you, O Lord. Alleluia. Alleluia. Alleluia.*

You like the service, boy?

The priest is at his elbow as he waits for his grandmother after the prayers—she is talking to a neighbour, a thin woman with a withered face. Standing together, they look like two dried barley stalks.

You like the liturgy?

The boy nods.

I see you following it, the priest says, combing his fingers through his beard.

In a minute, a bargain: he will be an altar boy, he will help with the services, wash the floor every week, clean the candelabra, scythe the grass in the small cemetery, anything else the church needs. And what will he get in return?

This is an honour, says the priest, scandalized.

The boy has seen the prayer books in a corner of the chapel. No one uses them; either they are unable to read or they have the prayers and hymns lodged in their memories. The boy has an inkling, though, a shadow of an idea that these marks, these scratches on a page could be useful. That they might even provide a means of escape.

I want to learn to read the prayer books.

The priest is startled, then pleased.

. . .

In the months that follow, the priest is kind enough towards him—he can spot a starved boy when he sees one—and gives him tea, bread and lard, sometimes even a glass of kvass. A man younger than he looks, etched with frustration, his longing to do great works, his devotion to holiness, all derailed with the denunciation of the Church. Exiled to this barren patch, he provides services to several of these small chapels, his vision slowly curdling inside him. But teaching this boy, he feels a faint echo of his original calling.

The boy's grandmother is wary, she is not convinced the boy has a grain of genuine piety. But the priest is the priest, a man with the grace of God in him, someone who should know. And the distinction of having her grandson singled out is gratifying. His father has no opinion, drunk most of the time now, hair matted, glassy-eyed, not enough in him to go after the boy, except to curse him and demand more work.

The boy tries hard to dull their suspicions, to induce at least a lack of curiosity. What is it they need, what will soften them up, or if not soften them—impossible—at least distract them? Food.

. . .

How long has the rabbit been here, in the growing dusk? A few hours, a day? Frozen with fear, long ears back, attempting to flatten itself against the ground. The grey-brown fur has been rubbed off its foreleg by the wire snare. He looks more closely at the bloody leg and realizes that the rabbit has been biting it with its incisors, a desperate attempt to free itself.

He makes the snares from wire, rusty scraps he finds at the sides of the fields or roads. Nooses that grow tighter with every struggling movement of the animal. He sets them out on the narrow paths left by the rabbits, the grass beaten down by their paws, using loose underbrush to block the ways around them.

He looks in the grass now, feeling for a rock. Here, a good-sized one, he hefts it in his hand. A strange exhilaration comes over him—as always—anticipating the impact, when the animal stops struggling, when its eyes glaze over. Now. He grabs the rabbit's neck and smashes the stone down on its skull. Immediately he is flooded by a sense of relief, an easing of the tautness, the hardness in his body.

Rabbit, his father says scornfully.

Meat is meat, says his grandmother.

. . .

The priest—wickery, mild, mournful. A weakness for Saint John of Kronstadt and sacramental *kagor* wine.

See, he says, pointing out the letters. Ah. Beh. Vey. Geh. Deh. Yeh. Yo.

The boy rubs his eyes in frustration, the words seem sealed into the page. And they are in Russian, not Belarusian. *Blessed be the Lord my strength, which teacheth my hands to war, and my fingers to fight.* He is fiercely determined, though, clinging to the idea that deciphering these markings is a key to something, desperate to believe that there is a way out of this deadening life.

It will become easier, says the priest.

His expression is a mixture of wistfulness and something like greed. But he is patient with the boy, working through the verses slowly. And once in a while, he gives him a kopeck from a small pouch he wears beneath his cassock.

At night, under his thin blanket, the Cyrillic letters swim in the boy's head, almost taunting him. *Ah. Beh. Vey. Geh. Deh. Yeh. Yo. It will become easier.*

. . .

Get up, screams his father. You miserable piece of goat dung. You are trying to read? You are too stupid. You will never learn to read. And what good is it, anyway?

Thwack. The board hits him on the back, on his legs. The boy tries to scramble away, but his father grabs him.

Who do you think you are? Goat dung. Pig dung. You think you can make yourself better than that?

Thwack.

Stop it, says his grandmother. Stop it.

She stands in front of his father and slaps him, hard enough to leave his cheek reddened, his mouth gaping open in surprise, the boy gaping, too.

The priest has chosen him, the priest has decided to teach him. That is enough.

The makeshift lessons go on.

At eleven, he begins growing so quickly, so intensely that it makes him weak sometimes, as if his strength, his energy, were being siphoned off for this purpose. His body is unfamiliar territory now, he is often surprised by his own large hands—nails split and dirty, palms calloused. Perhaps it is the rabbit—he keeps some of them for himself, skinning them and roasting them over small fires, often burning his fingers or his tongue as he pulls the meat off the bones, gulps it down. Then his growth stops as suddenly as it began, leaving him tall enough, but slope-shouldered, still thin.

The priest is becoming more gloomy, more mired in the vinegary ruin of his hopes. The boy's youth tantalizes him, gnaws at him. He paces restlessly, he prostrates himself, he reads by the hour, absently pulling hairs from his beard. He mutters parts of psalms, his eyes blank.

My wounds grow foul and fester because of my foolishness, I am utterly bowed down and prostrate; all the day I go about mourning. For my loins are filled with burning, and there is no soundness in my flesh. I am utterly spent and crushed; I groan because of the tumult of my heart.

The boy can feel his eyes on him as he goes about his chores, as he empties the censer, sweeps the altar, cleans the icons with vodka and water. He knows all of them now, these icons, he knows every crack, every stain. Solemn-faced Saint Efrosinia with her small, pursed mouth, descendant of Vseslav the Sorcerer, holding her two-barred jewelled cross, her hand raised in blessing. Pale-skinned Archangel Michael, framed by his grey wings. Saint Cyril, eyes morose, a book under one arm. The paintings are coated with linseed varnish, and the priest has shown him how to wipe the candle soot and dirt off—very carefully—with a rag and the vodka mixture.

One day he finds the priest holding up his hands as if they were unfamiliar, as if they belonged to someone else. He bangs them against the wall, and then clutches his head, moaning, swaying, berating himself, a stream of condemnation, muttered prayers for absolution. There is something almost sly in his despair, though, as if he sees other failures ahead.

At other times, he is unnaturally elated, fingering his cross. *Purge me with hyssop, and I shall be clean. Wash me, and I shall be whiter than snow. Fill me with joy and gladness; let the bones which Thou hast broken rejoice.*

The boy moves around him cautiously, warily. But this man is his link to a larger world, to unimaginable places. Places the priest has been, has seen—Minsk, the monastery in Grodno, Mogilev, the St. Sophia Cathedral in Polotsk.

A godless place, Minsk, says the priest.

Just as well, thinks the boy.

In that moment, he decides on Minsk, this is where he is going. Sooner or later, one way or another, he will get there. If he has to walk all the way, if he has to crawl, he will get there, away from this wretched existence. In Minsk, he will eat until he is sated, he will wear clean clothes, he will have a paid job, even a girl—warm-skinned, sleek-haired, breath like wild fennel—a girl eager to please. He hungers after these last things as much as he does the food, the thoughts of them drumming in his head.

At night he dreams about the food, though, hard dreams, about sitting down at a table loaded with thick stew, hunks of caraway bread and butter, buckwheat and blood sausage, soft white cheese. The food so close he can smell it, his mouth filled with saliva. But when he starts to eat, the food dries up, shrivels before his eyes until all that is left is a handful of stones and husks.

There is no rabbit meat in these dreams, no rabbit and mushroom stew, no rabbit sausages, no haunches of roasted rabbit. He is sick of the gamey meat, of skinning them, gutting them, cracking their joints. But it is better than hunger, better than the weasel gnawing in his stomach, and now it helps to mollify his grandmother.

. . .

Summer. He is fifteen. The flax fields are smudged with pale blue, the cart bumps and rattles along the rutted road. In the distance, plumes of smoke curl where a farmer is boiling milk.

He finds the priest asleep in the little room at the back of the chapel, his hair dishevelled, a glass with the dregs of sacramental wine beside him. His cassock has been pushed to one side, and he sees the small pouch.

Now, he thinks. Now.

Quietly, very quietly, he picks up the knife they use for the communion bread, edges towards the bed. The priest snorts suddenly, mumbles something, and the boy jumps back.

He waits until the man is still again, until his stertorous breathing is even, then he edges over once more. The thin leather strap holding the pouch is tougher than he thought, and he saws at it frantically. The priest stirs, starts to roll over, but one last slash and the boy has the pouch.

In a second, he is out the door, as the priest begins to sit up, holding his head groggily.

He jumps into the cart, and begins whipping the horse up. The horse rears, and then lunges forward.

The last thing he sees is the priest, staggering into the doorway, his mouth open as the boy drives past.

The drumming in his head now is so loud he can barely think. Minsk. Minsk. Minsk. Minsk.

FIVE

Better wit than wealth.
JEWISH PROVERB

A top spinning on its point, around and around, a whirling blur. A dreidel out of season. Now wobbling, teetering for an impossible moment, then falling, clattering onto the table.

She picks it up, spins it again. And again and again and again.

She is still stunned by the suddenness of her firing, disoriented by the loss of her cases, the clients—the files halted mid-work, the half-finished thoughts, the half-framed pleadings all cut off instantly. The loss of her ongoing loop of talk with Nate, the familiarity of its rhythms. She misses it all. She even misses Louis, as if the person who had done this was a different entity, a manic spirit that had taken hold of him when his back was turned and then released him almost as quickly.

A sense of uselessness hovers over her, so easily redundant. Her cases? Perhaps without her around, they are having a raucous party—plaintiffs, defendants rising off the pages of their files, mingling together, brushing up against each other, their causes of action rumpled, their pleadings slurred.

What did you do? says Gus, alarmed. They are sitting around the table, and he has his gouty foot up on a chair, an ice pack wrapped around it. The dog is lying underneath the chair, having elderly dreams of chasing something, every so often her legs jerking.

Nothing. Nothing that would explain this.

There must have been something, says Rudy. He is boiling herbs to make a tonic, and the kitchen smells like stewed grass. Consumed by his health at the best of times—the fainting has seen to that—he has a shelf full of herbs and remedies. Something that she discovered as a child, taking out the small jars and bottles, running her fingers over them, reciting their names as if these alone might have some power—milk thistle, cat's claw, gotu kola.

Now she realizes that Gus and Rudy are clinging to the idea that she is in the wrong, that she must have committed some lawyerly blunder, not because they think she is so careless, but because it would mean she could put it right. Without blame on her part, there is no solution. Only Malcolm is on her side, shameless Malcolm, someone who has been fired himself more than once. Secretly pleased she has joined these ranks, by the small vindication it offers him.

Not her fault, he says, pouring rye into a glass, circling the ice in it.

The others turn to glare at him. What does he know? Nothing, nothing at all.

Malcolm—always a liability, she thinks wryly.

Was he like Malcolm? she asked Gus once.

Who?

My father.

Gus looked as if he was about to strangle on his own tongue.

Maybe a little.

Now, as she looks around at them, she wants to say: *you don't understand.* But she doesn't understand herself. She sees the outlines of it, the overall shape—the conversation with Louis, the conversation with Owen—but the harshness of his response is still mystifying.

And if none of them understand, they all know this: they need her income. She has gone from being an unclaimed child, discarded by another life, to a source of support. The legacies of Gus and Malcolm—the house is swamped in liens and mortgages, several times they have come close to a forced sale.

Gus, inept, his half-baked schemes producing only debts, fretful creditors, writs of execution. And Malcolm? Always an erratic source of income, often contributing nothing, and now he is in a prolonged dry spell, his targets becoming less credulous. Too many skeptics, he says, as if this were a failing—a crisis of faith on the part of the easily fooled. His strategy is to generate a certain fondness for each of his marks in turn, offering them warmth, respect, solace—whatever his keen eye has seen they need, whatever they crave most. This fondness—half-genuine—means he almost admires their self-preservation, despite the effect on his money supply.

Rudy, though, Rudy is an illustrator, making elegant drawings for medical textbooks—blue lungs branched like root systems, unnaturally lustrous organs, sinews flowing down arms and legs. A good income once, but the field has overtaken him.

It's all software now, he says.

No longer the same need for his fine pen nibs and coloured inks, his ability to draw a true line, the precision of his shading. Now he wrestles with pixels and vectors, mourning the loss of something he could touch with his flat fingertips, reduced to working part-time.

The mortgages, he thinks, a few days later, sitting up stiffly from waxing the kitchen floor, folding his cloth over.

The mortgages, thinks Gus, hammering a stake into the earth.

The mortgages, thinks Malcolm, looking up from the racing results.

All the thoughts circulating through the house, winding around chairs, under tables, over counters, up the staircase—all these thoughts have become one thought: *the mortgages.*

She is in the kitchen, peeling blood oranges to make a salad, something to do, to make herself feel useful. The recipe is from Nate, and Rudy has already turned up his nose at it. Showy, this salad—the oranges, the torn red lettuce, the green-yellow of the avocados—but the dressing has walnut oil and coriander and she is not convinced that it will taste good. This is a recipe that does not require the oven, though—a finicky old gas hulk, the pilot light lit with a match. She pares the bitter pith off the orange segments, then cuts them away from their membranes. Fussy, time-consuming—this is why I don't cook, she thinks—but then she remembers that time is something she has now in abundance, that she is surrounded by large quantities of time, lying in piles around her. So much time, it is merciless; if she had any more it might bury her, minutes, hours, days closing over her head. She bites into an orange piece absently, the tart-sweet juice filling her mouth.

Next the avocado—scraping out the flesh, chopping it into cubes, running her tongue over the knife afterwards. Then the dressing—grating the rind off a lime, adding honey, vinegar, salt, the walnut oil and coriander, shaking it up. She smells it, looks at it doubtfully, thinking about their mouths becoming dry and puckered. Gus, walking by the kitchen, a caulking tube in hand, sees her there and stops, surprised. More than surprised, disturbed that she is doing something as unusual as making food, that it has come to this—further evidence of disarray.

And she is in disarray, no doubt about it, certain assumptions—unknown even to herself before this—in shambles. That she is not the kind of person who gets fired. That Louis is not the kind of person who fires people, at least with so little cause. That the supply of fairness in the world is larger than this.

But perhaps fairness really is a scarce commodity, she thinks. She has never been under the illusion that it was widespread, but perhaps it is even scarcer than she thought. A finite quantity, rare as mineral dust. Tiny amounts, sprinkled here and there, and between them, a shortage, a fairness wasteland.

Still, no matter how wary she is, how little she expects, it never seems to be little enough to avoid being blindsided. And all her efforts to control the shape of things, to negotiate with happenstance—to appease it, to distract it, to deceive it—seem futile.

Ah, says Drozd.

You cannot possibly think these situations are comparable, she says. Even you could not be so deluded.

She shakes her head, attempting to shake him out of it. Go and bother someone else, she thinks.

A breathing space, says Nate. Enjoy it.

Advice he would be wholly incapable of following himself.

He has been nonplussed by her firing, too, although he tries to avoid any sign of it.

Dolce far niente, he says, something he picked up from an Italian cookbook. The sweetness of doing nothing.

Nothing. He thinks she should be revelling in this absence of routine, the lack of any need for getting up, for suiting up. At least for the moment, for a few days, she should be enjoying the idleness of it all, the release from the sheer effort of working. But she is not sure she is able to do this. *Dolce far niente*. Perhaps she will have to move to Italy as well—this nothingness might come more easily living in some sleepy town with white houses, clay tile roofs, eating bread and figs in the sun. Perhaps she will have to trade this piece of her life for one belonging to someone else.

. . .

She is watching him, watching his narrow house. This edition of Andrew Jarvis, the first one on the list. Sitting in the café across the street, she has become a lurker, an observer, someone waiting.

Or a stalker, she thinks ruefully.

Of course, she should knock on his door, introduce herself, behave in some suitable way. But this would be a morass of a conversation, one she is still far from sure she wants to have. Why did you leave? Why did you stay away? Who are you? Who am I to you? If anything.

Perhaps these questions are unanswerable, anyway.

Then why is she here? Some fitful, uneasy curiosity? Some impulse to complete an outline of herself? Or is she merely thumbing through a catalogue of possible lives, looking for one with a father in it for the purposes of comparison?

. . .

Show yourself, she says to him. She has been there for almost an hour and she is restless. It has never occurred to her how extraordinarily patient a shadower, a stalker has to be.

And then suddenly he is there, walking out the front door. Just like that.

He is not the right age, though. This is not him. This is a man in his twenties, blond stubble on his jaw, stocky. A son? A visitor? At least stalkers know who their quarry is.

But this man seems unlikely to be even a relative. The wrong shape to the face, the wrong colouring, all wrong, no trace of the man in the photograph. Not impossible—a son could have inherited other looks—but less likely.

There he goes, setting off down the sidewalk.

She is half-relieved, half-disappointed, spared—or deprived—for the moment.

But there are others, others to find, to watch.

The rest of the list, sitting in her pocket, turns into a handful of gravel.

. . .

That evening. Gus is working in the garden, a faded green shirt, a bulbous nose, a cigarette behind his ear. His domain, a place where he rules supreme—Rudy and Malcolm have no interest in it. Although he is a negligent ruler, absent-minded, ignoring it for weeks while leaves shrivel, vines begin choking other plants. Then he goes out, trowel in hand, and submerges himself in it for an hour or two, cutting back creepers, tying up monkshood, watering it all with a leaky hose. Surprisingly, flowers emerge from this neglect—tough flowers, like hellebore, stonecrop, phlox.

The evening light is lingering now, spring well on its way. She starts to weed in a desultory way near where Gus is working.

Here, in this place, he is someone else—a seeder, a buncher, a lopper, bringing unlikely beauty into being, at least for a day or two, a week or two. She often helps him like this, has worked beside him from her first week in the house, digging in the loamy soil with a spoon. A refuge for her, a child of the city, or at least its lower levels—urns filled with cigarette butts, newspaper boxes with scrawls on their windows, cats crouching underneath parked cars. As a six-year-old, she filled up teacups with water and dirt, while he spread mulch or dug bone meal into the earth. Once, she caught him looking at her speculatively, as if he were wondering whether she might need an application of bone meal as well.

At the moment, this place is a tangle of bleached grass, the dried skeletons of last year's plants, patches of yellow trout lilies, windflowers migrating across the ground in untidy blue swaths. One of the vines has overtaken the fence, climbing up a pole to the overhead wires, winding along them, sending out runners hanging down—a towering green curtain.

They work in silence for a few minutes in the amber light, the earth on her hands smelling like iron, like leaf mould. A starling is calling *seet, seet* from a tree.

A breathing space. A pause in an unbroken line of jobs and school, scarcely a gap in all that time. Could this be a respite of sorts, a temporary truce with her own chronology?

No. She simply feels stranded, adrift. A breathing space, yes, but an unnecessary one. An unwanted one.

Although she must remember—must keep firmly in mind—that her job was not without its problems.

You're going to have to cobble together something that works.

Did he doubt her ability to do this, was there more than one reason he fired her? But what did he expect? That she would be able to fix all the gaps in the case, produce some new doctrine that would take care of its weaknesses? *The doctrine of insufficient evidence. The rule of shaky inferences. The principle of close enough.*

This case, she had said to Nate the week before. All these people—teachers, journalists, peasants, the torture, the killings. So many of them Jewish.

Not the ever-popular chosen people, he said.

I really do need a second opinion, another set of eyes.

An hour, he said, relenting. I can give you an hour.

He started in on the box, pulling out documents, skimming rapidly, intense, absorbed. From time to time he passed his hand over his bare head—a habit, as if he were looking for his hair. The hour elongated, then stretched into two, three while she worked on other cases.

Finally, he shoved a document back into the box, grimacing.

Not strong enough? she said.

Not nearly strong enough. If the rest of it is like what I've seen. Not nearly strong enough, even on the balance of probabilities.

The balance of probabilities. The legal test in the case, at least at this level, at this stage of the proceedings. A soupy test, not *beyond a reasonable doubt,* but a lower threshold. Which side, which claim was more likely to be true? Which claim was more probable than not? An attempt to round up disorderly facts, to organize the intuitions of judges.

It reminds her of one of Gus's schemes, though. *The balance of probabilities.* She imagines him stacking up a number of probabilities, making a teetering pile of them. Then adding more, one by one, until some point, the precise point, the balance point. Right before the pile falls over.

Now, she thinks: perhaps I'm better off without these cases, without this case.

No, no, say the spiders, aghast. Don't say that.

Two women are carrying on a conversation in the garden a few houses over, and one of them laughs, a brittle laugh. The light is fading now, dusk is beginning to gather.

One consolation: if she is off this case, she is less likely to be killed by a bomb. This thought not as cheering as it might be, though, since the others are still on the case, still in the building.

Nate rubbing his head, Louis and his books, Isabel holding up her hands—her refuge now something of an illusion.

She hears a small rustle and looks up. A tortoiseshell cat, an interloper, is picking its way around the snowdrops. It sniffs disdainfully at a clump of them, keeps on prowling. Then it jumps onto the garden chair and turns its head towards her for a second, and she has a glimpse of brilliant yellow eyes.

She stands up from where she is weeding, stretches, and begins wandering around, pulling up some twitchgrass, some seed husks turned to paper. A sulphur butterfly lights on a twig and pauses, moving its damp wings.

Has Rudy said anything? says Gus abruptly, his thick fingers hooked in the pruners.

About what?

Nothing, he says quickly. A bit of news, that's all.

News? Rudy never has news. Malcolm, yes—usually another scam. Listen to this, he says, as he describes his latest plan just this side of the law, or so he hopes, without caring enough to find out. Fireproof, he says. Gus, yes, occasionally he has news, another bankruptcy, reported unwillingly, his face shut down. Rudy, no.

What news? she says, reaching for the trowel.

I'll let him tell you.

There is no point in pushing him, he is as stubborn as paint.

She yanks a weed out viciously, taking a crocus with it.

A shout—a child in the distance—and in one silky motion the cat leaps onto the fence and disappears on the other side, its ginger-and-brown tail the last to vanish.

She turns to go inside, rubbing her hands together to brush off the coarse dirt.

The sweetness of doing nothing. On the way in, she kicks over a garden chair.

. . .

They grind the poppy seeds until they are powdery, then add the butter, vanilla, honey, eggs. This is the filling for the dough, a floury lump on the cutting board. The girl is sitting next to it on the counter, kicking her heels, once in a while poking at it tentatively.

Outside, the day is dark and wet, the rain coming down in grey needles, but the kitchen is warm with light, all the brighter against the gloom of the windows.

Purim. The Festival of Lots.

Lots? says the girl, shaking her head of dark curls.

Haman drew lots—sticks—to decide which day to kill the Jews of Persia, says her aunt.

Haman? says the girl.

The vizier to King Ahasuerus. Now whirl your *grager* to blot out his name.

The girl whirls her noisemaker, delighted by the clamour, by this idea that a name—a person?—could be wiped out by noise.

Her aunt puts her hands over her ears, and then sits down heavily, holding her lower back.

Some advice for free, she says. Don't get into a fight with your kidneys.

Why? says the six-year-old.

They're bandits, says her aunt.

She takes a sip of cold coffee and stands up again, pulling a rolling pin out of a drawer. She dusts the cutting board with flour and then scoops up the ball of dough, flattens it onto the board. Now she is rolling it, first one way, then another, the dough spreading out as she gently pulls it and rolls, pinches it and rolls, pats it and rolls.

Here, she says to the girl, handing her a drinking glass. Cut out some circles.

This is harder than it looks, not all the edges separate cleanly enough—*press harder*—and a few end up stretched and torn as the child tries to pull the scraps around them free. But soon they have twenty-three circles, and they add a spoonful of poppyseed filling to each one, folding the sides up into a triangle shape. *Hamantaschen*. Into the oven, set the timer.

When they're done, we'll take some over to Marvin and Ida.

Now they wash the dishes, the girl standing on a footstool, hands in the soapy water, an apron wrapped several times around her small body. Then the drying with the dishtowel, the wiping of the counter and waiting, as the kitchen slowly fills up with the spicy-brown smell of the baking.

Why did he want to kill the Jews? says the girl. Haman.

Who knows?

Did he kill them? All of them?

Does it look like it? says her aunt, gesturing to the two of them with the dishtowel. We had Esther. She outwitted Haman—whirl your *grager*. She talked the king into protecting the Jews. She was a real talker.

She opens the oven door to check the edges of the *hamantaschen,* letting out a cloud of fragrant heat.

That Esther, she says. She was something.

Why did he want to kill the Jews? says the girl again, eating a shred of raw dough. Can he kill us?

She is starting to sound alarmed, her face is screwed up a little.

No, no, you're safe now. Nobody can kill you now.

Where is Esther? says the girl, thinking that it would be good to know, just in case.

Long gone, says the aunt. But you're still safe.

The girl looks at her doubtfully.

The timer dings.

. . .

Apologize, says Nate.

They are sitting up on the bluffs, white sandstone cliffs beside the lake, three hundred feet high. *Danger: Bluffs unstable*, says the sign, the chalky walls prone to rockslides. But they are sitting back from the edge, they are drinking wine and eating cantaloupe wrapped in prosciutto. *A necessary precaution, says Nate. If it was up to you, we would be eating soda crackers.*

The sun is low in the sky, a sky made soft and smoky by pollution. A horizon full of pink-gold light, towers of clouds reaching towards the atmosphere. Farther down, the sun has laid a watery path across the middle of the lake, a path that seems to lead right into the sun itself. Not Der Blaue Reiter, she thinks idly. Something neoclassical. Maybe August Becker.

He really does seem to feel betrayed, says Nate, so an apology might help. And maybe this has been a cooling off period.

Who would have guessed that someone so self-possessed, so confident, would be so sensitive? she says. Does he seem cooler now?

No, he admits. He seems irritable.

He had another one of those misplaced moments, he adds, almost casually. He looked like he was dropped into the wrong spot without any warning.

They have avoided talking about this much, they want him—they need him—to be intact, undamaged, in good working order. They cannot afford to have him lose his place, cannot afford to think that these are anything more than momentary lapses—the symptoms of a low-grade fever perhaps, or a particularly rough flu. Symptoms that will disappear as quickly as they began. Twice now, though—this is not a good sign, this is difficult to ignore.

Could it be some kind of concussion? she says.

They consider this, ticking through what they know: he doesn't play sports, he has said nothing about an injury, nothing about a fall, an accident.

Not much of a silent sufferer, either, says Nate—we would have heard about it if he had been hit somehow.

The only thing likely to hit him is a book, she says. For a second, she can see his books falling from their shelves, raining down around him, his arms raised to ward off the blows.

The symptoms: almost none. No sweating, no paralysis, no sagging on one side of the face. Whatever this is, these moments when time seems to abandon him, it must be a quiet condition.

Even now, though, they avoid talking about other possibilities, more lethal problems of the mind. Tumours hiding among white fibres. Aneurisms ballooning out of artery walls. Things that might cause dislocation, confusion, that might turn memory into lace. No, too early to be talking—even thinking—about them. Only two incidents.

Although these are only the ones they know about, the ones that they have seen.

Do you think his wife knows? says Nate.

Carla—effervescent, her red hair a constant surprise, her fingers stained with oil paints. But this is more than high spirits, this effervescence is a strategy; she uses it to shape the atmosphere around her, to keep it at a breezy tone and pitch. Alert to small shifts in Louis's moods, she would have noticed something like this. Although only if one of these moments had occurred when she was around.

Would he have told her? she says.

No, they both think.

She takes another piece of cantaloupe, the taste of the melon, the salty, fatty ham together in her mouth.

Another possibility, something even more disturbing. The possibility that Louis is not the problem, that some gap in his grey matter has opened up a rare view of things. A view of sudden shifts in existence that are truly occurring, some fluidity normally hidden from sight.

Einstein, she says to Nate. He argued that the distinction between past, present, and future was only a stubborn illusion.

Well, I'm in favour of it, anyway, says Nate.

She swallows some wine.

What about that apology? he says.

She will need to work up to it, or perhaps work her way down to it. Even the idea produces a spurt of uncomfortable pride. Perhaps this was her problem, she had not been deferential enough.

The cloud towers are drifting into mauve and grey ribbons, edges glowing from the sinking sun.

Nate is talking about another one of his cases, a man who tried to rob small stores using unusual weapons—a lamp, a vase, a broom.

They gave him money because he was waving around a lamp? she says. Perhaps I should see what I can do with a toaster.

He was also six foot four and yelling.

Your NKVD case is going forward, too, he adds, giving her a quick glance.

She straightens up.

Owen says the new deputy minister is more interested in the case. They really think there's more to it. And the same MP is still harassing the Minister. Although they don't want to pay for another lawyer to get up to speed, so this might be the moment to go in and grovel to Louis.

She realizes that Nate has neglected to tell them that he had been through part of the file as well, and she feels a rush of fondness towards him, unexpected, unwelcome. Without any warning at all, he seems suddenly—startlingly—endearing.

Nate, she says to herself. Remember who this is. Remember that he is missing some of the ingredients of humanship. Remember that his moments of kindness can be quickly extinguished by that ticking ambition.

He is already too many things to her. A foothold—his rubbery sarcasm. A thought process—that nimble mind. A critic, even a stern critic, mostly of others, sometimes of himself or her. Exasperating, disarming.

But these are known quantities—habits of his, things that are familiar. Things she has even adopted, not as her own, rather as shared operations, joint labours. Adding anything else into this mix—especially something unpredictable—would be a form of lunacy. This is a man who bounds along the surface of his life, who avoids getting wet at all costs.

Although perhaps he is becoming better at this business of being a person. She looks at his eyes now, greyish-blue, clever, warm. The colour of iron, of rain. And he can be utterly disarming, a brother-in-arms.

No. This is not something to pursue, or even to acknowledge. This is something to be ignored, to be kept at a distance. She is simply at loose ends, her emotions scrambled by the firing, she is deluding herself.

This is nothing, anyway. A humming, a surge of bass notes. Something that can be pushed aside.

He gestures towards the bottle of wine in her hand, and she pours some into his glass, watching him as he leans back and takes a swallow, his throat exposed. She feels an urge to stroke his windpipe, to trace the lines of his collarbone. *The bone most frequently broken,* Rudy said once—he reads the text that goes with his illustrations. *No need for it to be hit dead on—it can be broken by falling on a shoulder, a hand, the impact travelling back.*

Ignore this. Stifle this.

Why?

Because she knows him, he is too fitful, too haphazard with people—they swim in and out of his focus. Because it might ruin their friendship, even their working relationship—if they ever have one again. Because he is entirely plausible, entirely convincing, until the ruthless side of him turns up, like a prankster of some kind. Even then, it seems like an aberration, an exception, too easy to explain away. Until the next time.

All good reasons. Very good reasons.

This is nothing, anyway.

. . .

She wakes up suddenly, her mind still crowded with pieces of dreams. She tries to catch hold of them, to hang on to them, but they evaporate too quickly, vanishing around corners before she can see what they are. This makes her feel a little lost, as if these scraps are small parts of herself that are disappearing—strange, fine parts that are too fleeting to survive.

But Nate's breath is on her shoulder, his warmth beside her—he seems unusually real, even in his sleep the pores on his skin, his shoulder muscles stand out. Perhaps she can borrow pieces of his dreams, perhaps they are hardier than hers, less likely to dissolve so quickly. How will she know if they are worth borrowing, though? What if they are bad dreams, what if they are ugly, threadbare?

She rolls over.

No. His dreams would be like him. Last night—a dry sweetness in the palms of his hands, his fingertips, his lips—something that seemed to expand, to rise and fall. His eyes hazy, as he touched and stroked her skin, exploring the hollows and bones of her body, sliding between her legs. Then his face twisted with urgency, as he pushed himself inside her, as she clutched his back, so many sensations at once, all exquisitely different, the rhythm of his movements making her gasp and arch.

Afterwards, she fell asleep suddenly, dropping into a quiet stream of darkness.

And now?

She looks around. His place is crowded with things, even the air seems full—traces of his cooking, garlic, blackened peppers. He is a collector, an accumulator of odds and ends—objects, clues, beliefs. A sepia photograph of elderly twins. A figurine of three mice riding a giant white radish. A quirky theory of combustion.

Look, he will say, showing her a wind-up ostrich stalking around in a circle.

She has wondered—even before this—if she is part of this collection, lurching around on wind-up feet. But she swipes away the thought each time. If it isn't entirely untrue, it is untrue enough.

And now, she thinks, now for the hazards. The possibility that this delicate, tentative web between them will evaporate, that they will stumble over unlovely things about each other, that they will fall down holes of yearning and misunderstanding. That they will find quarrelling more appealing, more satisfying than peace. That there will be a host of injuries, large and small.

But these things seem remote now, at a great distance. Instead, she is filled with a soft euphoria, she is saturated with him, with a curious delight in him.

Nate, she says to herself again, to remind herself. *Nate.*

But he has already become someone else.

Perhaps she can get a clearer image, not of him, but of this thing between them instead, its edges, its furrows and folds. Something distinctive, unmistakable, spelled out by their arms and legs.

But this, too, is formless, this tender fog, impossible to grasp. If she waits awhile, it will take on shape, its contours will be revealed. In the meantime, its shapelessness is tranquil, mesmerizing.

. . .

Surely her exile will not be permanent. Surely Louis is trying to teach her a lesson. Of course he will relent.

No sign of it, says Nate wearily. He has spoken to Louis again, urging him to reconsider. *We need the help. She knows the cases.*

Isabel tried, too, says Nate. She cornered him in his office, and gave him hell in that withering Spanish accent.

This is a foolish thing. You know yourself this is wrong.

Louis is adamant, though, unmoved.

Why? Leah says.

I have to be able to trust the people I work with.

Trust. An unruly thing, changing shape from moment to moment. Always a risk to trust some person, some circumstance. A necessary bet, though. Otherwise, paralysis would set in—people unable to take another step without some assurance that the ground would not collapse.

But trust doesn't require mindless obedience, she says. Trust doesn't require docility—if anything, a failing in a lawyer. Law is too tricky, too many-sided for that. Even trust is too tricky for that.

You're fired, he says again.

Owen. Is it possible he might intervene on her behalf, might explain that he had put her on the spot? But asking him would be dangerous, might only stir up the situation further. And why would he intervene, this man who is an expert non-combatant? A man who is above all cautious—only ever engaged to the extent he can retreat.

I underestimated how quick he is, she says to Nate. I admit it. And my attempts to sidestep the issue—not very adept. Perhaps his conclusions suited me. Perhaps Louis has some reason for being annoyed. But this?

From Louis, a man normally so hard-headed, says Nate. Self-satisfied, yes, but not a martinet.

More than that, she says, thinking of his flickers of warmth.

A four-year-old at the office one weekend, running up and down the hall, windmilling his arms, shouting gleefully. Louis scoops him up and begins singing to him, a children's ditty, his voice surprisingly musical, the child quieting down. He turns around and sees her, and stops singing abruptly.

He has his moments, says Nate cautiously.

Do you think this is another sign of some brain problem, some neural slipperiness? she says.

Possibly. Or maybe you hit a sensitive spot. A valuable client, too, a source of future cases.

Or perhaps he is more of a dictator than I thought. Maybe I'm better off without him, she says.

But she doesn't really believe that.

. . .

Her mother is humming again, so faintly as to be almost imperceptible. *Fiddle dee dee, fiddle dee dee, the fly has married the bumblebee.*

. . .

A job, this is her goal now. No more *dolce far niente.* But this is a daunting proposition without a reference. She needs an explanation for this event that is wholly inexplicable, something she can offer a potential employer.

We had a difference of opinion. Insubordinate, they will think.

We had a misunderstanding. Stupid, they will think.

I made a mistake. It must have been serious.

I did nothing wrong. She sounds like a client.

He was a difficult person. She sounds petulant.

No one will want a junior who might sidestep directions.

Why not start your own firm? says Malcolm, so pleased to have her in the ranks of the fired that he is full of useless ideas.

It takes too long, she says. Too long to build up a client list, too long to produce an income.

Could she evade the questions, claim to have done something untraceable for the last year—a lengthy trip? Ah, lies, there they are again, but she is without the desperate circumstances of her clients to justify them. And she has almost a physical distaste for lying herself, real lies, that is, not white lies. Something growing up with Malcolm had instilled, watching his lies ricochet around them.

She has nothing like his knack, his skill with them, either. A lie like this would call for agility, for practice. Deceit is a muscle as much as a skill, she thinks, something that requires strengthening, maintenance. And a good lie needs commitment—to vigilance, to consistency, to specific details, to auxiliary lies. Things even Malcolm was often too lazy to provide.

But perhaps her reluctance to lie is only a form of squeamishness. Maybe she is indulging a sense of integrity at the expense of her uncles, an income, she thinks. Is this really a matter of her concerns about virtue, about doing right? Or is it possible her preoccupation with the idea of *doing right* is part of a bribe, a bribe to luck? Does she secretly think that if she promises to be good—whatever that might be—this will ward off any strokes of random disaster? A modern form of superstition. Or a form of moral protection money.

Then she realizes that lying about a trip is not possible in any event. Too many lawyers, potential employers have seen her in court over the last year, with Louis and without him.

There are other jobs, though, other lines of work. Perhaps she can get a position in something else. But part of her rebels at the thought. So unwilling to come to terms with law at first, she is reluctant to abandon it now. And people, potential employers would be puzzled, so many of them impressed—in spite of themselves—by law. Why would someone abandon this, they will think—had she been expelled, even disbarred?

If there are some people who are impressed by law, she thinks, there are others who are fascinated by it. No matter how many laws there are, they want more, and no amount will satisfy them, will relieve the craving. They are addicted, they want laws about everything—sexual acts in ravines, purple loosestrife in marshes, bulk spices. About barking dogs, about keeping rats, about where the cremated ashes of dead people can be scattered. They are intoxicated by the extraordinary trick of power that law offers, the possibility of changing the constellation of things, of changing the results.

She is startled to find that she is becoming one of them.

. . .

The strings, she says, as her aunt pulls the bedcovers over her small body, turns on the night light. The ones holding up the birds. What happens if they break? Do the birds fall out of the sky? Or do they float on air?

Flying, floating, falling, says her aunt. You think those are the only possibilities?

. . .

Val, small, round-faced, quiet as milk, rooting through the kitchen cupboards for tea. She is everywhere, smelling of light sweat and talcum powder. Soothing, a little white moon of a person. A voice faintly husked by smoking, she begins doing some of the cooking, baked apples, leek and potato soup, custard pie, food as quiet as she is. So mild a person, so innocuous, but threatening to break apart this small sphere of existence.

Leah has had her suspicions, she has seen the signs in Gus—the minute upgrades in grooming, a new razor, a polished belt buckle, a different soap.

Don't leave.

I might not get another chance.

They would never say things like this, this is not the way they talk to each other. This is not the way Gus talks to anyone, but she has learned to avoid any unnecessary words with him. The result? Their conversations take place in a mute language that runs under the surface, a language full of stale repetitions.

Don't leave.

This might be my only chance.

Is he really thinking about it?

They all think about it sometimes. About separating themselves from this mismatch of people, marooned together by inertia, by a lack of money, by doubts about what else might be possible. More than that—by all the unseen filaments that grow between people, slowly, silently over the years, whether they want them to or not.

The rules of affinity and consanguinity, says Nate.

So far these thoughts of leaving have usually amounted only to half-formed calculations, vague daydreams—nothing as concrete as an announcement, a departure. At least not since Malcolm came back, *decree nisi* in hand. But Gus is the most likely defector now—the most presentable, the most apt to be liked or adopted by other people. He has friends, too, the bowling team, the pub.

Don't leave.

Val's cooking is certainly an improvement, she has to admit this, even though she is still resentful. *You can't buy Gus with food,* she wants to say to her. But perhaps she can. Even she herself has a hard time resisting—she eats a piece of shortbread irritably, annoyed at her lack of self-restraint.

Be fair, she says to herself. Be objective. Isn't Gus entitled to this?

No. Maybe. But who gets what they are entitled to, anyway?

Be smart, then. Be patient. These things have blown over before. Give her a chance, she means well.

Or perhaps she is taking advantage of his burly good nature, trying to wriggle her small moon self into this counterfeit family.

She's turning him into a spaniel, says Malcolm.

Jealous, he is strongly of the view that if anyone should have a girlfriend, it should be him, the man who even had a wife at one point. But he is such a blend of sincerity and deception, he loses people as quickly as he attracts them. A day trader in people, a speculator in human beings—not someone who can sustain even a friendship.

Isn't she something? Gus says, surprised into talking.

Yes, says Rudy, who almost flirts with her himself in his own rusty way.

But Gus leaving would be a disaster. She tries to be glad on his behalf, but feels only dismay.

Of course, she has thought about leaving herself, of course she has. This is the expected thing, the usual thing—children grow up and leave. Although perhaps these are children who are not charged with ensuring certain people will not vanish, who are not involved in a loss prevention operation with respect to particular human beings.

What about that guy? says Gus silently.

What about him? Wiry hair, blunt as a bone. Off to the International Court in The Hague, a prestigious internship. A man who needed no decoding, no solving—an easy, knowable person.

So easy that even this break—announced calmly—seemed easy, instinctive at the time. Together for seven months, gone now for three months, she has occasional moments of achiness. She tries to keep him locked away in a vault in her psyche, but even there, he is mouldering gently, producing odourless gases that seep through once in a while.

But if leaving is a possibility for her at some point, that *some point* is not now. Not this cluttered present. Not this moment in time—or the next, or the next—when a change like that would open up lines of contingency, lines of random circumstances. Things that might lead anywhere, that might land anywhere.

The doctrine of foreseeability. A man jumps onto a train leaving the station, boosted by a railway worker. He drops a package of fireworks, which then explodes, causing a coin-operated weigh scale to fall over and hit a woman standing on the platform. The woman sues the railway in tort and wins twice in the lower courts, then loses on appeal. There was no negligence in law because the railway worker could not have foreseen these events. Negligence in the abstract is surely not a tort, says Chief Justice Cardozo, if indeed it is understandable at all.

I know this is none of my business, she starts to say to Gus.

That's right, says Gus.

. . .

An apology. Apologizing to Louis would be a lie as well, but this is her lie to have, something private, about her own thoughts. Thoughts so crowded, so fleeting that anything might be almost true for a moment. And she feels entitled to this kind of lie, although she is not sure why. But how many apologies are entirely truthful?

I'm sorry, she says to the mirror, pushing out the words with an effort.

Too tepid. She will have to sound more convincing.

I'm sorry. I apologize. Wholeheartedly. It won't happen again.

Wholeheartedly?

Thoroughly. Thoroughly sorry. I truly regret this.

Does she? She certainly regrets the loss of her job. And apologies are peculiar creatures—many-headed, many-footed. *We regret to say*. Widespread now, everywhere, for small sins, sweeping injustices, for tiny blunders, vast tragedies. A massive traffic in remorse.

This idea that mere words can heal or repair something—where does it come from? That a ritual of speech can have such an effect. An appealing thought for a lawyer—a person who gambles everything on the power of language.

Drozd. What if he had expressed regret, had admitted his wrongdoing? She is becoming convinced of his guilt, his complicity. As flawed as the affidavits are, together they have a persuasive mass. What if he had apologized at some point, a genuine expression of repentance? Even if he were capable of this, what would be the effect? Would the dead bodies of people be transformed, skin growing back over their skeletons? Would their crumbling torsos begin solidifying, filling in with organs, nerves regenerating? Would the lives they would have lived reconstitute themselves backwards, like a living jigsaw puzzle?

No. Some things cannot be erased. Some things cannot be undone.

There is nothing to undo, says Drozd bitterly. You have no idea what it was like, what it took to survive.

Go away.

If undoing is not possible, if history cannot be turned inside out, an apology might still be useful, might still be a form of consolation. Although her own apology would be merely a gesture, a means to an end, something to pacify Louis.

I'm sorry, she says, studying her face, ensuring that she looks solemn, that no flicker of her eyes, no quiver of her mouth betrays her.

I apologize. I was wrong. It won't happen again. You can trust me. Your wish will be my command. Anything you say, goes. You two-faced autocrat.

No, no, I mean, I'm sorry. I apologize. You—

Just get it over with, says Nate.

. . .

The mortgages clear their throats.

. . .

Two women at a cafe, one with a pear and ice, the other with a ginger beer float. The woman with the float drinks some of it, but when she pours more ginger beer over the ice cream, a dead snail spills out of the bottle. She claims damages for gastroenteritis and shock. She wins in the lower court, loses on appeal, then wins again finally on appeal. The court rules that the ginger beer manufacturer owed a duty of care to the ultimate consumer. I do not think so ill of our jurisprudence as to suppose that its principles are remote from the claims of a civilized society upon its members, says Lord Atkin.

. . .

Not now, says Rudy.

He is brushing the dog, her tawny coat. He pulls the hair out of the brush, rolls it into a ball, then pushes the reluctant dog around so that he can do the other side, her toenails scratching the floor.

Now, says Leah.

It's nothing.

Now.

Just my arteries. Just a little problem with my arteries.

And? she says.

Clogged, they're clogged. And the cholesterol, the blood pressure—too high. Could have a stroke. Or a heart attack. Have to take some pills, watch the fat. Maybe take a few walks.

A stroke. Or a heart attack. She feels an unpleasant shift at the base of her spine.

It's nothing, he says again.

This from the man who takes gingko, she says half-heartedly.

Rudy, aging furtively—afraid that any admission, any recognition of it will make it more real, more concrete. Or will hasten its progress. There has been no hint of mortality before this, though, no sense of anything serious. Yes, he is passionate about his herbs, each one imbued with benefits, curative powers that he believes in utterly for a while, until his zeal begins to slowly deflate, until it collapses altogether, and he shifts his attention to some other remedy. But these remedies are for minor things—to lubricate his joints, to enrich his bloodstream, to cleanse his glands.

Maybe take a few walks. He is a driver, a driver's driver, someone who can devoutly summon up statistics on mileage, horsepower, torque, acceleration. He drives everywhere, even to the park several blocks away, letting the dog run around barking at sparrows until she is tired and then driving her home. The dark blue car is as old as the dog, shock absorbers worn out, metal body rusted through in spots. He sands the holes, fills them with putty and paints them, mixing the paint to match the colour exactly—camouflage—only to have the putty fall out again a month later. Often they have to jump-start it, she and Gus pushing it down a slope in the street while Rudy steers, the car stuttering over and over until the engine coughs and catches—each time a moment of small triumph.

All of this is not because he is particularly fond of the old machine, they owe each other nothing at this point. If he had any money, he would buy something newer, sleeker. He does the bodywork because he is afraid of being pulled over and sent for a vehicle inspection, an inspection the car will surely fail.

She watches him now, making quick, nervous strokes with the brush over the flaps of the dog's ears, her feathered legs, her golden flanks. Even in her old age, this dog is gravely beautiful, in the animal-like way denied to people. Rudy is brushing too hard, though, and she twists and turns to get away, and then lies down in silent resistance, one paw over her white muzzle while he concentrates fiercely on her plumed tail.

Suddenly, she has the urge to touch Rudy's arm, to reassure him. But she knows this would be a mistake—he would flinch irritably, and move out of reach.

. . .

Keep an eye on him, she says to Malcolm. Let me know if you see a problem, if you see anything different.

She is worried about Rudy, worried that something might happen to him while she is out of the house, that his heart might seize up, that he might be staggering around, dizzy, nauseated, while she is off buying eggplants or looking for grout. Or going to work—soon, she hopes.

Malcolm snorts.

I mean it, she says.

Why me?

Because you live here.

Gus lives here, too.

She doesn't say: *but you don't care enough to lie to me.*

. . .

One, two, three, says her mother, pointing to each candle flickering on the cake.

One, two, three, says the girl, kneeling on her chair.

She watches the candles for a few seconds—they are beginning to melt, small beads of wax running down to the icing.

Don't wait too long, says her father.

She puffs up her cheeks, her chin determined, then blows, the flames wavering under her breath.

Presents, says her father.

From her mother: a simple game, fingerpaints, gumdrops.

From her father: a clutch of helium balloons, hovering under the ceiling, trailing ribbons.

She is timid, reverent among these riches.

Come outside, he says.

He shows her how to take a balloon, to hold it by the curling ribbon, to make a wish.

A wish? What is a wish?

Something you want.

But at this moment, this instant, she has everything she can possibly imagine.

I'll wish, then, says her father. Now let it go.

They watch the balloon soar up into the atmosphere, shimmering in the sun until it becomes a tiny dot in the sky. Now she is amazed, her eyes round, hands outstretched for another balloon.

Her mother raises her camera.

. . .

Mint is growing wild in the garden, tiny blue spikes filling up empty spaces, strangling the other plants. Good for headaches, says Rudy. And memory. And digestion.

She is drying some for him now—for lack of anything better to do—spreading it out on shallow pans, setting them in the oven at a low heat. Two hours, it will take.

An hour in, she checks to make sure that the herbs are not turning into charred twigs. No, they are still surprisingly green—and the oven is surprisingly cool. A low heat, but this low? She touches the side of the stove absently, and then realizes that it has stopped heating up entirely, that it is cooling down.

This old oven—there is a reason she usually avoids it, only Rudy knows its whims, its moods. She opens the door, peers into its black depths, and spots something. The blue gas flame has gone out. How long has it been? This is the problem.

Simple enough. All she has to do is relight the pilot light. Even she knows that.

What? says Rudy, aghast. No, no, no.

But he is not there. He is taking a walk.

She strikes the match, pulls open the door again, and reaches in to touch the flame to the pilot line.

A flash, a boom so loud it is almost soundless.

Then she is huddled on the ground, on the other side of the room, her hand, her arm blistered, her shirt half-melted. Shaking so hard her teeth are chattering. The room around her is silent, a deep, thick silence. And everything in it has slowed down—when she raises her hand, it moves sluggishly, leaving trails in the air. This is not her hand, not anymore, it is someone else's hand, suspended in the silence—the skin tight, shiny, red.

Gus is there now, saying something. Crouching next to her, his mouth, his lips are slowly moving.

Speak louder, she thinks. I can't hear you.

His lips move some more.

Speak louder.

. . .

Sometimes people have to invent their own fates, she thinks, long, looping lines of events. The traditional Fates—the ancient women creating the stuff of destiny—must be growing tired, they are neglecting their work. Clotho, who spins the thread of life; Lachesis, who measures it; Atropos, who cuts it. Yes, they are the daughters of Themis, the goddess of divine law—they should know better for that reason alone. But they are too careless, too treacherous—only a fool would allow them to have their own way.

SIX

Gratitude is an illness suffered by dogs.
JOSEF STALIN

Wide cobblestone streets, lime and chestnut trees, car horns. Wrought iron balconies, the smell of petrol, red and yellow trams screeching along rails. Linen factories, tinsmiths, exhaust fumes, a clock tower. Minsk, 1938. Nothing like he has imagined, nothing like he could possibly have imagined; he has no store of pictures in his mind for this place, these crowds of people.

Women in shin-length dresses fitted to their bodies, a few with red lips, furs around their shoulders. Some of the men with polished shoes instead of boots, here and there a fedora. Walking singly, in couples, groups, some of them striding, some of them strolling. The hubbub, the foreign smells, the sheer busyness are overwhelming—it is all he can do to keep from gaping. That this had been going on, that these people had been lining up for kvass from barrels on wheels, that they had been buying malt dough or sour apple pies at the very moment he had been spreading muck on the fields or wrestling with the plow is unfathomable.

But he is here now, in this place free of the stench of rotting potatoes, and he can already see small possibilities hidden in this landscape. The curve of a woman's hip, the smoky aroma of grilled meat drifting into the street, a man putting on his hat in the sun, his fingers placed around the furrow in the crown. Glimpses of a new existence, already drawing him in.

He sells the horse and cart quickly, buys some used trousers, a shirt, a comb, a razor, scouring the shops for them—supplies of almost everything are short. He rents a corner in a weekly room—illegally—three other men in it, mildewed wallpaper curling up at the seams. An electric bulb hanging from the ceiling—a revelation, but only until six o'clock, when the power often goes off.

The next day, he begins searching and asking, applying and offering. Everywhere—a tannery, a distillery, an iron foundry, a machining shop. *Look, how strong I am, how quickly I learn.* But they are not hiring, or they are not hiring him—some of them skeptical about his claim to be sixteen, or sizing him up as a farm boy, too callow.

He is startled and angered by these rebuffs. They have no idea what a hard worker he is, how fast he is, how long he has been waiting for this, how much he has earned it. He keeps on going, plodding from place to place, attempting to conceal his resentment. *Come back next week, we might have something then.* But his supply of kopecks is already running low, and he is becoming more desperate. He cuts back on food—he is used to this, but it seems more painful now, after days in which he tore into loaves of bread, or wolfed down dumplings with bacon, letting loose his hunger. Another few days and he will lose his corner of the room as well, he will have to sleep out by the river. And the weather is becoming colder, trees littering the ground with chestnuts, the wind poking and prodding him through his thin clothes. Now he tries the shops, going from store to store, asking if they need someone to do anything, anything at all. *I learn quickly, I can read letters and numbers.* No work, they say, not bothering to tell him that if they did need someone, it would be someone with more manners, who could lure in customers, cajole them to buy. Not someone who hammers out questions, and then grunts his answers.

A sign overhanging the sidewalk—a spool of thread, a needle dancing beside it. A small shop, the place where he bought his shirt and trousers when he first arrived.

The smell of cedar greets him—to keep the moths away, says the tailor, to keep them from eating holes in the bolts of cloth. A thin man, wire eyeglasses hooked behind his ears, his fingers long and fine.

No, no work, he says. He tries to keep his face straight at the thought of this young man threading a needle, sewing a seam. A small girl—three? four?—sidles out of a backroom and slips her hand into his.

He looks the young man up and down sharply.

At least I can give you something to eat.

The backroom is lined with shelves, pieces cut to patterns stacked on some of them, chalk marks showing. Linen, twill, broadcloth. Spools of thread in every possible shade take up another shelf. Several irons of different sizes sit beside a tailor's form, a form with a half-sewn vest on it bristling with pins. The black treadle sewing machine is under the small window, the words *Kompaniya Singer* across the top in gold writing, partly rubbed away.

The man clears a place, moving aside baskets of needles and bobbins, basting thread, long scissors, a jar of white sizing. Then he ladles out a bowl of garlic and barley soup from a pot on the wood stove, cuts off a chunk of rye bread.

Soup mit nisht, we call it, he says. Soup with nothing.

The little girl curls up on the man's lap, wide-eyed as the young man gulps it down. She begins chattering in a small, piping voice, making quicksilver movements with her hands.

Do you like buttons I can draw pictures I have a velvet hair ribbon how old are you?

The young man looks at her dumbly.

Pay no attention, says the man. Her mother died a few months ago. The blood-spitting disease.

He says this in a way that suggests the words are unfamiliar, that they are strangers in his mouth.

When the bowl is empty, he begins rummaging through one of the shelves, pulling out an old jacket, a rip in the side sewn up in precise stitching.

The owner left it two years ago. I doubt he'll be back for it now, he says dryly.

He holds the jacket for him to put on, as if he were a customer, then straightens it, pinching the material over the shoulders.

Good fit, he says. Then he pushes him out the door.

Place to place, a cabinetmaker collective, a shoe factory, a slaughterhouse. Most are brusque, dismissive.

Eventually he finds himself beside the river, the Svislach, and he sits down to rest for a moment, tired. The stone embankments are patched with yellow lichens, a twisted willow hanging over the water. One of its branches is so heavy that it has split the trunk, a gash of white wood showing. A bowlegged man is poling a boat, leaning into the pole silently, lifting it and then sinking it down again.

Any work? he calls out to him.

The man shakes his head, leaning into the pole again, sending the boat gliding underneath the bridge, the green water swirling around him.

Nothing for him here. He stands up and turns back towards the main streets.

Then.

Only a week.

A small glassworks, sweeping the floor, moving pallets, stoking furnaces for a few kopecks, next to nothing. But enough to keep his corner of the room for the moment, for a few meals of lard and *kasha*.

And the place is warm, too warm, the furnaces stoked to small infernos. He sweeps up the scrap glass, the cullet, washes it, spreads it out to dry. By the second week, he is feeding it into the clay crucibles. How long does it take to melt, to go from solid to molten, from cold to hot, to two thousand degrees? Hours before it is hot enough, before the glassblowers can gather the melted glass on their pontil rods. This means there are always crucibles in rotation, the furnaces roaring and wheezing all night.

Be careful, says one of the men. Even a drop on the skin can burn down to the bone in a second.

Sometimes he stops for a minute to watch them—the head glassblower, a fish-eyed man, morose, but a master of breath and shape. He picks up a glowing blob, rolling the pontil back and forth on the bench, cradling the hot glass in a hollowed block of applewood. Then he lengthens it by swinging the rod around in a circle, picks up more glass, rolls, swings and begins the first blowing, the red-hot glass blooming out. More rolling, swinging, heating, cradling, a ceaseless effort to keep the fiery bubble from dropping off the rod. In a moment he inserts the shape into a hinged mould, and when he blows this time, the glass inside expands into the shape of another green wine bottle.

The man straightens up, wipes the sweat off his forehead with the inside crook of his elbow, his eyes bulging a little. A minute later, the bottle comes out of the mould, and he cracks it off the rod, smoothing the edges, the neck, the lip. After that, it goes into the annealer to cool down slowly, gradually. *If it cools too fast, it shatters.* And then on to the next bottle and the next.

Crates of bottles, jugs, jars, flasks—the glassblowers are swift workers. Several times a week, he sweeps out the van, unloads the empty crates, loads the full ones, rides along to help with the deliveries, to drop off the bottles at their destinations. All over Minsk, across the river, along the banks, into the low hills, the smell of the spruce trees, the red-barked pine trees in the air. From time to time, they go to nearby towns as well, Barysaw, Kojdanau, Nesvizh.

Another month, says the manager. But I make no promises after that.

Three months, he says, a few weeks later.

The young man is fascinated by the van, how the driver handles the wheel, the gears, the pedals, how he controls this large machine so nonchalantly. The driver, who would rather be sleeping in the back, notices his interest, and shows him what to do. A few weeks later, he pulls over to the side of the road on the way to Stowbtsy and they change places so the younger man can drive. His hands on the wheel, all that power sitting on the axles, even the rough sound of the engine are gratifying, and slowly, over the next several months, he becomes determined to hold on to this, to get it for himself. *The man is lazy, shiftless, this should be mine*. Once he is driving most of the time, even in the crowded streets of Minsk, he tells the manager. The next day, the sleeper is fired. Then the young man asks for his job as well as his own.

After that, the other workers draw away from him, their faces stony. Even before then, he was not liked, although they had to admit that he was quick, useful. But he had made no effort to strike up an alliance with anyone, and now they are wary. Too late, he realizes that some other ties might have been useful. More than useful, in some cramped part of himself, he wanted their regard, their acceptance. Or at least to avoid their scorn. No longer, though, now he is angry again—although he is often angry, a crawling, prickly rage never far from the surface. What does he need them for, anyway?

He eats his dinners by himself at a place near his room, whatever they have—soup with goose blood, offal pudding. Even so, it is more than he had on the farm, and his body begins filling out—he is no longer as gaunt. As he becomes stronger, though, so do his sexual urges, a stringy itch when he was exhausted all the time, now something that torments him, waking him up in the night.

. . .

She is young, although not as young as he is, her eyes too small, her features too spongy, too uneven to be beautiful. But her brow is clear, and her hair gleams where it picks up the light of the oil lamp. She is wearing lipstick, rouge, and is dressed only in a pink and black lace slip. *Aksana,* she says, her name; when she talks, her breath smells of anise pastilles and onions. She is practical about the exchange—what does he want? Certain things cost extra. *Just as usual,* he says, without knowing what that is. She pulls him onto the bed, the bedclothes stained with semen. His fingertips are thick-skinned, but he winds his hand around her arm, kneads her breasts and belly, surprised that all this skin, this flesh, is in his hands.

She is almost as clumsy as he is, pulling at his penis, moaning in an unconvincing way. At first her touch prompts a wave of shame and nausea, then suddenly he seems to be watching himself from a distance, his ears plugged, his mouth clamped shut. The nausea retreats and he watches himself push inside her, rocking frantically against her slight torso, his spasm of release fast, a blink of pleasure. Afterwards he watches her breathe, the skin of her fragile neck, her eyelashes, her hair twisted up at the base of her skull. She opens her eyes to see him staring at her, and she laughs, naturally and clearly.

He is mortified, anger surges in him, anger and contempt—for her, for himself. He has a glimpse of twisting and snapping that thin neck, of her head lolling off the pillow, lifeless. Of hitting her with the base of the lamp, blood seeping out from under her hair.

Here, she says again. He looks up. She is standing beside the bed. She has wiped herself with a cloth and is holding it out to him.

. . .

Stars over the city, dots of light in an inky sky. Underneath them, far below, street lamps offer up a mellower glow, a boon for someone who is almost night-blind. And in a place where there is so much to see, to hear.

They are drunk, these officers, five of them in serge uniforms, black boots. One stumbles in the street, another is singing loudly, tunelessly, his tunic ruched up over his belt. The young man watches them as they lurch around, holding on to each other's arms, shoulders. A bottle of vodka goes from hand to hand and they join in with the singer for a few lines, a ragged chorus.

The republic told us not to close our eagle eyes
We cut the enemy's claws
We blunt the enemy's teeth
We are the defence of millions

One stops to urinate in the gutter, and another guffaws.

NKVD, says a man next to him. All that vodka, down Russian throats.

Let them have it, he thinks. Who better? Let them drink a case.

He is impressed by them, by their authority, their arrogance. By the insignia on their collars, the leather straps from shoulder to waist, the revolvers on their belts. They know who they are, what they are. They know they are people who command, not people who obey. Even drunk, they walk as if they have an almost visible force coiled behind them. As he watches them, he has only one thought in his mind: *I want this.*

. . .

More orders come in for wineglasses, bowls, vases. Even in scarce times, there are people who need these things, who can pay for these things. Two of the glassblowers prefer them, these orders, there is more artistry, more skill required. More colours as well, not merely the never-ending green and amber of bottles and jugs. They add minerals to the glass, copper for red, nickel for violet, cadmium for yellow. To make milky glass, opaline glass, they add bone dust. When they can get them, they use pigmented glass canes—shipments from Germany, the tags still attached. *Safran. Kobaltblau. Pomeranze.*

The canes stand in a tall box in one of the cabinets, a box with partitions for each colour lot. The young man wipes them clean so that the grit and dust that settle everywhere, even inside the cabinet, will not change their hues when they are melted. Even a little grit will darken the batch, they say to him.

Irisgelb. Silbergrun. Dunkelviolett.

They are muscular, the glassblowers, smelling of *mahorka* tobacco. Thick-armed from the heavy pontil rods. Coarse, jocular, they work in undershirts stained with sweat, or sometimes with no shirt at all, the hair on their chests damp. When they open the furnace doors, the heat blazes out, a naked sun trapped in each one.

But when they handle the glass, they become makers, moulders, jugglers, their coarseness gone for the moment, their blunt hands full of knowledge. Stretching, shaping, twisting the glass, they make living things out of it, flowing from one shape into another. A strange, volatile thing—liquid one minute, rock-hard the next.

The cane is added in small batches, the molten glass turns blue, amethyst, rose. Then they use tools to stroke it, pinch it, to push it in and out of the furnace. One of them talks to the glass while he works, coaxing, chiding it, murmuring endearments. *Come on, lapochka. That's it, my darling, that's it. No, no, no, not that way, no, no, no. Ah, that's it, now you have it. Now just a little more.*

These are special deliveries, these orders, packed in straw. *Ay, ay, be careful,* they say to him, reluctant to see this work handled by someone so awkward. He nods curtly. What do they think? He has not broken anything yet.

And not all his deliveries are for them anymore. It began when one of the receivers at a winery suggested that he deliver some wine for them as well—some bottles to their customers, along his usual routes. *A little extra for you, no one needs to know*. The work, the little extra becomes larger, and now he is seeing Aksana more often, eating more.

I know another man, says the receiver.

Another receiver, more wine deliveries. They pay him less than their usual drivers—too expensive, they say. Then they pocket the difference. *See how this is good, good for everyone.*

...

Aksana is telling a story, the story of how they will be, now that he has more money, when he has even more. They are lying in her bed afterwards, while she straightens her chemise, puts herself to rights.

We will live in a house, we will have a Victrola of our own, we will go dancing every night. I will have a red silk dress, a necklace of black jade, we will have fine furniture—she stops to consider—of dark green velvet. We will drink wine out of thin glasses, we will eat meat every day off china plates. We will have a son, a daughter, and another son, and they will all live. We will have a maid, we will have a horse and carriage and also a car, we will have paintings on the wall. And we will have a *dacha* in the summer, like a Party official, with birch trees and a steam house.

She is seventeen, she has no idea how much these things cost. But when she talks in this dreamlike way, it all seems possible. For a moment, he is drawn into the story, for a moment he is part of it, he can see the massive fireplace, the overstuffed chairs around it, the patterned rugs. He can see the flames leaping and falling, then rearing up again, the brocades reflected in their glow.

Then he rolls off the bed, stands up, begins putting on his clothes.

Why would I marry a whore? he says.

. . .

A cold day, already darkening in the late afternoon. One of the unofficial deliveries. He parks behind a building, out of sight, and goes in to collect the boxes, pick up his pay for the last few days.

One, two, three, five boxes, into the back of the van. But before he can get into the driver's seat again, a man grabs him from behind, holding his arms behind his back. Another looms up in front, smashes him in the face. He can feel blood from his nose dripping down his mouth, his chin, he can taste it, an iron taste.

A piece of rope is looped around his neck and twisted slowly, cutting off his breathing. He yells, but nothing is coming out, he claws for the rope soundlessly, but his arms are still pinned. He writhes desperately in the man's grip, choking.

The money, they say. The money.

He nods towards his coat pocket, struggling for air, the street beginning to spin around him. They find it, then throw him to the icy pavement, kicking him in the back. He gasps and draws in a burning breath.

No more deliveries, they say. No more deliveries from here. You can bring the bottles from the glassworks, but no more delivering the wine. Or we tell the manager, tell him that you're a thief. And we will do this again. Only it will be worse.

Then one of the men takes the key from the door of the van and throws it in a long arc, a brief flash in the dusk, landing on the roof of the building. They kick him again, and disappear.

Good for everyone. Except the regular drivers.

Granat. Brilliantrubin. Kirshrot.

SEVEN

. . . whatever other qualities Jews may possess,
likable or the reverse, no one who knows them well can
deny that they are personally interesting.
ERNEST JONES, BRITISH PSYCHOANALYST, 1879–1958

Her hand, her arm are wrapped in gauze dressings. Every night, she unwraps them, rinses the weeping blisters, gingerly dabs on the ointment they gave her, and then winds clean gauze around them again. She takes the painkillers at the appointed hours, attempting to avoid any gaps when the pain might come skidding back.

A gas stove, they said in the emergency ward, nodding to themselves, not bothering to point out the foolishness of what she had done. Perhaps they were inured, oblivious to it, faced with the same or greater levels of idiocy every day. An ocean of folly that laps up at their doors, that they wade in from morning until night—the unwise, the careless, the ignorant, with a few unlucky people scattered among them.

Three weeks, they said. And your skin may be discoloured afterwards, reddened. Although it may fade eventually.

Stay out of the kitchen, says Gus.

Stay away from the stove, says Rudy.

Not like Val, the maker of pale food—lemon pies, soufflés, baked potatoes. She has taken this moment to fasten herself to them more closely, she is everywhere now, wiping baseboards, scraping ancient paint drips off the glass in the front window. If Leah sits down, Val is there shortly, settling into a chair beside her, as if they were about to share some confidence.

We need more butter, she says.

We, thinks Leah.

She is beginning to despise Val in a small, ungenerous way. Despite her resolutions to think better of her, to be more gracious, to be glad for Gus, when Val appears beside her she has to resist the urge to flee to another room. And her cooking is insidious, she thinks, this is her way of sidling up to them, slipping her arm into each of theirs. The others know it, too—dimly, faintly—but they are too enthralled to care. As if they had fallen for it, fallen entirely, as if one by one they had pitched forward into a massive vat of cream. They seem oblivious to the idea that this might mean Gus will leave, that their rumpled household might fall apart.

If he does leave, she thinks, they will become uncalibrated. Without him, Rudy will lose his balance, will become unmoored, and Malcolm, Malcolm will become intolerable. And then if she moves out—eventually—how will they survive, who will keep this small world together, who will take up arms in the feud against decay? Rudy looks after the kitchen, some of the cleaning, but only that—Gus is the fixer, the installer of small repairs, she is his assistant. They may not be very good at it, but without them, who will put up weatherstripping, poison the mice, seal the cracks? She pictures the others in a downward spiral, unshaven, the house deteriorating, sinks plugged, infestations of ants.

It's not your job to look after them, says Gus silently.

Whose job is it?

She tries to banish the idea of this constellation of people breaking apart, each of them spinning off into a lonely orbit.

What if they have to sell the house?

They probably will.

No.

. . .

He wants to see you, says Nate.

Why? she says hopefully.

He doesn't confide in me, he says, also hopefully.

Finally, they think.

. . .

Don't bother, says Louis, raising his hand to stop her, mid-apology.

He sounds almost amused. Does he still feel betrayed? So difficult to tell. If only he were easier to read. Perhaps Rudy could create a diagram of the inside of his head, one of his illustrations—a finely detailed landscape of his brain. The temporal lobe in dark pink, the cerebellum, the frontal lobe in turquoise. Or—although this would be harder—a graph showing the movement of his thought patterns, darting and whirling in his skull. And while he is at it, perhaps he could even pinpoint the source of his lost moments, some black spots on a brain fold, some plaque in his grey matter.

No, she will have to keep guessing. But if Louis is still holding a grudge, working with him will be difficult. She locks her fingers together and looks at him, surrounded by his open-flapped books. All those paper mouths, a chorus of sorts. Perhaps they will be consoling in some way, help to repair whatever muffled damage he feels he has suffered. Or perhaps he will read something forgiving, something benevolent.

What are you waiting for? he says.

. . .

She has a job again, a place, a paycheque. She wants to go sailing around the office, giddy with relief, running her hands along the surfaces of the desks. She wants to sit in her office, gripping the arms of her chair, sending it swivelling around on its axis.

I work here, she says to a client in the waiting room, who nods, puzzled.

I work here, she says to Isabel.

Si, says Isabel happily, her hair floating around her head, looking like a cynical angel.

For how long?

He will get over it, says Isabel. Look, he has already taken you back, no? He will get accustomed to having you around again. You will make yourself *esencial*—what is the word in English? Yes, she will make herself essential. She will make her memos small jewels of clarity and insight, she will create arguments that are so persuasive, she will fall for them herself. She will prepare facta that will insert tiny, delicate fingers into the minds of judges, that will shape their thoughts, their suppositions, their perceptions.

All you have to do, she says to him silently, is to pull yourself into position, fit yourself back into your skin. Retrieve yourself from the grip of this ailment, this disorder—whatever it is. Give that silver-haired head a shake, make all those synapses, all those neurons fall into place. Surely this is not too much to ask.

AFFIDAVIT

I, Pavel Makarevich, of the City of Minsk in the Republic of Belarus, make oath and say as follows:

1. In 1939, I ran a flour mill in the country outside Minsk, where we ground wheat and rye grains, using water power from the river that ran there. The mill had not yet been collectivized because it was small and out of the way, and I was paying a subsidy to a local government official. Five other men worked in the mill with me, grinding, packaging, storing, and delivering the flour.
2. I lived with my wife in one of the better areas of Minsk. However, my wife and I frequently argued, and often in the evening I would go out instead of staying home and meet a group of friends at a small bar, where we would talk and drink until late.
3. Business began to decline, as a result of the growing shortage of wheat. I was reluctant to lay off any of the men, as I had worked with them for many years. Eventually, though, the mill was losing so much money that I had to do something, so I laid off Bogdan Zayats, the worst worker. When I brought him into the small room I used as an office and told him, he became very angry and bitter, shouting at me.
4. Shortly after this, two NKVD officers came into the bar, and arrested me. They took me to the local NKVD building, where they demanded that I confess that I was a *kulak*, a well-off peasant. They ordered me to say I was a profiteer, and a counter-revolutionary agitator, and to name my friends as other enemies of the state. When I refused, they put me in an enclosed cell that was meant for four people, although there were already twenty-one people in it. As a result, we could

not sit or lie down. We were forced to stand, packed together so tightly that we could hardly breathe.

5. It was completely dark and extremely hot, with no water or food, no ventilation and no bucket for sanitary functions. The stench was very strong. Some prisoners told me they had been there for weeks, that their legs were swollen and blistered, and that the blisters had become infected.
6. At night, they brought in planks and bricks to build layers so that we could lie down. The distance between each layer was less than a foot.
7. Every few days, NKVD officers took me to another room, and beat me with a chair leg, an electric cable, or a rubber hose, screaming curses at me and calling me a *kulak*. Sometimes they would slam my head against the wall five or six times in a row. They knocked out two of my teeth with the butt of a revolver. One of them spat in my face and in my mouth. When I still refused to confess, they put me back in the cell, bleeding and bruised. It was still extremely hot. One of them said to me that if I did not confess, they would "cook" me along with the others.
8. During the time I was in the cell, at least two people were suffocated to death. Their bodies were not removed right away.
9. After ten days of this, I agreed to sign a confession. A younger man was brought in to write out the confession, and then I signed it without reading it. I heard the officer call the younger man *Stefan*.
10. The younger man was about five feet, nine inches, with wide cheekbones, dark brown eyes and hair. I have examined a picture of Stefan Drozd, attached to this my affidavit as Exhibit A, and he may well be that man.

11. The mill, my house, and all my possessions were seized, and I was deported to Tomsk Oblast in the north of western Siberia.
12. I make this affidavit in good faith and for no improper purpose.

Sworn before me this twenty-third day of October, 2009, in the City of Minsk. Ivan Stasevich, a Notary Public in and for the Republic of Belarus.

Another nightmarish story. The identification is a little better, but still not enough. *He may well be that man.* And how many people are called Stefan in Belarus?

The spiders wake up again, all talking at the same time.

Stop, she says to them. Slow down. Take a breath. Think about this, consider it for a moment. Close your eyes and imagine this. Could describing these horrors be an end in itself, not merely a means to a deportation? Perhaps setting them out in writing transforms them into something more concrete—not only memories, pieces of thought, now they have a physical form, even if it is only ink on paper. Now they are tangible, they have outlines and edges, they can stand on their own. The testimony of ruined lives, miserable deaths.

And then, because of that, is it possible that this case is not really necessary? Do you really want law to start meddling with all this, to start cutting and stretching these memories to fit into its own categories? Perhaps these documents can clear a place in all the babble instead, can stand as eloquent tributes in themselves.

Nonsense, says her aunt.

Nonsense, say the spiders. What about responsibility? What about accountability? What about punishment?

But this case is only a deportation. Yes, that can be a death sentence for some people, many of their refugee clients. Here, though, will there even be a trial at the other end of it? In

Belarus, the country that still has an NKVD of sorts, now the KDB, the Kamitet Dziaržaŭnaj Biaspieki.

We only ensure there will be no execution, no capital punishment, Owen says. We obtain diplomatic assurances on that because we have no death penalty. Whether there is a trial is not our problem.

Even if there is really more to it, even if he might have been involved in international human rights violations, or crimes against humanity?

Even then. Criminal prosecutions are too difficult, we've lost a number of those cases. So we revoke their citizenships instead.

Whose job is it to provide a reckoning, then? Whose millstone is he?

His own country.

Which country is that? He has lived here over three times as long as he did in his country of birth.

But he should not have been here. And we can only do so much in the real world, a world of arbitrary borders, accidental landings. He stole his place here, and we want it back.

. . .

This time she will speak to the man, she will nerve herself to say something. This man, her next Andrew Jarvis. She has moved down the list, begun watching again, outside a small set of flats. And yesterday, she spotted him, a dark-haired man with a sprinkling of grey, emerging in workboots. Not only spotted him, followed his car to a warehouse in an industrial park, a place with unearthly blue siding—distributors of hard goods, according to a sign. Does he look like her uncles, like herself? He is not unlike them, anyway. And he is the right age as well—middle-aged, perhaps a little older. How would someone feel at that age, confronted with a child they abandoned?

Middle-aged, Louis said once, the word dripping with scorn. An idea he despised, possibly because he qualified.

But these are weathered people, she thinks. Seasoned people, people who might have discovered their own strengths and flaws by stumbling over them. People with scar tissue from prolonged exposure to the absurdities of being. People who might welcome a daughter into their lives.

And if not, then at least she will know.

Know what?

More than she does now.

This is how she will do it: She will walk up to him on the sidewalk and say hello—casually, lightly. Then she will ask him if he has a minute, there is something she would like to talk to him about. Yes, she could telephone or write, give him some warning. But she wants to reduce his chances of saying *no. No, I won't talk to you, no, I don't want to see you, no, I have no explanation, I have nothing to say.*

Not this morning, though. And perhaps not another morning, when he might be in a rush. Some evening, when he is almost home, when he will be in no hurry. But not quite yet—she is not entirely ready, not absolutely ready, she will need to brace herself, to fortify herself for this odd encounter. She will need to talk herself into this again.

. . .

Carp, whitefish, pike. Glistening on the cutting board. The fins, heads, bones, and skin go into the pot with carrots, onion. A pinch of sugar, says her aunt. Go ahead. Maybe two, your fingers are small.

While the broth heats up, they drop the slippery fish bodies into the grinder. Grey coils fall out below as her aunt turns the handle. They add them to a bowl with matzah meal, black pepper, eggs, parsley, then pat the mixture into pale ovals.

Her aunt hovers over the cooking broth, tasting it with a spoon, skimming off the foam. Then she slides the gefilte fish in, a stir from time to time to prevent them from sticking to the pot.

Now we wait, says her aunt, sitting down, holding her back. This recipe is from the old country, it takes its sweet time.

The old country? says the girl, her legs dangling from the chair.

Where are you people from? The question asked by a curious parent in the hallway, after she had said something, used one of her aunt's Yiddish words.

Where are we from?

I'm from here, says her aunt. You're from here. Your grandparents? Some *shtetl* in Lithuania.

You people.

Later, they arrange the gefilte fish on a plate, put a slice of carrot cut into a flower shape on each one. In the middle, her aunt sets a fish head, goggling with radish eyes.

Isn't that something? says her aunt, although she is suddenly tired again, she has to sit down.

A Seder with Marvin and Ida, the neighbours, every year. Slow, comfortable, remarkably kind, these two. Ida will make up the Seder plate—*charoset,* roasted egg, *karpas,* bitter herbs. Marvin will chant long lines of Hebrew—*this is the bread of affliction*—and they will make little stacks with matzah pieces, horseradish and apple-walnut paste. At the end, they will sing looping, hypnotic songs—*one goat, one goat which my father bought for two zuzim*—that will swirl in her head for days.

Time for a nap before we get dressed up, says her aunt.

Leah pokes at the fish head.

Can he still swim? she says.
I doubt it, says her aunt.

. . .

The white fog is still there, her relationship to Nate still soft and blurred. She tries to restrain herself from looking for tiny cues of intimacy on his part—unable to decide what she is hoping for. Even the smallest gesture suggesting closeness makes her draw back, alarmed, but any hint of distance leaves her forlorn. And what does he want? He is unhurried, unworried, but his physical presence is more palpable. And he is slightly stranger—as if he had been replaced with another version of himself, but with a number of subtle differences. There is something more inquisitive about this version as well, like a man suspended in the middle of asking a question.

Still, she is peculiarly happy, she finds herself content with all this formlessness, at least for the moment. They slide into a rhythm of going to his house several times a week, bringing Thai food back with them, exploring each other's bodies, their fingers, their breath still smelling of lemongrass, cilantro. There is a largeness about him, something about his size, his heavy shoulders, the length of his back, the weight of him on top of her. She can feel this largeness slowly seeping into her—in some way making her small body larger as well.

Eventually, she thinks, eventually they will begin writing tiny stories of themselves on each other. There is no way to stop this, no way to prevent it. Then later they will add to these stories, they will alter them, fine-tune them, fill them in. But for now, there is still white space, still room for possibility.

That night.

She is lying in bed with him, one of his collection of objects in her hands—a small frame with an outline of a woman's face inside, a profile. The front of the face is made up of a thin chain, so that shaking the frame changes the profile—one minute an enormous chin, tiny mouth and nose, the next all lips.

He puts down his book and watches her for a moment. Then he takes her hands, turning them over, studying them seriously. The burns are healing, scabbed over now, her nails are short, uneven.

Look, he says tenderly. Your thumbs are different lengths.

He holds them up so she can see. I'll fix that for you.

He presses them together, recites a mock incantation.

What's the matter? he says when she laughs. You don't think I can do it?

Yes. Yes, she wants to say. I think you can do it.

. . .

Owen, in person. They are in a boardroom, black leather sofas along the sides, an oak table, muted grey walls. A sober room, except for a framed print on the wall at one end, a view through a window, a field of grasses, a field after that, a quilted landscape of greens—sage, olive, moss. The wind is blowing in through curtains, lifting them so lightly, so carelessly that they are almost floating. Like a Wyeth, she thinks. She finds it distracting, her eyes drawn to it, this picture that promises so much freedom, such breezy escape—she can almost smell the fresh air.

She pulls herself back to the room with an effort.

It's a little disconcerting, isn't it? says Owen. I keep looking at it myself during meetings—I can almost see myself with one leg over the windowsill.

A surprise—this is a man she would have thought was truly wedded to his job. And someone who personifies civility, the way he talks, the way he listens—elliptical, careful.

Louis agreed with your assessment of the evidence, he says.

Naturally he would have called Louis, why would he have accepted the opinion of junior alone? She realizes this is a tactful way of explaining what happened, how Louis heard about their conversation.

But here you are, he says, pausing slightly, making the point that he had angled to get her.

Yes. Although he did it under the guise of cost, she thinks, he covered himself perfectly. And her contract is only for the length of the case.

Still, there is no doubt he is a man who does what he can, the good that is available to him. And he does it gracefully, sincerely. His weakness, his failing is that he limits this good—the available good—so narrowly. Only those things that will have no effect whatsoever on his work, his prospects, no possibility of consequences to him. In a world of endlessly colliding circumstances, so little is left, so little fits within these limits.

But he is asking her about the gaps in the evidence now, the additional testimony they will need. They talk for a few minutes, and she feels the riffles of his courtesy spreading out around her. She suspects this has little to do with her, that this is how he talks with everyone. Is he cautious about treating people differently on the basis of their importance? He must have seen the quick rise and fall of numerous politicians, dignitaries, officials. Better to cultivate everyone, no matter how insignificant they seem at the moment—a discreet formula for reducing risks, an insurance policy. Regardless of the reasons, he does it so well, it is almost impossible not to like him, not to enjoy this flow of cordiality.

And perhaps there is some substance to it, something of a reflection of himself, not merely a strategy. Perhaps it shows some fundamental niceness—not niceness in the usual shallow sense, but a deeper, hardier form.

We need someone to interview potential witnesses in Belarus, he says now. To make sure we get the evidence we need this time, someone who knows the law, the evidentiary thresholds. And we're still trying to track down whether he was involved in some kind of mass killing. We usually use our own lawyers and historians, but we're still overrun with secondments and maternity leaves.

She imagines Minsk as a grim place—crumbling buildings black with age, side by side with squat apartments from the Soviet era. Institutional department stores with bare shelves, tired-looking merchandise. People in drab clothing, lineups for buying bread or meat. Trucks rumbling through narrow streets. A place of shortages, scarcity—colourless, chilly.

I'm looking forward to it, she says.

. . .

You weren't interested in going to Belarus? she says to Nate.

Among other things, he says.

. . .

All Men shall be Ready to Pursue Felons

And forasmuch as the Peace of this Realm hath been evil observed for lack of quick and fresh suit making after felons in due manner, it is provided that all men generally be ready and appareled at the commandment and summons of Sheriffs and the Cry of the Country to sue and arrest felons, when any need is, and they that will not so do and therefore be attainted shall make a grievous fine to the King.

. . .

The racetrack is a strip of dizzying light beyond the shade of the stands, the sun so bright she can barely see for a moment, until her eyes adjust.

A racetrack? Hopeless, says her aunt, shaking her head.

Nothing like the trots, says Malcolm defensively. He says this as if having drivers, their sulky carts, made the races more welcoming to children than the thoroughbred races. And for once, Rudy and Gus are on his side—they are weary of arguing with him when they need him to look after her.

Malcolm is in his element here, this is his natural habitat. He loves the antsy, expectant crowd, the sense of excitement hovering over the stands. The glee they feel in winning, kissing their tickets, crowing, leaping up on seats, arms outstretched. Or the disappointment, the collapse of anticipation until the next race, when it begins all over again. And for him, an endless number of people to become fond of—and then fleece.

At first, she was caught up in the jarring glory of the horses as they rushed by, the thudding of their hooves, their muscles bunching and releasing, their sleek coats—bay, black, chestnut—gleaming in the sun. The moment when the gate car folded its wings and the horses lunged forward, manes and tails streaming out, sulkies flying behind them—carts that weighed less than a sack of rice. Then hurtling around the track, the drivers in their coloured silks leaning back, hitting the shafts with the poppers on their whips.

But now she has been here too many times, she is restless, this is not like the books she reads about horses, full of mild peril, the endings buoyant. This place is race after race, the smell of roasted peanuts, stale beer, horse bodies rushing past, again and again.

Have a little flutter, Malcolm says today, to keep her interested, as if he were grooming a future mark. He knows she has ten dollars from Rudy, he is remarkably alert to the presence of money, even a small amount. But he refuses to let her decide on the horses herself. Spice Blossom, she says, racing card in hand. Every Man Jack. Ladyslipper.

Stabs in the dark, he says, smoke drifting from the cigarette between his thumb and first two fingers, cupped by his palm.

Stubborn as Gus by now, she goes off on her own.

On Spice Blossom, win, place, or show.

We don't take bets from kids, says the man.

It's for my uncle, she says, pointing him out.

A loyal customer, a crony.

Tell him just this once, says the man, looking around.

The gate car closes and the horses thunder past, the drivers splayed out on the sulkies.

Spice Blossom, snorts Malcolm. Not in a million years.

The announcer, a rich, swampy voice, running a continuous line of words. *At the quarter, it's Seascape in the lead, with Coal Harbour coming up on the outside, Breathless on the rail, a damp track out there today, folks, still Seascape in the lead, but there goes Ladyslipper punching through the pack, moving up, now it's Seascape, Breathless, Coal Harbour, and then Ladyslipper, and Ladyslipper coming up on Coal Harbour, then Every Man Jack and Spice Blossom, the rest of the field trailing at the half.*

Now Ladyslipper moving up on the outside, Breathless still on the rail, Coal Harbour in the pocket, Seascape still in the lead, Ladyslipper passing Coal Harbour, at the three-quarter pole, it's Seascape, Breathless, Ladyslipper, and Coal Harbour, all going well, then Every Man Jack, Spice Blossom, the rest of the pack trying to close the gap.

Oh, no, no, this is bad, look at that, Seascape is down, the horse is down, the driver on the track, we've got an accident, Breathless running into him, two horses down now, Coal Harbour swerving into Ladyslipper's cart, this is a bad one, we've got horses loose on the track, repeat, horses loose on the track, three men down, no, one is up now, two, where's that ambulance, what a pileup, hold your tickets, repeat, hold your tickets. Only five horses left in this race, although we've got Ladyslipper up and running without a driver, what a mess, all the drivers up now, coming into the stretch, there goes Every Man Jack in the lead now, then Spice Blossom and Ask Around, Spice Blossom moving up, head to head with Every Man Jack now, Ask Around behind them, the driver out there trying to catch Ladyslipper, Spice Blossom and Every Man Jack nose to nose now, but Every Man Jack is coming back strong, opening up, he's back in the lead and it's Every Man Jack at the finish.

At long odds, she does well, even for second place. She is jubilant, flinging up her arms the way she has seen other winners do. He gives her thirty dollars and pockets the rest. She protests, incensed, but knows that trying to pry more money out of him is useless.

Only later does she think to ask: Why did he fall? The first horse?

Malcolm shrugs. Could be anything—running injured, track conditions, bad luck. They'll probably put him down.

What?

If he's got more than one broken bone, or maybe a compound fracture. The others, too. Maybe not Ladyslipper, she seemed to be fine.

She is aghast. She has been hugging her little victory pile to herself with secret elation, a fortune for an eight-year-old. But now it is tainted, it has death spattered all over it.

I'm never coming here again, she says fiercely.

. . .

Now. More documents, more affidavits, more papers.

Mass operation 00447. Concerning the punishment of former kulaks, criminals, and other anti-Soviet elements. First category: particularly vicious, engaged in counter-revolutionary activities. To be executed. Second category: showing less active opposition, but nonetheless arch-exploiters with an innate tendency to destabilize the Soviet regime. To be sent to labour camps.

These words, she thinks now. These violent, cartoonish words. People suffered, people died of these words.

AFFIDAVIT

I, Jacob Akselrod of the Republic of Belarus, make oath and say as follows:

1. I was a shopkeeper in the *shtetl* of Zaslavl, a business I took over from my father. My small general store stocked a variety of goods, including calves' jelly, wax for softening boots, kerosene, flax cloth, pocket knives, scissors, dishes. One night a week, I taught at the local synagogue, where we had seats on the eastern wall, and once a month, I travelled to Minsk to buy supplies for my store.
2. I often did bookkeeping on the side for other merchants while my wife looked after the store. She was a good wife, neighbourly and modest in her clothes, and always busy, cleaning and baking, growing and pickling cucumbers and beets, washing and mending our clothes. We were unable to have children for a long time, a source of considerable sorrow, but eventually we had a small daughter and later a son. After so much time, they were very precious to us.
3. Our house was on a small parcel of land near the Chernitsa River. One of my non-Jewish neighbours approached me to buy this land, as he wanted the river access. I refused, as my family had lived there for many years, and he was offering too little for me to buy a similar house.
4. The following week, two NKVD officers came to my home and arrested me. I was charged with making Trotskyite remarks and illegally promoting the Jewish Labour Bund. I

was taken to a building in Minsk where an NKVD officer ordered me to confess that I was an enemy of the revolution and that I must name others who were enemies.

5. I refused to confess to any of the charges.
6. He then beat me with a rubber truncheon on my head, testicles, and ribs. When I fell over, he kicked me in the stomach and in the kidneys.
7. He told me to confess to my propaganda against the Soviet Union and against Stalin, and to name my confederates. Otherwise he said he would turn me into a piece of dung.
8. He made me stand on top of a bench, my arms bound behind me, forcing me to keep my legs straight. Then he knocked the bench out from under me so that I fell on my face on the concrete floor. He called this *the parachute*.
9. Several times he placed a loaded revolver in my mouth, and pretended to pull the trigger.
10. He presented me with a *kharakteristika* from a witness, my neighbour, who said that I was guilty of anti-Soviet agitation. This was untrue.
11. After this, he forced me to stand for five days and nights. If I fell over, he and another officer would take turns pouring snow water on me or beating me until I stood up again.
12. Finally he said if I didn't confess, they would arrest and rape our little daughter.
13. After this, I told them that I would confess. A younger man was brought in to write down the confession. I have been shown a picture of a man called Stefan Drozd, attached to this my affidavit as Exhibit A, and although he is much older now, he is similar to this younger man.
14. I signed a confession that I was guilty of propaganda and agitation against the Soviet Union. When they insisted that I name my fellow agitators, I gave them false names. When I

signed the papers, however, they had changed these names to others, names that I didn't know. I signed anyway because I was afraid for my daughter.

15. My house was confiscated, and eventually sold to the neighbour who wanted it. I was sent to a labour camp in northern Russia, and my wife, my two young children were sent to a special settlement. The labour camp was little more than a marshland. In my barracks, the amount of space for each person was less than the size of a grave, it was so cold that it was barely above freezing, and food was provided at starvation levels. I was often beaten there, sometimes by the commandant when he was drunk.
16. My son died of typhus within a few months in the special settlement, and my daughter died of the same illness a year later. My wife gave her scant rations to our sick children, and she died of starvation and cold shortly after my daughter.
17. When the commandant of the labour camp discovered that I knew bookkeeping, he began using me to keep similar records there. He then increased my food ration a little. I believe this is the only reason I was able to survive, and also why I was eventually released.
18. I make this affidavit in good faith and for no improper purpose.

Sworn before me this twenty-third day of November, 2009, in the City of Minsk. Ivan Stasevich, a Notary Public in and for the Republic of Belarus.

The identification is still weak, the brutality still harrowing. They still need a clearer connection to Drozd. All this paper, and it is not enough—to have a case, they need something tighter, something more. And she badly wants them to have a case, she has become attached to these people.

Is it the Jewish thing? says Nate.

Yes. No. Maybe.

Don't get too self-righteous, says Louis. There were quite a few Jews in the NKVD, especially in the beginning. Administrators, bureaucrats. Mostly purged by Stalin later—members of the intelligentsia. And in the end, simply because they were Jews.

These people, though, the people who inhabit the affidavits—she is afraid that if they lose this case, it will be another blow to them, a repudiation of their suffering.

Although perhaps we are too obsessed with remembering, she thinks. With fixing circumstances in time, with capturing moments—hours, days, months—and locking them up. Perhaps we should be obsessed with forgetting instead. Maybe there is some essential language of forgetting—some grammar of oblivion.

Is it possible, she says to her aunt, that the value of remembering might expire at some point?

No, says her aunt. For a person, maybe. For a people, no.

. . .

What about the White Queen, the one who could remember the future? she says to Nate.

I wouldn't rely on that.

. . .

This is it, she can see him coming down the street. Early evening, the rain has stopped, but the air is damp, alive, claret-coloured streaks in the sky. He looks tired, his face is creased like an old paper bag, his stubble is greying. A dusty shirt, sweat stains under his arms, a jacket slung over his shoulder. He is carrying something in his other hand, something giving off a hot, meaty smell—dinner, she assumes.

When he is past her, she will leave the car, begin walking behind him. In a few steps she will catch up to him and start chatting in an offhand way, as if she were a neighbour making small talk. Then she will come out and say it, say it in some way or another:

I think I might be your daughter.

Do you remember having a daughter?

How would you feel about having a daughter?

Surprise.

What? he says. Wearily, he hitches his jacket up higher over his shoulder.

Who are you? What are you talking about?

She repeats it, feeling sheepish.

What daughter? I don't have a daughter. Get away from me.

A long time ago. You were married to my mother, Miriam.

Is that a hesitation, a second, less than a second?

You're insane, he says.

I'm Leah, the baby you had, she says more loudly.

He glances quickly at her face, and then back.

Get out of my way, I don't know what you're talking about.

They are almost at his door, he has his key out.

This will only take a minute. She slips in front of him, in front of the door.

Get away from me.

Are you sure? Are you sure you don't remember my mother? A photographer. Are you sure you don't recognize this hair, these eyes, this mouth?

He glances swiftly at her again, and then away.

What did you do to your hands? he says more pleasantly, nodding towards her bandages. He reaches around her to twist the key in the lock.

Burns, she says. Painful, but getting better.

A shame, he says. Now the door is open, but she is still in front of it.

Suddenly he grabs her, shoves her to one side, and she loses her balance, falling heavily onto the hard-packed ground.

Get away from me, you crazy bitch.

He slams the door.

. . .

So, says Nate. Was it him?

Who knows? she says moodily.

What about the others?

What about them? she thinks. This attempt to fill an old void, to get her hands on some part of a father—a dry-skinned elbow, an ear—is rapidly falling apart. Instead of providing some rustle of insight, there is only more confusion. Instead of some element of certainty—even a ragged, partial certainty—there is only more doubt. And some chagrin. And a tiny jolt of fresh hurt.

This is it. She is swearing off Andrew Jarvises. At least for now.

. . .

These documents — this case — is giving rise to an old urge in her, an urge to lodge a complaint. To argue with an omnipotent being, to lay the damage at someone's feet.

At least one advantage of having a god, she says ruefully, is the possibility of a hearing of sorts.

An odd view of religion, says Nate. What you really want is an umpire. Or a genie. Or possibly a scapegoat.

Her aunt had an occasional God—only sometimes, she said, as if she mislaid him from time to time. No prayers—I don't beg—but I make requests, give advice. Usually ignored, I have to say.

This God was personal, though, not some ineffable, unknowable spirit. A god as fallible, as unreliable as a Greek deity.

Believe me, I have my reasons.

The war, the camps—obscene horrors, beyond comprehension. A collective *Shema* interrupted mid-sentence. The sound of stillness echoing for the length of a missing heartbeat, for the length of a missing breath.

And a god revealed as careless, fickle—one who had shrunk in size, forfeiting his former claims.

Where was he? Lazy? Lost? Taking a nap? says her aunt.

The logical problem of evil, a classic problem in philosophy. Or an evidentiary problem—evil as proof, proof that any godhead is either incapable or indifferent.

Whatever evil means. A host of evils, perhaps, jostling each other for territory, breathing out some terrible rot. Or different degrees of evil, a range of malevolence from the petty to the catastrophic.

Where would Drozd fit on this scale?

Evil, snorts Louis. We're talking about law.

Law, his primary faith, the synagogue a distant second. His sacred texts—the presumption of innocence, the burden of proof, the right to remain silent. Tools of the trade, but for him, something more compelling, more transcendent—things to be prized in themselves, that inspire allegiance. He is convinced of their virtues, and perhaps convinced that they confer those same virtues on him by extension. If they are lucid, meaningful, then so is he. In some way, these rights are part of him—elements of his own constitution.

She understands this, she is so often captivated by doctrines herself—their gravity, their patina, even their pits and scars. If there is anything that deserves some sense of fidelity, some form of belief, it might be them.

But they are not saving Louis from anything. He seems to be developing a tiny fracture at his core, something almost unnoticeable. Unnoticeable, except for the microscopic fissures that are beginning to spread out from it.

. . .

How long will she be away?

Two or three weeks, says Owen, depending on how it goes.

She suspects that Malcolm has forgotten about keeping an eye on Rudy, that he forgot almost immediately, within seconds after she spoke to him. And he and Gus—neither of them is likely to remember the signs of a heart attack.

Drafting Val is a mistake, she knows this, even as she does it, catching her one day in the hall. Val is delighted, far too delighted at this apparent thaw in her resistance, something that makes her all the more uneasy. Now they are co-conspirators, the two of them against the men, Val seems to suggest. Her delight is mixed with a hint of triumph, and Leah winces inwardly. But she is still worried about Rudy, picturing him clutching his chest, his body crumpling.

I could move in, says Val hopefully, her small moon face avid.

No, no, she says hastily. She wonders again why Val is so eager to win them over, to acquire Gus, this terse man. She understands why he is smitten—Val often has a cloud of damp warmth around her, as if she had just left her bed after a deep sleep. And she fusses over him, replacing the laces on his bowling shoes, washing his comb. But what does she want? Perhaps, like Gus, she feels her chances are running out. How old is she? In her fifties, her milky skin starting to break down into facets, her neck creased, her nails ridged and yellow from smoking.

For the moment, though, she will keep an eye on Rudy.

Your mother would have approved, says Val.

What?

She sees she has gone too far.

The way you take care of them, she says lamely.

You know nothing about my mother. Nothing.

Even less than she knows.

. . .

A little wild, her aunt had said. But she took you everywhere. Always wore those pearls, too, although she wasn't a pearl kind of person. Seed pearls, she said. And she loved that camera of hers. Click, click, click.

Seed pearls, she thinks now. She pictures her mother throwing them into the garden, where they would reproduce madly, a swath of pearl plants with silver flowers.

She has a photograph, well-thumbed. Not beautiful, but close enough that people must have looked at her twice when they saw her, glimpsing something in her face they almost recognized, then shaking their heads when they realized their mistake.

She liked the sauce. So much that she drove when she was drunk, even with her six-year-old child? Where were they going? What were they doing? Was she that careless? That impulsive?

. . .

A winter of snowfalls, the year Leah turned ten. Snow piled up on streets and yards in mounds, the cumulous drifts softening and whitening the landscape. Masses of cold stuff floating down and attaching to branches, bushes, turning into pillowy layers on the ground. Clothing a dead vine winding around a telephone pole, as if the pole were wearing a feathery boa, guy wires rimmed in white. Caps of snow covered the arms, the backs of the chairs in the yard, choked the gutters, a dogwood—branches uplifted like a dancer in fifth position—holding up a white pile.

As soon as the walks were shovelled, down it came again, one thick blanket after another. It was a fluke, an imperative, a redrawing of the city. It was all people thought about, dreamed about, talked about. Snow, they thought suddenly, waking up in the middle of the night. Snow, they said absent-mindedly when they passed each other on the street. All the forms of it, the endlessness of it, wrestling with it as it progressed through different stages—the powdery snow turning into starchy mounds, then into the grey-streaked mountains left by the night plows. Picking their way over it unsteadily when it melted down and froze into snow rubble. They talked about the small avalanches sliding from roofs, or the layers of snowfalls that were building up silently—wet snow, floury snow, sleet, snow pockmarked by rain. Each layer solidifying on top of another, as if they were new geological formations.

She spent hours outside, climbing snow dunes, burrowing in it, rolling in it, sometimes lying still in it, watching her breath curl upward in the steely air. She and the snow had become allies, complicit, lost in the white landscape they were shaping, hollowing out snow caves, making troughs, building snowmen that leered accidentally at passersby.

She wondered whether the snow might get so high that it would bury them, the first-floor windows blocked by it pressing against the panes. They would have to swim through it, windmilling their arms to create a path, snow filling their boots, melting into slush. And if it became high enough, she thought, they would have to tunnel out the sidewalks, making snow columns to hold up snow ceilings, cutting holes in them to let in the cold light.

One weekend, at her aunt's house, she opened the door to find the world coated in ice—the steps, the wires, the trees, their branches dazzling in the sunlight. Glazed stalks poked out of the snow, ice needles hung from the porch roof, a bush had turned into a small ice fountain. The brilliance of it, the sheer beauty was overwhelming, almost frightening—the landscape both harder and more fragile, more likely to break. She slithered and slid her way into one of the caves she had made, and sat there in the dark, arms around her knees.

After a while, her aunt came out, a coat over her dressing gown. She crawled into the cave beside her, and sat there for a minute.

What are you doing? she said finally.

I'm hiding, said the girl shyly.

An honourable tradition, said her aunt.

. . .

Glass. Were we to dwell on the many curious relations that glass bears to scientific principles, either as a consequence of them or as an aid towards their development, it would take us far beyond our limits.

EIGHT

The Pope! How many divisions has he got?

JOSEF STALIN

November. A year now at the glassworks, months of feeding the furnaces, of sweeping broken cullet, the hissing and clanking of wet blocks and pontils. As he walks home, the wind comes barrelling down the street like a fist, whirling up dead leaves, pushing people off stride, their eyes stinging. The street lamps cast a yellowish glow against the evening sky, the smell of tar and diesel lingering from the day, and he pulls his jacket up against the wind.

A commotion down the street. He cranes his neck. A thin man in a black suit is running, dodging in and out of crowds, doubling around a tram. After him, stouter, panting, a man in a uniform—*militsiya,* local police—shouting as he runs.

Stop him. Stop him.

The thin man is closer now, and Drozd leaps into the street, grabs him. The man twists in his grasp with surprising strength, but he holds on.

The man turns towards him, his glasses broken. The tailor—the soup, the jacket. The man begins to say something, but the officer draws up, gasping for breath.

Vermin, he says between gasps, his hands on his knees. A traitor. Hold on to him.

In a minute, he has caught his breath, and he leads them down the street, Drozd still gripping the tailor with both hands. The tailor has taken off his broken glasses, and he stares at the young man, his black-brown eyes willing him to turn, to loosen his grasp.

My daughter, the tailor says quietly.

The young man looks away from him, feeling a faint prick of something old, something unidentifiable.

Soup mit nisht, we call it.

This man, he has done something wrong? he says to the officer.

A Bundist, a Jew, he says. An enemy of the revolution. Isn't that enough? And when I tried to arrest him at his place, he ran.

He notices the prisoner staring at the young man.

You know him? he says. Maybe we should put you in a cell, too. Maybe you're a counter-revolutionary. Or a Bundist too.

No, no, says the young man hastily, kicking the prisoner's legs.

At the *militsiya* headquarters, the prisoner is taken away, his face set into a mix of fear and stoicism.

I'm looking for work, says the young man.

We don't hire the likes of you, says the officer abruptly.

I'm strong and fast, he says. I can drive. I can help you with the prisoners. Or anything else. I can wash the floors. I don't need much money.

Go away, says the man, who is bored by this already.

I can read and write.

You? You can read and write? says the man sarcastically. Read that, then.

He points to a sign on the wall.

All officers must report to the serzhant at the beginning of the shift.

. . .

What's this? says the captain—a pitted face—looking at the young man contemptuously. A thief?

He says he can read and write, he read the sign on the wall.

The captain studies him.

How old are you?

Eighteen, says the young man, as boldly as he can.

The captain raises his eyebrows.

. . .

When he tells the glassworks director, the man seems relieved. No one else says a word to him, not goodbye, not farewell, not godspeed. Nothing, nothing at all.

. . .

The bookstore, an old, woody smell. He gapes at the rows of shelves stuffed with books, more than he had ever imagined. Some of the shelves are bowed under their weight, and the books spill over, stacked on tables, piled on the floor. He is hoping to find something to expand the number of words he knows, to learn as much as he can in a hurry. All around him, people are peering at the shelves, fingering the volumes, almost stroking the pages. But they are better dressed than he is; he feels clumsy, an intruder in this place, his hands and feet suddenly too large again. He grabs something–anything–off the top of a pile, pays for it, and flees.

That evening, he opens it up, begins studying it carefully, the black print marching across the page like distant people across a snowy field. To his disgust, it turns out to be a school book about geology, filled with incomprehensible ideas, words he will never use—*mantle, crust, continental drift*. But if he concentrates on the smaller words, the shorter sentences, it is useful enough.

And if his halting reading now is based on rock formations and psalms, he is still more literate than some of the *militsiya* officers in his squad. Even though he is only a clerk, an errand boy, someone who does what he is asked, any task that needs doing. He delivers messages and papers, keeps lists of prisoners, brings the officers hot tea and cigarettes, cleans their boots, banging off the dried mud. A surprising number of them crave sweets—curd buns, sugared cranberries, biscuits—and he scours the stores for these, bringing back what he can find.

All the while, he studies them surreptitiously, deciphering their ranks, names, the procedures they follow. He will not make the same mistake he made at the glassworks, he will make himself one of them. He will form alliances, he will use these links between people—how they talk to each other, how they think about each other—for himself.

He helps them fill out their reports—a waste of time, they say—although he can see that some of them have difficulty with the words. They are not embarrassed by this; if anything, some of them see reading and writing as a little suspect, unmanly, too close to the despised elite. The real work of a policeman: arrests, convictions for the steady flow of thefts, assaults, armed robberies, now and then a murder. Sometimes they are pressed into service for the arrest of a traitor, or a *kulak*, but these are usually the province of the NKVD.

Several of them are lazy—he spots this early on. Plodders, some of them, too, although this is all much of the work requires. And closer up, he sees that a few of them are less than well turned out—a frayed collar here, a missing button, a stain on a tunic. But together, they know almost everything that goes on in the city, they have their own internal maps—the gambling, the brothels, the warehouses, the municipal officials taking bribes.

Sometimes they even have their fingers in these things, but they are all immersed in the city, an extension of it. A living part of its noisy streets, they are on a first name basis with these neighbourhoods—their eyes hard with knowing, their ears filled with the murmur of a thousand conversations.

They tolerate him—he is useful, he is no threat—they talk in front of him as if he was not there. They gripe about the food shortages, about the latest housing directives, the queues. They have no particular hostility towards the men they arrest; often they know them, especially the petty offenders, the swindlers, the ones with contraband, the small-time thieves. Nuisances, they consider them, reserving their strength for more serious crimes.

The captain is foul-mouthed but gregarious, a man who spends his time fostering his links with the people who matter, who have influence—this committee member, that regional administrator, the chair of the district council. Playing whist with the head of prosecutions, drinking with a group of local judges. A master of subtle favours and bargains, he has developed a network of people—and things—as intricate as a local economy.

Better for us, the men say to each other, taking comfort in the idea that he might be able to protect them from political swings and shifts, from the fitful whims of bureaucrats. And it means he has no time to be a hard taskmaster with them, to punish every rule infraction.

Drozd listens to it all, soaking up every piece of information, hoarding it as if it were money. He makes little headway on his plans to get to know them, though, to build alliances—they see him as of no consequence, worth nothing, and his overtures are too awkward, too patently insincere.

Then, a few months later, it all changes.

. . .

The man—arrogant-looking—is sprawled in the chair in the captain's office, nonchalant, his legs extended in his black boots. A khaki coat, dark breeches, his peaked hat with the NKVD insignia on the desk. Through the half window in the office door, they can see the captain looking strained, shifting uneasily in his chair. Now his voice is raised, his hands apart in a gesture of irritation, exasperation.

Always trying to take our men, to recruit people, says one of the officers.

But he says it with a thin skin of resentment, in a way that suggests he would like to be recruited himself.

They never have enough officers, says another. But we are short here as well.

The voices in the office continue on, lower now. One of the officers moves a little closer, almost involuntarily, the temptation to try to hear something overwhelming. But now the captain is opening a bottle of vodka, pouring it into glasses. The two men raise their glasses in a toast, and drink them back.

Then the captain is at the office door, crooking his finger at Drozd. The officers look at him with astonishment. The clerk? The errand boy? This is who they want?

In the captain's office, he tries to stand up straighter as the NKVD man studies him.

You sure he reads and writes? he says dubiously.

Wordlessly, the captain puts a directive in front of him, and he begins to read out loud.

Fine, says the man after a second.

Turn around, he says to the young man, making a twirling gesture with his hand.

He turns once, twice.

He will do.

The captain is scowling, though. This bargain—a clerk instead of an officer—is his idea, but he is still reluctant to lose him.

He makes himself useful.

You want to serve the revolution? says the NKVD officer.

. . .

Tonight the stars are black, silent, their light trapped behind murky clouds. But darkness is better for men who are sleeping. Although he is only half-asleep, struggling with his blanket, which has become tangled and twisted around his legs. He is dreaming that he is climbing out of the river, scrabbling at the riverbank, but the reeds in the water have wrapped around him, pulling him down, the mud sucking at his feet. He wakes with a jolt, and remembers. The NKVD. *The NKVD*. Not an officer, only a clerk, but still—the NKVD. Perhaps it will pay better, he will find another room, another step up, away from the stale smell of other men, the stink of their unwashed clothes.

Elsewhere in the city, under the darkened stars, in another house: a young woman in a pink and black camisole, exhausted. The last client gone for the evening, a rough man, but he pays well. She is mumbling in her sleep, fragments, dreaming of clothes, the *dacha*, the children she will have. Under the bedclothes she throws out her arm, turns over on her side. *And they will all live.*

Even without the clouds, the light from the stars would not have reached the tailor, down in a cell at the *militsiya* station. Lying on the foul-smelling floor, his body aching. He is dreaming of a daughter too, dreaming of the village where he grew up—a poor place, a place of hard earth and bare faith. And a swing—two ropes and a piece of fence board—under a hornbeam tree, the trunk splaying into root nodes. The ground beneath it scrubby, nearby a patch of campion, the buds on the silvery-grey stalks almost open. He and the little girl stand there, looking at the swing, until she puts her small hand in his and then, unable to contain herself, gives a silent wriggle. He picks her up and sets her on the swing, shows her how to hold on, wrapping her little fists around the ropes. He gives her a push, and the swing begins moving.

At first she is hesitant, uncertain. Then the motion begins to take hold of her, and then to enchant her, up and down, back and forth. A shy smile comes across her face. Higher, she says, and he pushes harder, up and down, back and forth. Higher, she says.

Hold on, he says. Hold on tight.

He gives her another push.

Her silky hair is flying out behind her, her small legs kicking the air, moving in and out of the shafts of sun. The tree branch is bent, the leaves brushing against the ropes as the swing rises, the sunlight filtering through them. Back and forth, back and forth, back and forth. He sees the blur of her dress as a small laugh bubbles from her, he smells the rotting acorns below, the powdery odour of the years drifting around her. This inquisitive child, this child with darting hands, this child so full of stories—the delicate lines of her face alone enough to break his heart.

. . .

These officers could not be more different from the *militsiya*. Russian to the bone, to the marrow of the bone, convinced of their superiority, contemptuous of this city, this country. A dead-eyed captain, morose, stained teeth, distant from the men.

The NKVD headquarters for Minsk *voblast*. The men think of themselves as ruthless, although even he can see that some of them are not. But these are also the ones who are rowdy, who crack jokes, who mock the prisoners, who invent crude nicknames for them. A good enough bargain, the others seem to think. And they are all convinced that they are the select, the finest—the eagles of the revolution. A low-pitched swagger hangs in the air.

Peasants, says the chauffeur bitterly. They think Belarusians are peasants.

He is cleaning the vans, they require constant sluicing out, wiping down. More often than not, vomit, blood, mud, urine. This is the garage where they take their breaks—the local recruits, chauffeurs, couriers, guards, the lower end of this machinery.

Some of them are better than others, says Drozd.

Who?

Sidorenko.

Sidorenko is a young officer, greasy-haired, beefy. Sometimes he imparts bits of information to Drozd through an almost closed mouth, although only when no one is nearby. If the other officers are close, he is contemptuous, dismissive.

Who do they think they are? says the chauffeur, wiping the door of the van.

An army, says one of the guards, his German shepherd curled at his feet. They think they are an army. Some of them were in the military before.

An army? says the chauffeur. Better than that, they think they are little gods.

He wrings out his cloth into a bucket, wipes his hands, and then lights a cigarette.

Bellyachers, thinks Drozd. Gripers. He wonders whether he should be talking with these men, then remembers his resolve to make allies.

They think they are so strong, so hard, says the guard.

But they *are* strong, says Drozd. They *are* hard.

Not all of them, says the chauffeur. Look at Nikonov. Or Plisetsky. Spineless. And what makes a man hard? A uniform? You would look hard with a gun, too.

He rubs his forehead with the back of his large thumb, cigarette between his fingers.

Drozd looks around apprehensively.

They never come down here, says the chauffeur. Never.

. . .

More paperwork, more errands. He fills out forms, files documents, tags evidence, brings the officers whatever they want. With each edict, each directive, he becomes more fluent in the language of this twisted system. *Kulak. Saboteur. Class enemy. Follow the true path. Stay alert. Trust no one*. The words are seductive, their belligerence, their echoes of betrayal. *Trust no one*. But even the daily memos are codes for a better life. *Monthly rotas. Care of uniforms. Winter hours.*

He watches the officers closely again—if anything, more closely. He sees who mutters to someone under his breath, who snickers at someone's jokes, who nods or makes knowing gestures of derision, of malice. He fixes these tiny moments, this information in his mind, saving them for the day when they might be useful or necessary. The more he does for them, the more he attempts to earn their respect, though, the more disdainful they become.

These things take time, he says to himself. They do not know me yet. They will see. A little more time, and they will see how valuable I am, that I am made of the same cloth as they are.

If they think they are little gods, though, they are little gods that drink. He has seen his father swig *samahon* endlessly, but even so, he is impressed by their capacity. Drinking is forbidden during the day, although the hour of vodka creeps backwards from time to time. And almost every night, they are out, drinking until their tongues thicken, their eyes become slits, their hands clumsy—knocking over glasses, dropping bottles.

A different form, a different manner of drunkenness for each one. Sidorenko becomes gradually tight, edging into it slowly, more and more loutish. The *serzhant* shows no signs of being affected at all until, suddenly, he is unutterably exhausted, he falls asleep where he sits. Another officer becomes first acidic, then silent; Plisetsky becomes clammily sentimental.

We are the defence of millions.

Who can blame them? says the captain dourly, arguing with someone on the telephone. They need something. What they have to do to get these traitors to confess.

What they have to do. Impossible to avoid hearing the sounds from the interrogation rooms—the screaming, the crying, the pleading. Even a strange smell, as if fear and pain had their own scent, mixed with the acrid smell of floor cleaner.

Physical measures of persuasion are very effective, says the directive.

You will get used to it, says Sidorenko in a low voice. Sometimes it takes a while, but you will get used to it. None of them are innocent. None of them. If they are arrested, they are guilty. Otherwise, it would be a disaster—the officer made a mistake, a mistake he cannot afford to make.

He mimes a quick slashing motion across the front of his neck, so fast it is almost unnoticeable.

And the shame, the weakness of not getting a confession, he adds.

Confessions. Everything revolves around them, the core of the work. They are powerful, adaptable—they work backwards to justify the arrests, the interrogations, they work forwards to justify the sentences. Usually there is no other evidence against the prisoners, unless it is the confession of a previous suspect naming them. But this lack of other evidence does not suggest innocence.

Not at all, says Sidorenko. This is proof of the cunning of these traitors, these saboteurs. How well they cover their tracks.

The young man is impressed with this airtight way of thinking, the simplicity of it—every angle connected. It makes sense to him, a clean, hard sense. He is less convinced by the idea that this is part of something loftier—the fight against the turncoats, the spies, the treasonists, to protect the revolution. This is not how he thinks, the idea of lending himself to something like this, but he adopts it as part of the currency of the place. And the idea that if there is a fight, it must be ferocious, absolute—that the rot must be cut out—this, this is persuasive.

Drozd, says the captain, a few months later. He is standing by a cabinet in his office. At ease, he says. New duties for you.

His tone implies this is an honour, an elevation of some kind, although there is no more money, no other title. And his eyes are as dead-cold as ever.

A shortage of officers.

Now he will be working more with the prisoners, writing down their confessions, their denunciations of friends and families. He will be going in and out of the interrogation rooms now, something new. He will assist the officers, taking down statements, reading them back before they sign. The men are more literate here than the *militsiya*, but his help will speed things up.

This is how I am trusted, he thinks.

One step closer to being an officer. His withered sense of pride inflates.

. . .

The man is naked, propped up on a chair, his body blotched with bruises, one arm twisted at an awkward angle. His face is swollen, an eye almost closed.

Another one ready to confess, says Sidorenko. He is tired, sweaty, rubbing his shoulder, running his hand through his greasy hair.

Take this down, put it in the usual language. He says he engaged in anti-Soviet agitation, sabotage, and terrorist activities. He says Dzmitry Kuzmich was also involved, that he did these things as well.

Drozd writes it down laboriously on the pad he has been given, couching it in the formal terms of other confessions.

Sign it, says Sidorenko, propping the man up further, putting the pen in the man's hand and curling his fingers around it. The man, barely conscious, scrawls something.

Take him back to the cells, and then clean up in here. The night cleaners can wash the floor, but wipe the rest of it down, straighten it up.

The blood on the truncheon. Half-mugs of cold tea. Lengths of rope.

Take the coat and the boots, bring them upstairs, but leave him the shirt, the pants.

He goes out, still rubbing his shoulder.

Get up, says Drozd to the prisoner.

The man makes an attempt to do it, and then collapses back in the chair.

Get up, he says more loudly.

The man is clearly feigning weakness. The clerk feels a surge of anger—he is being hindered in his new duties.

The man makes a small gesture with his unbroken arm, a gesture of helplessness, hopelessness. He makes another effort, but falls off the chair, barely able to put out a hand to catch his fall. Then he lies motionless on the floor of the cell, half on his side, half on his back, his eyes closed.

Get up, Drozd yells.

He erupts in rage, grabs the truncheon, and bangs it against the wall.

The man begins to shiver uncontrollably, and then stops.

Drozd half pulls the man up, looping his arm around his neck. The slack body hangs against his own as he drags him towards the cells. The touch of the man's naked arm against his neck, his sour breath, the smell of urine, is repulsive.

The man tries to say something, almost inaudible.

What? says Drozd. Perhaps he has more to confess.

The man whispers again.

What? says Drozd more loudly.

The man makes a small hissing sound. Drozd puts his ear closer to the man's mouth.

Lies.

. . .

Take the coat, the boots.

Plisetsky has disappeared. Overnight, he is gone, his chair empty, his desk bare, no other traces of him. As if he had never existed, never sat there, rolling peppermints around in his mouth, complaining about the prisoners. A blank space, a hole in the air.

The captain, his coarse face more impassive than usual.

A coat has been found, he says meaningfully. A coat with a name in it, one of the prisoners. The family saw it for sale in the market.

The officers look uneasy.

The person responsible has been punished, he says deliberately.

He gives nothing away, although he manages to convey knowledge and denial in the same breath.

I have received orders, he says pointedly. I have been ordered to ensure this does not happen again. No coats, no boots, no jackets, no clothing. No selling of possessions. It undermines our reputation, the honour of the force.

Silence.

Is this understood?

. . .

Piles of clothes, linen shirts, shoes, leather belts, wool jerseys, gloves. Wallets, rings, eyeglasses, watches, most of them turned into rubles. What are they to do with them, after all? Give them to the families of traitors, enemies of the people? What have they done to earn these things?

We deserve it, they say to each other. This is hard work, hard on the body, hard on the mind. Dirty work, we are fighting a war, we are on the front lines. Not like some fat-gutted bureaucrat, setting the price of wheat. We are the NKVD, the highest and first sons of the revolution. Away from our homes, eating rotten food, sleeping in cramped quarters. What we have to do. We need the money, for drink, for whores, for comfort. We deserve it.

At least we can still use their rubles—if not their wallets, at least the contents of their wallets.

Money has no name on it.

. . .

One evening, Drozd finds Plisetsky's badge, slipped behind a drawer in his desk. He pockets it quickly. Wherever the man is, he has no need of this.

. . .

What happened to the tailor? says Leah.

What tailor? says Drozd.

The one who gave you the soup.

Him? He was slime. Less than slime.

He was another human being. He was kind to you.

Human beings are worth nothing, a Jew even less. Pigs. And why does it matter to you so much? Who are you to judge me?

. . .

The doctrine of rescue. The owner and captain of a boat invited a number of friends on a cruise. One fell overboard into the freezing water, another jumped in to rescue him. Both died, but the owner was held not to be responsible. There is no general duty to rescue in common law, says Justice Jessop. One can smoke a cigarette on the beach while a neighbour drowns, and without a word of warning watch a child or blind person walk into certain danger.

NINE

If God lived on earth, people would break his windows.
JEWISH PROVERB

Minsk, a city dragging its history behind it like a sack of boulders. A place full of surprises, remade after the war by dreaming Russians. Avenues, they said when they woke up, their heads groggy. Colonnades. Obelisks. Monuments.

Now a place ancient and young, timeworn and eager. A city and its own younger brother, living together in close quarters. The bright air is strikingly clear, and in the distance, there are waves of undulating apartments in pale green or ochre stucco. A river meanders along, its surface scattered with dots of light. But behind all this, loitering in alleys, slipping around doorways, there are other things, hidden things: lucent warmth, grittiness, spiky courage—things liable to erupt in startling ways.

The investigator picks her up at the airport, a man in his forties, the skin shadowed around his eyes, his mouth finely curved, uneven.

Todar Pavlovich, he says, eyeing her disapprovingly.

He is a disapproving man—of her, the airport, his car, the city itself. Especially the city.

Rubble after the war.

He says this as if it was the city's fault, and he has not yet forgiven it—still holding on to a grudge about the disappearance of this building, that corner. But these changes, these missing pieces must have vanished before he was born—perhaps these are borrowed grudges, inherited from his parents as a child. Of course, a child can hold a grudge—even a second-hand one—as keenly as an adult. Something that can be orienting, steadying—almost sustaining.

The architecture—first Stalin, then Khrushchev, says the investigator moodily.

They pass an Orthodox church, white with blue cupolas dotted in gold, then a park of balsam and fir trees. A bronze statue, a man, stands with his coat thrown over his shoulders, a cane in one hand, poised mid-motion on blocks of granite, his eyes blank.

Yanka Kupala, says the investigator, in answer to her question. A poet. Died falling down stairs. Or maybe he killed himself after naming names. Or maybe he was murdered.

Too many choices. Reality should be less optional, less fickle, she thinks. Something solid, fixed to the spot, as faithful and unblinking as an owl.

The NKVD, they went after the writers, poets, artists, he says. Executed twenty-two of them in one night alone. A disaster for a small country.

Does she know any Belarusian artists? Soutine, born in a *shtetl* near Minsk, a man who painted the rabbi, and was beaten up by his son, an Orthodox butcher. But he moved to France early on. Chagall, of course, his father a herring-seller. A painter of acrobats vaulting from swings, of willowy couples sailing through the sky.

The investigator takes her to a bar, shelves of dimly lit bottles behind the counter. In a few minutes, plates of sausages and potato pancakes appear, the barman wiping his hands on his apron.

I cannot guarantee anything about these witnesses, says the investigator. He eats slowly and primly. I know the problem is identifying the man. But it is getting harder and harder to find witnesses who are still alive—they are dying like insects.

Flies? she says.

Flies are insects, he says severely.

What are you expecting them to say?

He runs through what they have said to him so far, adding in his own caustic remarks.

Any other prospects? she says. The researchers suspect that he was involved in executions, they want to track down every lead possible.

Maybe you should hear these ones first, before you send me on a wild bird chase, he says.

She resists the temptation to say *goose*.

After two glasses of vodka, he becomes expansive, begins talking about himself. He has a soft, guttural accent, turning his English into a line of low, rumbling words. When he talks about his plans, his ambitions, his usual disapproval recedes.

Chicago or New York, he says. I could work for a large law firm, I have seen the kind of work they do, who they hire.

His face lights up a little as he talks; this new side of him is so nakedly hopeful she has to try hard not to laugh. Perhaps working with him will be more agreeable than she thought.

He has done some work for a lawyer in Boston, investigating importers, exporters. It will lead to more, he thinks. The man was impressed with his thoroughness, his clarity. A man with influence and—the investigator rubs his thumb and first two fingers together.

Wealthy? she says.

Jewish.

She hesitates for a minute, while he goes on talking.

I'm Jewish, she says, interrupting him.

A second of revulsion, then his face reassembles and smooths out.

The pitfalls of a name that gives so little away.

A stealth Jew, says Nate.

You should have told me, said a new boyfriend over and over. Someone who had drifted off shortly afterwards. *You should have told me.*

She never seems to get used to this, it always surprises her. Who did they think she was before? Who do they think she is now?

Sometimes people look at her reproachfully, as if she had been working undercover, and had unfairly caught them out. *You don't look Jewish,* they say, then wish they could stuff this inane sentence back into their mouths.

Ashkenazi hair, says her aunt.

You know what I mean, the person says silently, as if they shared some heavy-nosed, olive-skinned understanding.

The investigator is fully composed now, but more distant than before. Or perhaps she is more wary of him. They will both brush this aside, act as if this moment never happened.

Tomorrow, the first interview, he says, the witness has moved to a place outside Babruysk. The interpreter and the KDB officer will meet us there. Do you want to rest now, prepare for tomorrow?

A KDB officer will be at the interviews, Owen had said before she left. A diplomatic requirement for permission. We have to do this through governmental channels. They were fine when we were after Nazi war criminals—if anything, they were helpful. It might be a different story this time.

Yes. It might. The Belarusian KDB—the inheritor, the keeper of the NKVD legacy.

Her hotel room is small, old-fashioned, the wallpaper striped in brown and cream. An uncomfortable-looking chair is drawn up to a desk—three gold foil-wrapped chocolates, an orange, an overripe plum arranged in a row on it. A narrow wardrobe on the other side, a samovar of hot water in the corner. The bedspread is tired-looking, but clean, and the room smells like crumbs.

She sits down at the desk, tries to concentrate on her questions, to read the short profiles the investigator has given her. But she is too restless, her thoughts flitting around, and her burns are nagging at her—healing, but itchy. She wants to get out, to see this place, Minsk, to hear it, to be in it.

The night is warm, spring drifting into summer—people hurrying home under the street lights, carrying parcels, bags, umbrellas. She watches their faces as she walks, looking at them as long as she dares—their expressions tired, distracted. A tight-lipped man, a woman smiling at something to herself.

As she passes the street lights, her shadow changes, shrinking on the sidewalk, then stretches out again. The street signs with their Cyrillic lettering are impenetrable to her. She has a brief glimpse of what it might be like to be illiterate, an existence without written words, surrounded by graphic silence.

She wanders into a grocery store. The smell of curdled milk, shelves of dark bread, a small meat counter—chicken breasts with pimpled skin, pig trotters. Rows of white and green cheeses, honeycomb, jars of pickles—peppers, tomatoes, onions. Packages of dates, figs, apricots tied with hemp. A tank of fish in the corner—hake? carp?—the water dirty, the fish grey and whiskered, primeval-looking. Another display case has varieties of pickled cabbage salads, green, purple, scattered with carrot shreds or small chunks of pork. An entire wall of vodkas.

None of this makes her hungry or thirsty at the moment—the oily pancakes are sitting heavily in her stomach. But she is tempted to buy something, if only to become involved in this purposeful scene for a moment, to be purposeful herself. To be someone other than an observer. Some vodka, perhaps, something to keep in her room. She studies the rows of bottles, but the language defeats her again, and she picks one at random.

A line, but not a long one. Two women are talking in front of her, they look like a mother and a daughter. The younger one is lively, laughing, the older one saying little. Behind her, a man and a woman seem to be bickering quietly, but the rest of the line waits patiently. When she reaches the cashier, she pulls out her money, looks up inquiringly.

But the women is shaking her head, flicks the bill with her finger.

Wrong language. Wrong currency.

. . .

Yes, says the investigator the next day, his disapproval slipping again for a moment. We are the kings of vodka—Russian vodka is nothing. Nothing. We have vodka with pepper and honey, vodka with cowberries, birch leaves, bison grass. Vodka filtered through black flint or platinum. Every kind you can imagine.

. . .

The countryside, grey and damp, the sky iron-coloured. A thin mist over the fields, blurring the spears of mauve-and-pink wildflowers in the ditches. In the distance a peat fire, the smoke smudging the horizon. A stream follows the side of the road for a while, a gleaming snake, and they pass fields of young flax, rapeseed flowers, separated by stone fences. A rowdy flock of swallows goes by, the birds diving and rolling in the air.

Past Babruysk to an old farmhouse, a sour cherry tree blooming in front, piles of worn tires, bleached sacks. The door is answered by an elderly woman, a small birthmark on one of her cheeks, flossy white hair.

Sardechna zaprashayem, she says. Welcome. She offers them bread, salt, honey, tea.

An older man sitting in the corner nods to them, his face framed by bristling white brows, one sharp eye. The other is a puckered scar, a few age spots on his skin. On his lap, an old cat kneads the blanket over his knees.

The floor is covered with a woven rug, and the shelves on the wall hold rows of jars—runner beans, yellow peppers, onions, relish. A whole shelf of dark beets alone, floating in brine, like jars of pickled rubies. On the other side is the fireplace, surrounded by white ceramic tiles, a metal firebox below. And over in the corner, soft cheese in a cloth, hanging over a bucket, a giant larva.

The KDB officer is already there, young, square-faced, a dark blond crewcut. He introduces himself tensely. The interpreter—*call me Polina*—is livelier, her glossy black hair pulled back into a clip, her fingernails bitten down, her voice with a stretchy, violin-like quality. She mocks the officer a little, as if his stiffness was a personal dare. He does his best to ignore her, although his eyes follow her around the room as she sets up a recorder, puts out lapel microphones. She ignores his eyes, although she moves her hips a little more than necessary. But when she puts on her headset, clears her throat, she is serious, capable.

Testing, she says. Her voice changes as she begins to recite a strand of words in a slight singsong.

When she is satisfied, they begin.

Tell us what happened.

I was named by someone, says the man in a raspy voice. I am not sure who, even now. Although I have my suspicions.

He glances at the elderly woman, who nods at him—*go on.*

My father and mother were Ukrainian Jews, from the Homyel *voblast* in southern Belarus—there were many of us there. I was born in Homyel city, but moved to Minsk to get a job. I married my wife—he gestures to the woman—and we had three boys. I worked in the municipal archives as a senior clerk for eleven years, never a complaint. Some of those years were good years for Jews in Minsk—we had the State Yiddish Theatre, *heders* and *yeshivas* everywhere, a hundred synagogues. Almost half the population, we were, Yiddish was one of the official languages. Can you imagine?

No. She makes an attempt to imagine this, to envision walking down streets, mingling in crowds, knowing that she was surrounded by Jews. A tiny sense of relief comes over her, a relaxation of muscles, the loosening of a hidden tension—a tension she hadn't known was there.

But then it all changed, says the man. They closed the synagogues, they banned the *heders* and *yeshivas*, they went after the kosher grocers, the Jewish tradesmen. They banned the Sabbath. We could see it happening, but we never thought it would get worse, each new measure was a shock. We steeled ourselves to bear each change, thinking that it was the last, hoping that it was all temporary. Clearly this cannot continue, we thought. A new government will come in. Or they will come to their senses. Then in 1938, three NKVD officers came to my apartment, and told me to confess that I was a traitor, a wrecker, a member of the fifth column, that I was sending information to the Bund.

Never, I said. Impossible. I am entirely loyal to the revolution. I would never do such a thing. What information could I possibly send anyway? The marriage register? Tax records? I know nothing important, there is no military information here, nothing worth anything.

But they arrested me despite this, and took me to the NKVD building, where an officer beat me with a club around the head and ribs, beat me until my clothes were covered in blood.

The old man coughs, a wet cough that seems to shake his frail body, and then spits into a basin beside his chair. The woman gets up from her chair, pulls aside a grubby curtain under the firebox to reveal logs, some old pans. She takes a log and adds it to the fire, stirring it up.

The next day, says the man, the officer beat me again, this time with a chair leg. He hit me so hard on the side of my face that he took out my eye.

He gestures to his puckered socket.

He made me crawl on all fours, he forced me to bark like a dog. He threatened to beat me with barbed wire. He told me he would kill me, he would shoot me in the head if I did not confess. If I confessed, if I named others, they would send me to a forced labour camp, but at least I would not be executed. He made me stand for five days without sleeping, without sitting or lying down, *stoiki,* he called it. When I could not stand up any longer, when I kept falling over, he would beat me again. He brought in a younger man, a clerk, so they could take turns.

Finally, I confessed, although I still refused to name others, to this day I have never named anyone else. The clerk wrote up a confession, which they forced me to sign, admitting that I had attempted to create an uprising, that I was a spy, that I was guilty of anti-Soviet agitation. Then they sent me to a labour camp.

In the labour camp, I had to cut down trees with an axe so dull it took hours to get through the trunk of one tree. The rations were so scanty, I had to catch rats and eat them to stay alive. Most of the prisoners had dysentery, frostbite, scurvy, lice—the lice alone almost drove me mad. People died every day from tuberculosis or typhus, every day there were more bodies. I was not released until 1948.

She asks him about the NKVD officer, the clerk.

They were men, they were police, the elderly man says, shrugging.

Did you recognize either of them at the time?

No.

Did they refer to each other by names?

Not that I remember.

Did they have any identifying numbers or badges?

Not that I remember.

She shows him a photograph of Drozd. Was he one of the men?

The man squints at the picture, turning it this way and that.

Yes, Todar showed me this, he says in his cracked voice. I think it might be the clerk, I think it might be him. Although he was much younger then. And his hair was different. His eyebrows were thicker then, too.

This is important, says the investigator. These men should pay for beating you, for sending you to the labour camp, for what they did to other people as well.

The KDB official raps sharply on the table.

If you are not sure it was him, do not say that it was.

The man looks at the official as if seeing him for the first time. He takes in his uniform, his insignia, his scowl. Then he seems to shrink a little.

I might be mistaken, he says. These things are difficult to say.

He looks down at the cat, strokes him a few times, and coughs again.

She almost groans. What had she expected in a place where facts had been malleable for so long, where they had become saleable commodities? Things that could be created, exchanged for survival, for protection, for relief from torture or death.

She asks more questions, but the man becomes vaguer with each one.

On the way back, she watches the countryside flow by, the countryside where Drozd grew up. Is there anything here, some element in this terrain, in this soil that gave rise to him, that poisoned him, deadened him? But this sleeping landscape seems placid enough, lovely—a light rain falling, the soft grey mist still there. Clumps of ghostly birches, the fields stretching out, blurred into delicate greens beside the road.

She closes her eyes for a minute, puts her head back against the seat.

These stories—first the affidavits, now these recitals—are wearing her down. Their details are beginning to creep into her everyday life, when she dozes, when she dreams, into any gaps in her thoughts. *When I could not stand up any longer. Where the space was the size of a grave. When every day there were more bodies.* And they leave an imprint of sadness on her, spongy impressions on her arms, her legs, her mind.

But the testimony of this witness would not help them much. His evidence would not survive even the mildest cross-examination.

You'll have to do better than that, says Louis.

. . .

Does he expect you to snap your fingers, conjure something out of thin air? says Nate. No, ignore that, he probably does.

From a distance, Nate seems to have expanded, spread out, drifting through the telephone. She is still waiting for this thing—whatever it is—to assume a real shape, to cohere and harden into something with edges, folds, corners. She is puzzled by its formlessness, but not impatient—she has fallen into this as softly and easily as rolling over. If she starts trying to shape it herself, to impose some form on it, she might end up with a version of her past relationships, instead of something with its own unique contours. But soon, very soon, she hopes that it will become more tangible, a thing she can press against her face, clasp to her chest. Something that she can touch, that she can wrap around herself, that she can hold in her hands.

She feels a warm, silvery cramp in her chest.

Are you still there? he says.

. . .

She is crouched beside the row of leafy plants and her legs are beginning to ache. The basket in front of her is only half filled with strawberries.

Law school, the end of second year. Nate has persuaded her, has convinced her she will have a good time. *We need to get out of the library, we need the fresh air. And I have a recipe for jelly, strawberry with basil.*

But the sun, at first a welcome warmth, is now hot, drilling across her back, and her hands are sticky with juice. She stands up, shakes out her legs, and moves to the next row. Here she tries pulling the glistening berries off in handfuls, but she crushes too many of them this way, the smell almost spicy. All she has to do is fill this basket, she reminds herself. But the basket is filling so slowly that she lifts it up to see if there might be a hole in it.

She rubs the back of her neck, then stands up again to stretch her legs. Nate, in the next row, his basket almost full, looks up at her.

This is too much like work, she says.

Only a row or two more, he says encouragingly.

Let's make less jelly.

What a thought.

One more row, she says.

Three, he says.

She picks up her basket as if to throw the strawberries at him.

You wouldn't dare, he says doubtfully.

A long, slow arc, brilliant red in the sun.

. . .

An hour, a day, week. How long has she been sitting there, in this room or another, Polina's singsong running through her ears? Watching the investigator study his fingernails, the KDB official tapping his pen. The investigator is a smoker and the familiar smell makes her more receptive, she feels she can listen to almost any story, no matter how weak, how flawed, with a nicotine-stained equanimity. So far: a farmer, a welder, a mathematician, a teacher. Each with a harrowing tale, each with only the most dubious identification of Drozd.

They are compelling despite this, so different from each other, but alike in their underlying bluntness, their clarity. As if the horrors they experienced had burned away an outer covering, and left them with a shell-hard core. Undaunted afterwards, persisting in creating new lifetimes for themselves. Even now, they continue in these uneven duets with the world, still closely—valiantly—coupled to their lives. What kind of fortitude, what kind of nerve does that take?

Not many possible witnesses left, says the investigator. So many of them were executed, or they died of their injuries, or died in the labour camps, or died since then, infirmity, age. Not many left.

She is surprised at how fiercely she wants to win this case now, something that has crept up on her. She is convinced there should be some moral compensation for the destruction this man helped to wreak, some redistribution of circumstance and consequence.

Particularly since there is no sign of any remorse on his part, no sign of regret, nothing that might be a form of atonement. Unless living an ordinary life, a humble life, the small virtues of it, a thousand tiny moments over time, unless these things have their own redemptive force.

No, this is not enough. At least in his case.

Perhaps this is not the way to think about it, though, the idea that someone's good deeds and bad deeds are linked at all. Or that there is some formula, some equation that can be applied to come up with a tally, an accounting. A moral netting out. Particularly since *good* and *bad* must be ever-changing configurations.

Some things are unredeemable, say the spiders. Some people owe a permanent debt to justice.

But justice requires evidence.

We're not alchemists.

. . .

The doctrine of frustration. A man rented a music hall ("God's will permitting") to hold a series of fêtes and concerts, including a quadrille band, a wizard, tightrope performers, rifle galleries, and boats on the lake. The music hall burned down before the event, and the man sued the owners for failing to provide the hall. The Court of Appeal found that the owners were excused from their obligations in the same manner as if a painter commissioned to do a portrait had been struck blind. The perishing of the hall, said Lord Blackburn, made the thing impossible.

. . .

There's no one else, Ida says again.

Sure, says Marvin, and begins setting up the rented mourner chairs.

She was my closest friend. I owe her this. And those uncles are hopeless.

Sure, says Marvin.

The shiva. She is eleven, almost twelve, she refuses to sit in one of the short chairs, to be there for the Kaddish. She refuses to wear the torn black ribbon.

She wouldn't want this, she says. She wouldn't want this.

Her voice is thin, she is shocked, reeling inside.

Yes, she would, says Ida wisely. She puts her arm around the girl, who stays stiff for a second or two, then shrugs her off.

Then I don't want it.

The prayers, the hand washing, the candles. In her dazed state, the girl feels as if a small cloud of Jewishness has engulfed her, something unknown, murky—not her aunt's familiar rhythms.

Marvin winks, an empty gesture, as if they are on the same side, even though they are not. But she knows he means to be kind.

She still insists on staying outside, refusing to talk to people, throwing a ball against the side of the house—off the wall, off the paved driveway.

Thud. Thud. Thud. Thud.

Leg under the ball. Leg over the ball. *One, two, three alairy, kick the cat out of the dairy.*

I'm so cold, her aunt had said. I'm so cold. Tell that nurse to bring me another blanket. I'm so cold.

Her laboured breathing, the tremors in her hands.

Thud. Thud. Thud. Thud. *Seven, eight, nine alairy, meet me then in January.*

Ida plays music—wistful, beautiful songs—to entice her inside. Marvin raises an eyebrow—during a shiva?—but she shrugs. *What's the harm?*

Nothing will bring her in, though, except to eat and sleep.

Between the thuds, she hears voices she knows. Here come the uncles now, in a clump, walking up the front path. Nervous, they have banded together for protection, Gus smoking hard.

She agrees to go inside with them, only because they look so worried, as if they might be subjected to some ritual against their will.

Finally, says Ida reproachfully to them.

They sit at the dining room table, dark mahogany so burnished she thinks that plates might slide right off it—she imagines them skating around its surface, people grabbing frantically for them with both hands.

Sweet potato kugel, says Ida, setting out dishes and forks.

They are drowning in a mountain of kugel dishes—noodle, cheese, potato—people bring it every day. As if this starchy dish were a cure for mortality, a remedy for death.

The uncles glance at the covered mirror on the wall, look at their plates suspiciously. Then Rudy begins nibbling on his piece, and Gus starts eating with his eyes closed, a test of his mettle.

Delicious, Malcolm says, smiling at Ida, and she pats her hair involuntarily.

Come home, says Gus.

Soon, says Ida. She'll be home soon. It's good to mourn.

She puts her arm around Leah again.

But Leah is not mourning. All her energy is focused on shutting it out of her mind, sealing it away.

The yellowing skin. The muscle cramps. Her metallic breath.

Why the hell don't they heat this place? her aunt had said.

Someone had brought a box of teas to the hospital for her, tea samples in small round tins, a metal tea egg with a small chain. Every day, Leah brewed it—the nurses let her use their electric kettle—as precisely as possible, according to the instructions.

She put fresh cold water in the kettle, she shut it off as soon as it boiled, she added a teaspoon of tea to the tea egg. Then she carefully steeped it—three minutes for white tea, two minutes for black and green tea. They were working her way through the box: Oolong, Orange Pekoe, Assam, Darjeeling, Ceylon White.

This one is supposed to be malty and smooth, she said, reading the description.

Her aunt made a sound, half cough, half laugh.

I'll drink it later, she said. Leave it on the tray table.

Thud. Thud. Thud. Thud. *Seven, eight, nine alairy, sitting in a cemetery, ten, eleven, twelve.*

Midway through Darjeeling, on the way to her aunt's room, a nurse headed her off in the corridor.

I'm so sorry, honey. Let me call someone for you.

Incomprehensible. Unimaginable. Unbearable.

An ocean of pain swamped her. Her mind snapped shut.

Outside, a flock of starlings burst into the air, twittering fiercely.

. . .

Rain is coming down in warm gusts as the investigator parks the car. She has slept badly, her eyes feel roughened, tired.

This is a good one, you will see, he says. But he has said this before each witness, so she only nods.

Irina Novik. A doctor, although she is in her eighties now, and no longer works. *This is a country, a place of old women,* they say, the men dead before their time—executed, worked to death, blown up in wars. She lives in an apartment, she is standing in the doorway, a dress of blue linen, a cardigan on her shoulders. Her black eyes watchful, the skin translucent over the veins on her hands, the rings on her fingers sunken into the flesh.

The place is dirtless, whip-clean, all blues and greys. Fabric has been tied over the chairs and sofas, making their surfaces softer. The KDB officer looks larger, stiffer here, out of place in his uniform.

A pot of coffee, an apple torte. The woman limps as she walks, her ankles swollen.

The investigator explains again: This is for a foreign court case, no, not here. They are looking for information.

The woman keeps turning her rings around, looking at the KDB official.

You should speak freely, says the investigator. She is a lawyer—he points at Leah—you have the protection of the law.

Nothing will happen to me?

Nothing will happen to you, says the investigator.

But how does he know? Leah thinks. How can he be sure?

The KDB official is frowning on the other side of the table.

The woman pours out the hot coffee, wiping the drips off the bottom of the spout with a cloth after each cup. After the last one, she pauses for a few seconds, holding the coffee pot in mid-air. Then she puts it down abruptly, with a sigh—a deep, balloon-like sigh, as if she had been holding her breath for decades.

We lived in a village near Minsk, she says abruptly. My father was a group leader at a *kalhas*, a collective farm, and also looked after the draft horses. My mother worked in the kitchens there—that was where they met, and eventually they had five daughters. I am the middle one, the oldest one died last year. My father loved the taste of mushrooms, so my mother would gather them for cooking.

Mushroom picking is big here, the investigator says to Leah. The silent hunt, they call it.

Polina frowns at him, and the woman continues.

It was September, a warm September, rainy. Good for the mushrooms. My mother had heard of a small copse on the outskirts of Minsk between the Ring Road and the Zaslauje Road that had many mushrooms. She took us there, the children, we all had baskets. We picked all afternoon, the light was fading, but there were so many patches of them, we wanted to pick as many as we could.

We were getting deeper into the copse when we heard the noise of shooting. Get down, snapped my mother, get down, get down. She was annoyed, she thought there were boys shooting grouse or hares. *They should not be shooting here*. Then the shooting stopped, and after a little while she let us stand up again, and we went looking for the last few mushrooms before the sun set.

A moment—Polina makes an adjustment to a microphone and then nods.

I found a clump of chanterelles apart from the rest, and then another and another, until I was separated from my sisters. As I was turning to go back, I heard voices. I went towards them, and saw a clearing through the bushes, through a wire fence, where two black vans were parked. Several NKVD officers were shovelling sand into a pit and smoothing it over. I could see a hand, a foot sticking out of the pit, before they pushed them down and buried them. Then they left in the vans.

The KDB officer is rigid, his pen tapping twice as fast as usual. Be careful what you say. Tap, tap. Make sure it is the truth, that your memory is not tricking you. Tap, tap.

The woman looks at him, anxious but stubborn as well. Now that she is finally telling this story, she is not willing to stop, perhaps she is not even able to stop.

I know what I saw, she says doggedly.

Not a word, my mother said later. Not one single word, not a word to anyone. If they knew you were there, they would kill you.

A few days later, we were coming back from the market and we saw a man sitting by the side of the road, his back against a tree, reading a newspaper. As we went by, we saw that the man was a dead body that had been propped up. Someone had dug up a body in the night and posed it like that. My mother and father looked at each other, and then my mother said again: *not a word, not one word.* So even though I heard other stories over the years, I said nothing. But now things are different.

This forest, says the investigator. Where was it?

It was Kurapaty. Kurapaty forest.

The investigator turns to Leah. An NKVD execution site. Where they took people to kill them, not only from Minsk, from other places in Belarus as well.

She sits very still.

No, says the KDB official loudly. It was an execution site, but it was the Germans who killed people there. All those rumours, this is all they are. It was the Germans, they were German-style executions. Russian guns? They used Russian guns they had captured when they invaded. Don't forget, this woman was a child, she is confused, it was so long ago.

Why do you say the men you saw were NKVD officers? she says to the woman.

They were wearing NKVD uniforms. We would see groups of officers in the street sometimes, even I knew what the uniforms looked like. And it was several years before the Germans invaded, I was seven or eight. The Germans came when I was ten.

There, says the official. You will take the word of a seven-year-old child?

I remember, says the woman. And I know what I saw.

Did you see the faces of the officers? says Leah.

Yes, when they were shovelling, they went in and out of my view between the trees, the bracken.

Leah shows her the photograph. Was he one of the officers?

She studies it carefully and then puts it down on the glass coffee table.

No, she says.

Are you sure? blurts out Polina, then begins fiddling with her headset to cover her confusion.

Yes, I'm sure.

Leah feels herself sag. Of course. This case. This hapless case. What had she expected? She will be suspended in this limbo of missing evidence forever.

One more try.

Have you seen this man before at all? she says. Anywhere?

Yes, says the woman.

Where?

At the graves, Kurapaty. As I was saying.

The KDB official tenses up again, raises his voice. But you said he was not one of the officers.

He was a driver, he drove one of the vans.

. . .

Kurapaty. A carpet of wood anemones, white flowers stretching in every direction beneath the spruces, rows of black crosses between them. She is standing with the investigator, the forest dim and green in the morning light.

If spirits really do depart the dead, if there are phantoms of some kind that rise from bodies, this forest must be thick with them, she thinks. A city of dead souls, elbowing each other, stepping on pale, cold toes, jostling for position. Thousands of bodies, hundreds of thousands. Officially, only thirty thousand.

But nobody believes that, says the investigator.

No surprise, then, that these spirits might be crowded. A fifteen hectare forest tomb.

Have they left some residue of their thoughts, their emotions here, some substance cast up at death? Some essence of being that arose at the very moment of passing? Unlikely, perhaps, although even a scientist might grant that unknown—as yet—things such as this might exist. In a world of quantum physics, of sound waves, of particle theory, perhaps other unseen forces should not be ruled out too quickly. As a matter of science, was the idea that such a large number of deaths might leave their mark somewhere—a mark that might one day be as measurable as radon or carbon dioxide—so impossible?

Either way, a profoundly melancholy place.

Congratulate your researchers, she says to Owen. Give them a hand. Give them a raise. Tell them their intuitions were impeccable.

This was a war, says Drozd. If they were troops killed in battle, thousands of soldiers, nothing would be thought of it. This was a war, a battle to protect the revolution, these were the casualties of the other side.

Jus ad bellum. The just war, war as a natural right. Out of fashion in principle, persistent in reality.

Persons taking no active part in the hostilities shall in all circumstances be treated humanely. Fourth Geneva Convention.

The rules of war. Clumsy. Honourable. Absurd. This mass slaughter, this bloodbath is permissible. This one is not. Soldiers, yes, even conscripts. Civilians, no.

They were all enemies, says Drozd. Attempting to destroy us. And some of them were not really people. Jews are not really human. This is a proven fact. They are closer to animals. They are filth. And the others were scum—the *kulaks*, the traitors. It was a war.

Do you really believe these things? she says.

Yes, he says loudly.

Then why were you hiding the bodies?

. . .

Is there anything to the argument that it was the Germans at Kurapaty? she says to the investigator.

No, it is pigwash, he says.

Hogwash, she says silently to herself—but at this point, he can call it whatever he likes.

Even a commission set up by the Communist Party found it was the NKVD, says the investigator. That the shootings took place between 1937 and 1941, part of Stalin's purges. Before the German invasion in 1941.

What about the idea that they were German-style executions?

Shooting people at the graveside was not invented by the Germans.

. . .

If Kurapaty is not full of crowded spirits, if it is only earth clinging to old bones, there is still Dzyady, the feast of the dead. When deceased ancestors visit the living, a gentle gathering.

Superstition, says the investigator, but he seems tolerant of it—indulgent rather than his usual scorn.

A relic of a time when the boundaries between this world and the next were more flimsy. A day when relatives of the dead sweep their graves, pour vodka around the headstones, leave food. A moment when they invite the restless dead into their houses. *Come in, come in, welcome, warm your cold bones by the fire.* Hoping for a dreamlike word, a gossamer touch from a departed brother, a husband, a mother. Places are set at the table for them, honey, barley porridge, eggs, blini laid out. The table is circled three times with a candle, and the doors and windows are opened, the names of the dead are called out. *Come in, come in, make yourselves comfortable, come and be with us.* They drift in, smelling of sweet death, they settle down, silently companionable.

At the end of the evening, they return to the everlasting, unless a particularly amiable one is kept around. And for the others, if they seem reluctant to go, if they want to settle in where they are? They are swept out with a broom.

Now, on Dzyady, people come to Kurapaty, says the investigator. They collect near the Luch watch factory, they march slowly past Kalinoŭski, past Lahoiski Trakt, past Mirashnichenka, then on to Kurapaty, clutching their crosses and banners.

What do the dead say to them, their rustling hands, their whispery voices among the trees?

We are here. We are waiting.

TEN

You cannot make a revolution with silk gloves.

JOSEF STALIN

I have started a child, says Aksana, stroking her belly tentatively. Her stomach is still flat, the hairs below it curling, no sign of any burgeoning underneath. The oil lamp casts wavering shadows on her skin, a play of light gold, dark gold.

He is flooded with irritation. *Why tell me?*

Then he pauses for a moment in the act of buttoning up his shirt. A child. A slip of a person, someone he has fathered, who might have his eyes, his mouth, his head. A son, who might give him more substance, who might make him seem older, who might look up to him. For a moment, he can see a dark-haired boy, clean-limbed. My son is strong, he could say to Sidorenko.

Then he remembers—this could be anyone's child.

I need money, she says reluctantly, picking at a seam in the green coverlet, smoothing it down, picking at it again and smoothing it down. Money to get rid of it.

Why ask me?

I'm asking all my patrons, I'm asking each one to give a little.

What about him?

He gestures with his head towards the floor above—the man who runs the place, fleshy, red-faced.

He will not pay, he will only throw me out. He says he can find another girl easily.

I will speak to him.

She shrinks back on the bed, her dark-blue eyes clouded with fear.

Then he will throw me out because of that.

Not when I am finished.

The man is more corpulent than ever, his hands pudgy.

Take care of this, barks Drozd, flashing Plisetsky's badge.

Of course, of course, says the man, changing tack mid-air, about to reject any request. Now he is ingratiating, his face wobbling—half-afraid of the man, half-hoping for business from other officers.

Aksana looks at him wonderingly when he comes back down. She makes much of him, stroking his head, rubbing his back.

This little victory warms him. He stores it away in his mind, and over the next few days takes it out to examine over and over, nursing the moment of the man's sudden deference, Aksana's surprise. No matter how many times he does it, though, no matter how much satisfaction he gets from it, he ends up with the same thought.

He needs his own badge. He needs his own uniform. He needs his own gun.

. . .

The prisoner, says Sidorenko. Someone has to watch him.

They are short-handed again, two officers have gone back to Russia without replacements. The captain has become terser, more dour. Men needed all over, he says shortly.

The possibility of a war in Europe has been scratching at the edges of their existence. Still nothing more than a foreboding, a wind drifting in from the west, carrying faint traces of oil, smoke. But there is a sense of expectancy, of uncertainty—a foreshortening of the possible future.

Make sure he does not sit or lie down, says Sidorenko. He has been standing for four days now, I have been working with Bazhanov. Soon he will break down, soon he will confess. But Bazhanov is sick today, so this is your chance. If he starts to collapse, throw snow water on him. I will take over again in the morning.

Who is he? What has he done?

Another *kulak*. He resisted the farm collectivization, had labourers to plant and harvest his grain, to look after his livestock. Bull-headed. Refuses to admit his crimes. And our numbers are low.

Refuses to admit his crimes.

Article 58. Any action aimed at overthrowing, undermining, or weakening of the power of the worker and peasant soviets or the economic, political, and national achievements of the proletarian revolution.

Too undefined, too broad to be good law, says Leah, shaking her head. Constitutionally suspect. The doctrine of vagueness.

It covers everything, says Drozd smugly.

Our numbers are low. The estimates from headquarters—the crowds of traitors, out to destroy progress, to take the bread out of people's mouths. The renegades who must be found, interrogated, executed, or sent to labour camps. The pressure is intensifying, the possibility of a war making it more urgent. The sheer number of bodies required is relentless, they are sometimes reduced to rounding up thieves, beggars, vagrants, priests. Fear has begun slipping into their conversations, their decisions, their reactions.

Fear. His old acquaintance, something he knows. An expert, he is familiar with all its shapes and sizes. And now the signs of it are becoming unmistakable—he can hear their hesitations, he can see their doubts, he watches their restless hands. Underneath the swagger, he can sense it—fear of denunciation, fear of the regional directorate, fear of new crimes or failures. Fear of allegations that might reach out and grab them, that might send them spiralling into their own machinery of torture and confession.

Trust no one.

But this is to his advantage. He starts quietly, repeating a spiteful comment to one officer, a word of praise to another, a line or two from a telegram on the captain's desk to a third. Then he watches the effects, adjusts his tactics. He becomes a conduit, a purveyor of small tidings. Most of the officers are wary, but the condition of fear makes them hungry for information, and they are not particular about where it comes from or who is peddling it.

Comrades. If this was ever anything more than jargon, there is little in the way of camaraderie left now. Some of them have kept their old alliances, but many have been eroded or weakened. He is not surprised—he has always found the idea of friendship baffling. And a form of calcification has taken hold in certain parts of himself—has built up gradually—so that even if he understood it, he would be incapable of responding. But now, if he is isolated, they are becoming more withdrawn as well—an office full of suspicious loners. The squad itself a wolf in danger of eating its own tail.

This is your chance. The kulak.

The first night: he maintains a watch outside the interrogation room, through the tiny aperture in the door. The man shudders and sags in the cold, but stays upright through the evening, past midnight.

In the early hours of the morning, though, the man begins sinking, millimetre by millimetre, drooping, dropping in slow motion until he falls to his knees. Drozd unbolts the door and throws the bucket of melted snow over him. He screams and Drozd slams the door, waiting outside until the man is standing again. The room is so cold, he wonders if the man's wet clothes will freeze on him. He is determined that this man will get no rest, not even a moment of sleep, until he confesses. *Stoiki.*

A few hours later, the man is down again. He throws the snow water over him, the man screams again, but he stays down. Another bucket. Nothing. Another bucket. Nothing.

He is furious. He drops the bucket and grabs the rubber truncheon, begins hitting the man with it. The man curls up on the floor, attempting to protect his head with his hands, his arms.

This only increases his rage, the blood singing in his ears. The miserable traitor, foiling his efforts. Anger pours through him, a small grunt of it escaping with each blow. The feel of the truncheon landing on flesh, over and over, the impact rising up through his arm. But when he stops for breath, the man is still curled up on the floor.

He lifts the truncheon again, and the electric light—always unreliable at night—goes out, leaving the room in darkness. A darkness so complete, so deep, it might be a solid thing.

Night blindness. He can see nothing. He listens for the man's breathing, the rustle of his clothes, for any sounds of what he might be doing. All he can hear is his own panting. Perhaps the man is standing up, stealing noiselessly around behind him, poised to leap on him, to knock him down. Maybe he is gathering his strength to strangle him.

He is suddenly in a cold sweat, lashing out frantically with the truncheon.

Then the light is on again, and the man is still on the ground. Lying there, his mouth stretched open in a grimace. He looks more closely and realizes the man is laughing, a silent, mad laugh.

. . .

The next night: the man is still there, still unconfessed, but standing up.

I told him I would cut off his manhood with a saw, Sidorenko says, grinning, on his way out the door.

Several hours later, though, the man is drooping again, falls over once more.

One, two, three buckets of snowmelt. More screams, but he is still on the floor.

An old storage cupboard in the corner of the basement. Mops, brooms, pails, some small tools for minor repairs, a few screwdrivers, a hammer, some nails. A small handsaw.

Look, he yells in the man's ear.

The man opens his eyes dully, sees him waving the handsaw around.

See what will happen to you? To your manhood? Look at this edge, these teeth. They will tear your skin, your organ, your veins. You will bleed to death, no longer a man.

The man rolls over, tries to heave himself up on his hands and knees, and then vomits, a thin yellow stream. He collapses again. He makes another attempt, but slips on the water-soaked floor before he even reaches his knees.

He rolls on his back again. I confess, he says thickly. Then louder: I confess. Then he is shrieking, *I confess, I confess, I confess,* over and over, his eyes staring, an unusual light in them. The string of words becomes incoherent, he is raving now, twisting and jerking from side to side on the floor. He screams until he is hoarse, until his voice is nothing more than a croak. Then he is suddenly limp.

Drozd has to wrap his hand around the pen, write his name for him on the paper.

. . .

He feels cockier, confident now. This is the beginning, he says to himself. And Sidorenko does clap him on the back, surprised. Still, he takes credit for the confession himself, nothing in the report even showing the involvement of anyone else but Bazhanov. Drozd makes sure the others know, though, telling the chauffeur about it within earshot of an officer, telling a guard who he knows will pass it along. His standing has risen slightly with the officers as a result of his snippets of information, and this increases it a few millimetres more. When he puts tea down on their desks, one or two nod at him.

If it takes a while, he thinks, it will be worth it. In the meantime, he knows how to wait.

. . .

The dawn air is rinsed, the light slowly turning from pink to yellow, the black mustard growing beside the hedgerows swaying a little in the breeze. He tramps through the fields, past the small forest—still dim, only a few fingers of pale sun slanting into it. The river is cold—at eleven years old he has become something of a swimmer, but there is no need here, the water is only up to his waist. He climbs, dripping, onto a flat rock in the middle of the river, and sits down, his makeshift fishing stick in hand. An early plover trills its two-note call as he threads a worm onto his hook, a bent nail. He throws out the hook, hoping for a pike or a perch, and settles down to wait, scanning the river for any signs of fish.

As he waits, the water rolls and eddies around him in whorls. He is tired, he is always tired, and after a while he dozes off, still clutching his stick.

A few minutes later, he wakes suddenly, unnaturally alert. Something has changed.

The dawn mist is rising and a silver-brown bear is on the riverbank, head erect, ears upright, testing the air. Emaciated, fur matted along one side, it must have wandered down from one of the forests to the north, looking for food.

It stands on all fours for a moment, narrowing its small black eyes, and then dips its muzzle into the water.

A tug on his stick, and he grabs for it. The bear looks up at the sound, lays its ears back on its head, and snarls noiselessly. Then it lopes off into the forest.

Another tug on the stick, and he wrestles it out of the water, hauls it up—a perch is on the hook. It thrashes about, a shining muscle on the flat rock. He tries to pull it off the nail, but the twisting fish is hard to hold. Eventually, he works it off, but he tears some skin on his palm.

It hurts, he is bleeding, but there is no point in going home, it will hurt in the barn, it will bleed in the potato field as well. He will try for one or two more fish—one or two more before the sun will be up so high that the fish will go into hiding, clustering in the dark green shallows of the river.

The next day, his hand is red and throbbing. He knows better than to complain, and goes about his chores, favouring it as much as possible. But the following day his arm is swollen as well, and the day after that he is feverish, lying on the straw-stuffed mattress. He drifts in and out of sleep, a half-sleep, filled with bleary dreams so strange he is not even sure they are dreams. He sees a bear's head, grinning wickedly, its muzzle thickening and shortening. Then it turns into an enormous perch, head flattening, ears disappearing. The fish begins bleeding from its eyes, and starts to hit him with its energetic tail. Stop, he says, but his mouth is filled with blood.

Stop. Stop.

His grandmother is shaking him.

Drink it, she says.

He picks the mug up clumsily and takes a swallow, burning his tongue on the hot liquid. Then he falls back into his delirium.

When he wakes up a few hours later, he hears them talking.

Will he die? says his father.

Perhaps, says his grandmother. She seems indifferent.

His father swears. Useless rat.

I've put a poultice on his hand. There is nothing else to do.

He drifts off again.

Will he die? says the bear head, now more human than bear-like. Will he die? says the perch. He and the perch are deep in the river now, his breath a spray of bubbles floating up to the surface, the gushing of the water around him a sensation in his ears rather than a sound. He can feel the current circling his body, picking him up, swirling him around, carrying him along. The light above him is fractured by the green water, small, bright spears appearing and disappearing in the dimness. He dislodges some fine sand, the grit drifting through a shaft of sun in the water. Then he sighs and goes to sleep.

When he wakes up again, he is in the cemetery behind the chapel, the trefoil crosses on the graves streaked with moss. He is sitting on the ground, shivering, as it starts to rain. At first there is only a light pattering, a few seconds later the water comes sluicing down. He sees his arms, his legs, begin to soften at the edges, he sees them start to dissolve into the dirt.

He wakes up again—cooler this time, his arm less swollen.

Will he die?

Not yet, says his grandmother. Not yet.

. . .

A transport, says Sidorenko, handing him a key ring. Go and bring them from the cells. Take two of the guards.

Drozd walks down the corridor, opening doors, rousing the men inside them, shaking their limp bodies. They stand up unsteadily, their faces bruised and unshaven, hobbling on battered feet as the guards line them up in the hall.

What about the man in the interrogation room?

Get him too.

When he opens the door, he sees that the wooden bench that serves as a bed is empty. The man is hanging, hanging from a pipe in the ceiling, the noose a strip of cloth torn from his pants.

He recoils, jerking backwards. The guard looks on from the corridor, his mouth open, as the bundle twirls lazily back and forth on the noose. First one way, then the other way, one way and the other. A slow twist of death.

. . .

You will drive, says the *serzhant*, as if he is conferring a favour. The chauffeur must have gone home for the day, home to his wife, her placid manner, his dinner—she can make anything out of nothing, he says reverently.

Are they taking the prisoners to a transfer point, a place where a truck will be waiting? Or perhaps they are putting them on a train. There is a rushed, furtive air to this operation that puzzles him. And why are they taking the dead man, only a sack of cold flesh now, cut down and loaded in with the other prisoners?

But the chauffeur is still here, they are taking two vans. They load up the prisoners, along with some of the officers and guards.

The night is clear, the sky studded with white beads. He is following the other van, he can see its red brake lights bumping up and down on the rough road. They are driving out of the city—insects are blundering into the stream of the headlights, and a small owl swoops past.

Here, says the *serzhant*, and he pulls up in a clearing in the trees. An odd place for a transfer.

There are several men already there, standing with shovels, shielding their eyes against the headlights. They have dug two rectangular trenches in the clearing, piled the soil to one side.

You will be doing more digging, say the officers, as they line up the prisoners in rows at the edge of the trenches. Stand there while we get the shovels.

He watches the faces of the prisoners, still benumbed with sleep, squinting in the light. Some are bewildered, others are bleak, some scornful, some despairing. As the officers line up opposite them, he sees dawning comprehension.

Run, they yell. *Run*.

The men begin to scatter, but the officers are already shooting, their revolvers cracking, the sudden noise echoing around the forest.

Now the faces of the prisoners are agonized, astonished as they stagger backwards, most of them falling into the trenches as they die. Some are wounded, writhing on the ground, calling out the names of their children, their wives, their gods. One is trying to crawl away on his elbows, dragging his leg, part of his jaw blown away. The officers reload their guns, and begin to pick their way around the clearing, looking for anyone still alive, kicking at the bodies. Any movement, and they shoot the man in the head.

Watch this, says Sidorenko. A crawling man is still moving, slowly, painfully, fiercely. When he gets to the edge of the clearing, the officer shoots him.

Any bodies lying outside the trenches are hoisted up by their arms and legs and thrown in, along with the body of the prisoner who hanged himself. Then the *serzhant* gestures towards the men with shovels, and they begin filling up the trenches.

They are almost finished when the sandy surface of one of the pits begins heaving. A man with a shovel jumps back and calls out.

Take this, says Sidorenko, handing Drozd the gun.

Heavier, warmer than he thought. He walks over and empties it into the dirt. The heaving stops.

No resurrections here, says Sidorenko, and Drozd laughs.

. . .

We may however mention a circumstance very little known in common life, that there are certain kinds of glass that may be dissolved in water. All glass is, chemically, a silicate of some alkaline or metallic oxide; and according to the nature of this oxide, so does the quality of the glass differ. If potash or soda be the substance combined with the silicic acid or silica, without any third ingredient, a glass is produced which, though presenting the usual vitreous aspect, is easily dissolved.

. . .

If anyone is not really human, Leah says, it's you.

You know nothing, he says. You have no idea. No idea of the necessity, the urgency.

Clearly she is too slow-witted, she is not capable of understanding this. Not capable of realizing that there is even something fine about these shootings—this ability to create death out of life, to obliterate a human being, to erase a spark of existence in a second, half a second.

All with a Nagant revolver. The sleek power of it, the explosive force. He has never felt more substantial, more satiated, more complete. In this haze of death, he has never felt more alive.

ELEVEN

We do not want to take too many Jews,
but in the circumstances, we do not want to say so.

DEPARTMENTAL MEMO TO
PRIME MINISTER MACKENZIE KING, 1938

Good, says Louis. But one seven-year-old witness isn't enough.

She calls him from time to time to report, hoping for something beyond their present chilly truce. Let there be peace, even a shaky peace, she thinks, and he does seem to be thawing slightly. But now that she knows about this unexpected blind spot in his character, she worries she might stumble onto something else, put her finger on some other sensitive point lying under his skin. She is determined not to show this, though, she tries to carry on in the same way as before. He will pick it up in a second if she seems to be humouring him or tiptoeing around him, and even the slightest indication that he needs tactful handling would be fatal.

I know we need more, she says. We're working on it.

Strictly speaking, the investigator is working on it; she is hampered by the lack of language, the local connections, how utterly foreign she is. But she can see that he is working hard. The shadows around his eyes are heavier, and his face is tense, cagey, hair a little unruly, in need of a cut. He has spoken to the people who talked to the archaeologist, at least the ones who are still alive and not senile. He has spoken to the people they have suggested, and the ones they have suggested in turn. In the area near Kurapaty, he has resorted to stopping old people on the street—his head whips around when he sees anyone white-haired, anyone stooped over. Did you hear anything? Did you see anything? Do you know anyone who did? He follows up one name after another, attempting to run rumours down to their roots. What do you remember?

We knew about it, says one man in his eighties. Most of us. How could we not? The crack and boom of the guns in the night, the vans, the dogs. It was something unspoken, that lay beneath the surface. We kept it there, kept it silently so that it would be in the shadows, less dangerous.

But were you there? Did you see anything?

No. But we knew about it.

Hearsay. Even hearsay multiplied a hundred times is still hearsay.

We must face these facts, says the investigator. Most of the witnesses were shot on the spot. The rest were NKVD, not likely to come forward. But I will find you a witness. I promise this. I will find you someone.

And he does.

. . .

Rafael Benyaminov. His face is crimped with tiny lines and pleats, but his eyes are keen, discerning.

Arthritis, he says, the joints on his hands and wrists knobby and swollen.

Treskovshchina, Minsk *voblast*. A home for the elderly. His room is small and stuffy, shared with another man. Faded photographs on every surface—a woman with a lovely pale face in a black, high-necked dress, two boys and a girl in woollen stockings, a picture of men and women standing in front of a house in the snow—the likenesses marking them as brothers, sisters, children. An old radio, a pink tin ashtray, a package of baked milk biscuits beside the bed.

The investigator has brought him cigarettes, and he takes out two, puts the rest behind the radio.

There is a sitting room we can use, says the KDB officer stiffly. I have arranged for it.

The room is on the main floor of the building, the walls blue, armchairs with a pattern of ferns. It smells of laundry soap and leeks, and on the wall is a picture, a still life of plums spilling out of a bowl. A set of playing cards, a box of dominoes, a pair of reading glasses are scattered around, a half-done puzzle on an end table.

Nearly all women here, says the investigator. *A country of old women.*

Polina positions the microphones, the recorder, her dark hair pulled into a knot, her movements fluid and quick. Her dress is sleeveless, her arms angular, white, a vaccination mark on one. She glances at the KDB officer, wrinkles her nose, and salutes with mock formality. He nods tightly, but the back of his neck begins to redden, and she laughs.

These two. Leah has spent so much time with them now, with the investigator, that they seem oddly close, oddly familiar, even though she really knows so little about them. What she knows, though, she knows intimately—the noise Polina makes in her throat when she is exasperated, her irreverence. The way she conveys to the officer that she does not believe in him—or at least who he thinks he is—but does not necessarily hold it against him. The way the officer cracks his knuckles, his fastidiousness. The state of the investigator's stubble in relation to how much he had to drink the night before, his persistent air of reproof.

But she knows, too, how deceptive these things can be—the irreverent Polina has a subtle centre of gravity, the young officer has his hard side, the investigator nurses his hoard of aspirations.

Time to begin, he says now. Polina puts on her headset, and as always becomes brisk, efficient, starting her singsong introduction.

The man—a retired music teacher, he says—launches into his story immediately, the words running away from him.

My parents were well off, my grandfather had been a merchant and my father was the director of a wine co-operative. We lived in the High Market area of Minsk and they were active in society, my mother in the Jewish Ladies Club and distributing food to the poor, my father in the State Jewish Library, in a burial society, in our synagogue where he sang in the choir. My mother would have dinner parties where we would listen to concert broadcasts or readings by poets—Izzy Kharik, Avrom Sutzkever.

My older brother was a talented cellist and when he was twenty, he became a cello teacher. He was well-known and had many students for his lessons. He was the eldest son and I was the youngest—there were three sisters after him, so there were eight years between us, but he was always kind to me. He would pay me a kopeck or two to copy out sheets of music for his students, take me for walks in the botanical gardens near Chelyuskintsev Park on the Sabbath, buy me ices. He taught me the cello as well, although I did not have his talent.

In 1938, when I was twelve, three NKVD officers came to our house, and arrested my brother, my father, and me. They confiscated our prayer books, our *tallisim*, back copies of *Der Veker, Oktyabr,* sheet music. They claimed that we were using music lessons to spread anti-revolution sentiment and to procure money and support for the Jewish Labour Bund. This was nonsense—my father tried to stay away from politics, and my brother and I were only interested in music.

They took us to the NKVD headquarters in Minsk and locked us in a cell. It was very crowded and some of the people were ill, or had open wounds—the smell was foul. My mother came to see us the same day, crying, and told us she had called everyone she knew, everyone who might have any influence. The ones who were Jewish were willing to help, but there was little they could do. Even the rabbi said that he had no influence with the NKVD. The ones who were not Jewish, she said, were suddenly aloof, uninterested.

She brought her brother, my uncle, who was an advocate—they had bribed the officers to let them see us.

My uncle told us that he argued with the NKVD captain for our release, but the man had rejected his pleas, and then threatened to arrest him as well. He had also spoken to a Party official he knew, but was told that his hands were tied, he could not intervene.

Could not or would not? said my father bitterly.

Does it matter? said my uncle.

But we will keep trying, said my mother, her face working. We will devote every minute, every ounce of strength, every kopeck we have to getting you out.

I remember the way she said that—*every minute, every ounce of strength, every kopeck*. Then she began to cry again, and kissed us through the bars.

After a day, a guard removed me from the cell. At least they are releasing you from this hell, my father said, looking relieved. Locking up a child.

Instead, the guard took me to an interrogation room, where an officer beat me on and off for three days, demanding that I confess to certain crimes. He ordered me to say that the sheet music was coded with Bundist messages, he insisted that I name my father and brother as co-conspirators.

You are a musician? he said. I will make sure you never play anything again.

When I still refused to confess, he broke the fingers in my hand.

He holds up a wrinkled hand now to show his middle and ring fingers are crooked.

I was very frightened and in great pain. After a few days, I confessed to being a Trotskyite, something that was not true. The officer brought in another man to write this down, to have me sign it. But I refused to implicate my father and brother. In the end, though, they charged them with associating with Trotskyites—in this case, myself. I was horrified at how I had been tricked, and tried to withdraw my confession, but they ignored me.

His voice wavers at this point, and he hastily swallows some tea.

They put me back in the cell, and one evening they told us we had been found guilty by a *troika*, a panel of three officials that made these decisions. We did not have the chance to address the *troika*, to use an advocate, or to defend ourselves in any way. Then they loaded all the prisoners in the cells into vans, and drove us to a forest clearing on the edge of Minsk. There were two shallow ditches there, and they told us we would be digging them deeper as part of our sentences for forced labour. They lined us up on the edges of the ditches, telling us they were waiting for more shovels. Then suddenly they opened fire on us, bullets flying past.

The KDB officer tries to interrupt him, but the man rattles on.

A second, less than a second before the shooting, I had bent over to slap an insect off my leg, and the bullets only grazed my shoulder. I fell into the ditch, however, because another man fell against me, and I was pushed into it. He ended up on top of me, twitching for a second or two, coughing, and then becoming still. Blood from his head was running onto mine, but I was rigid with fright. From where I was, I could hear the officers walking around, shooting anyone who was alive. They missed me because I was covered by the dead man on top of me, and because I lay completely still.

Then dirt began coming down around me, they were filling in the ditch. I thought I would end up dying anyway, suffocating from the weight of the man's body, from the dirt. But his body fell in a way that created a small space around my nose and mouth, and I was able to breathe for a short period of time.

The dirt muffled the sounds after that, but I felt the ground rumble when the vans started up again, and then drove off. With my one good hand, I clawed my way out from under the dead man, out of the earth, and into the open air. I made my way slowly to my uncle's house, where my aunt washed my wounds and put salve and bandages on them. I could not bear to see my mother, to tell her my father and brother were dead. And to tell her it was my fault. After a few days, they said it was no longer safe to keep me there, and they sent me to a cousin's house in Brest—they would tell my mother after I was gone.

In Brest, I changed my name and over the next two years, as my beard began to come in, I let it grow to cover as much of my face as possible. I was fourteen when the Germans invaded, and I ran away from my cousin's house and joined a partisan camp. I spent the years from 1941 to 1944 as a partisan, trying to destroy German supply and fuel depots and attacking communication lines. In the end, I am not sure how much damage we were able to do, but we did what we could.

After the war, I became a cello teacher myself, in honour of my brother and father. I used my crooked fingers to hold the bow, my good hand for the fingering.

He stops abruptly, he seems to have run down, out of words.

She places the photograph in front of him. Was this man the one who beat you?

No, he says.

Was he the one who wrote down your confession?

He looks at the investigator, who moves his head almost imperceptibly.

Go ahead, he adds, when he sees the others looking. It is safe to talk.

Yes, he was the one. He was much younger then, but I remember.

Younger, she thinks, but older than his victim. If twelve is old enough to suffer, is sixteen old enough to be accountable?

Was he one of the NKVD men who shot at you? she says.

He glances at the investigator again.

Yes, go ahead, says the investigator.

He was there, he says. He was there.

The KDB officer begins barking questions. He was not an officer, was he?

I don't know.

Was he wearing a uniform?

I don't think so.

What time of day was this?

In the evening. I don't know what time.

Isn't it true, the KDB officer says more loudly, isn't it true that the people who tortured you, who shot at you were German troops, not NKVD?

No, he says. That is not true.

Are you sure that you remember properly?

The man flares up. You think I do not remember who arrested us? Who tortured me? Who killed my brother and my father? You think I do not remember? I would have to have a poor memory to forget those things.

. . .

When do I get the money? he says, as she and the investigator settle him back in his own room. He begins rubbing liniment on his swollen hands.

What money?

I will handle this, says the investigator quickly. I told him that if he would be testifying in court, there would be money for the travel fare, the travel expenses. To come and speak at the trial. I will explain to him how it works—please go on ahead.

. . .

Five o'clock in the morning. The telephone in the hotel room, an old dial set. Who would be calling her here? Nate? Louis? Not at this hour.

Val, her voice tinny.

Gus? What?

You mean Rudy.

No.

We don't know how long he was lying there, she says. He's in the cardiac ward now. They're going to do a bypass, but— Her voice trails off.

This is what she says.

This is what Leah hears: he's alive.

. . .

The air is heavy with the mingled breath and perspiration of so many people, so close together. The flight will be longer than usual—turbulence, says the pilot—they will have to fly farther north to avoid it.

She is beset with superstitions, omens. If she avoids drinking on the plane, Gus will survive. If she rejects the meal, he will recover. If she keeps her hands in her lap, he will be cured. And every object, every item has turned into a charm or amulet. Her paper cup has taken on mystical properties, the wooden stir stick a talisman. How quickly she has reverted to this, as if one inexplicable event has triggered an entirely different world, an ancient one with its own capricious rules.

Now this, she says to Nate, this is where a god might be useful again. A divine being to implore, to beseech. To hear my case.

For example. The appellant is a good man, a gentle man, a man who overcame his natural caution, his reticence to raise a child who was not his own. A man who read the books to her suggested by teachers, hesitating over some of the words, making his way through a list every year. A man who took her to swimming lessons—unable to swim himself—sitting fully clothed on a folding chair at the side of the pool while the other parents were in the water. Who listened seriously to her school tales of small indignities, tiny triumphs. A man with a quiet, obstinate heart, the same organ that has been starved of blood by a clot—now a lump of damaged muscle.

Why should he—of all people—have been chosen for illness, even death? Of all people.

Chance, says her aunt. Random chance. Haven't you been listening? Think of all the different kinds of luck. Blind luck. Fisherman's luck. Hard luck. Jewish luck.

Jewish luck?

Also known as bad luck. What—I have to explain?

Malcolm singing tunelessly under his breath. *I've got the left hind leg of a rabbit. Things are going my way. All I have to do is reach out and grab it. Things are going my way.*

But luck is not an answer; luck is part of the question itself. Or a way of saying: *there is no answer, no answer that makes sense, that has meaning.*

The thought barred from her brain: *it was supposed to be Rudy.*

Not that she would ever wish such a thing on Rudy. Never. Never. But this? This is an ambush.

Ask Rabbi Yitzchok, her aunt said once, when the little girl pleaded for another piece of strudel.

Who?

Levi Yitzchok of Berditchev. The lawyer for the Jews—he interceded for us with God. Dead now, but that wouldn't stop him. Better give him a try, because you're not getting another piece from me.

Rabbi. A request now.

If you look to your left, says the pilot, you'll see quite a remarkable view of Greenland. Usually the cloud cover is too thick, but we have an unusually clear day. You can see the fjords over there, and the icebergs floating down them.

He sounds a little elated, even a little awed, and the passengers look up curiously. Then they begin standing up, filing over to the aisle on the left side of the airplane. The aisle is quickly crowded, but something about the pilot's voice has made them subdued, unexpectedly polite and careful with each other, murmuring apologies or requests in low voices. They peer over heads, between shoulders, past the rows of seats on the left side, ducking and craning. No one tells them to return to their seats, or that the seat belt light has come on, or that they need to balance out the load, as if the crew, too, was suspended in this moment.

She can see the fjords carved into the snowfields from where she is standing, the mountainous icebergs, the Arctic water—shifting colours of white, green, turquoise, grey. The brilliant light, the eerie beauty of it are quietly exhilarating, they reach into her and touch something buried. For a moment, she forgets everything else, she feels a brief stab of gladness.

The passengers are hushed, transfixed by the sight. Then they seem to shake themselves, and begin moving back to their seats, slowly, silently, their faces bemused.

. . .

He is pale under his tan, a tube in his heavy nose. Too burly to be a natural patient, he seems out of place, as if he might have wandered into the hospital by mistake, as if he might have been nabbed by a particularly efficient orderly and hooked to an IV, electrodes slapped on his chest. This whole thing must be some misunderstanding.

She glances at the band on his wrist. No.

His eyes are closed, the lids swollen, but when he hears her voice, they open for a few seconds and then close again. His hand moves on the sheet, a half-gesture of greeting.

The drugs make him sleepy, says the nurse.

She wants to take that hand, to have something reviving, something life-giving flow from her hand to his. Something that will say to this shirker, this loafer of a heart muscle: *wake up, get moving, make an effort.* But she has nothing like that to give him, she has only a wild longing for his survival. And to hold his hand while he is so weakened seems to be taking advantage of him, an attack on his barricades of reserve. So she sits as closely as she can, her arm almost touching, and watches the monitor transmitting its jagged lines of information. Perhaps if she watches it long enough, these lines will begin to make sense, will become a language she can understand.

Your mother went home to change her clothes, says the nursing assistant.

My *mother*?

A sliver of hope leaps in her chest.

No, no, no. She must be talking about Val. *Val.*

But she is astonished to find that such a hope, such an absurd, strangled hope is still even imaginable, has been hibernating in her all this time.

How could this be possible? Is this what happens to the hope of a six-year-old, shocked beyond understanding, beyond any form of belief? Something deeply buried, desiccated after so many years, but still there. Or perhaps hope is always irrational—perhaps this is one of the things that makes it hope, makes it different from saner, more logical kinds of thought.

Time for the procedure, says the nurse.

A technician wheels in a white monitor on an extension arm, a curved keyboard, heavy cords looping around. The patient's chest is bared, a few grey and white hairs exposed. His skin, his flesh looks particularly defenceless, surrounded by the hard edges of the equipment. The technician attaches more sensors and places a dollop of gel—*this will be cold*—on his chest. Gus flinches, and then closes his eyes again. Then the technician picks up a wand and begins drawing circles in the gel.

Sound waves to the heart, he says, while he watches the monitor. When the waves bounce back, they form an image.

Sound waves. If only she had known this was how to assess his condition. Then she might have done it herself, making a clear sound, a bell-like sound near his chest perhaps, listening carefully for the echoes. And if she had been able to translate the results, Rudy could have drawn the image with his inks, a pinkish cross-section of the thoracic cavity. Something that might have revealed a weakness, a flaw, that might have sparked an alert.

The technician watching the screen looks thoughtful, then serious.

What is it? she says.

His doctor will discuss the results with you.

Don't leave, she says to Gus.

I might not get another chance, he says.

. . .

The physical world seems to be rising up against her, the corner of a desk catching her on the hip, a cabinet door reaching over to hit her forehead, a lower drawer stretching out to trip her.

How is he? says Louis.

Not good, she says shortly. Have you spoken to Owen?

Yes, and we think we have enough evidence now, enough to go ahead—with the last two witnesses, particularly the music teacher, and then the more circumstantial evidence, the records. The War Crimes Section has a couple of researchers who are doing more digging into the documents as well.

The music teacher. She feels a faint twinge, a sense of unease. He seemed credible enough, although she is not sure how to evaluate the credibility of someone remembering events from so long ago. What condition can these memories be in, when so many later memories have been layered on top of them? Although he must be right, if any memories would stay clear and fixed, surely it would be these—torture, the execution of his father and brother, his own strange almost-death. Buried in the arms of warm corpses, a stiflingly close view of mortality. A twelve-year-old surrounded by bodies, bodies with a last expression frozen on a face, a shout still fixed on a set of lips.

No one would forget that, no one could forget that. But the details might have become distorted over the years, perhaps even now they slide in and out of focus. Particularly a detail about the presence, the face of a particular person.

Memory can be embedded in the body. She has read this somewhere, that memory can permeate cells, become physical. The example: phantom pain. But what does this really mean? Do people become the physical embodiment of all their past experiences? Do memories twist and shape muscles, organs, blood vessels? Or perhaps they strengthen those things, nourish them. A moment of joy fused into lung tissue, an exquisite painting fixed on the surface of a cornea.

Good find, this evidence, says Louis. You may have a future here yet.

Maybe you could be more specific, she thinks.

. . .

Still thinking about your witness? says Nate, tracing lines on the back of her neck.

She is lying with her head on his chest, lingering in the torpor that suffuses her—both of them—afterwards. She is beginning to think of this act—the aching buildup of desire, the shuddering release—as a thing in itself, something apart from both of them, an entity of its own. Something that drugs them, leaving them in this languid haze.

Being here now is soothing, a quiet hole in time where no one is recounting horrors, no one is frighteningly ill. Where the ground is not shifting, at least for the moment—something that seems rarer than before. She runs her hand over the hairs on Nate's arm, the folds of the pale yellow sheet. Her wariness about this accidental—incidental—coupling is fading away. Sometimes she finds herself watching his hands, his torso for clues—attempting to make some sense of him from his body, to make sense of the two of them.

At the moment she is listening to the lazy thump of his heart, wondering if she could record it somehow. Record it, and play it back to Gus, to his own defective muscle, to jerk it into awareness, to remind it how to go about its duties. *Listen to this. Remember this? You can do it.*

The witness?

I wasn't thinking about him, she says sleepily. But I am now.

When do I get my money?

Is it really just the travel money? she had said to the investigator afterwards, looking at him hard.

Of course, he says, astonished that anyone would suspect otherwise.

First you were obsessed with finding enough evidence, says Nate, and now you're questioning what you've found. Based on what?

Nothing, really. That's the problem.

She is convinced now that Drozd was involved in torturing and executing prisoners, that he was involved in the executions in the forest. How much do the details matter then? Whether it was this prisoner or that one, whether it was this killing or that one, he was an accomplice to such ruthless brutality that these distinctions might be irrelevant. And he is only being deported, not imprisoned. Losing *a* life, but not his only life. A life he stole. A life that was denied to his victims.

No, no, no. This is wrong, this is a kind of slippage. She can almost see legal tenets dissolving before her eyes. There must be specific facts, there must be evidence, even for the balance of probabilities, that untidy test. This is a case about wrongdoing, not a quality of character. He must be guilty of something precise, knowable—something he has done, not something he is, not some innate evil.

Evil again. *Its own foul and hideous bulk.* Saint Augustine.

Protean, ever-changing, stretching to encompass new horrors. But if there is anything that counts as evil, surely it must be torture and killing. What kind of person takes part in these things? A spontaneous human mutation, someone born without the ingredients of a conscience?

Difficult to know, say the experts. A stunted amygdala, says one. An endocrine malfunction, says another. A damaged childhood, says a third.

People have miserable upbringings without becoming torturers or murderers, says Nate.

Brain chemistry. Faulty circuitry.

More chillingly: an inherent human tendency, some of them say, liable to surface in anyone in the right circumstances.

No, she thinks. Not anyone. And what about guilt? What about accountability? There must be a role for them somewhere in this poisonous combination of greed, callousness, self-interest.

Your job is to deport him, says Nate, not to inspect his inner workings.

Still. What happened to the normal human brakes on cruelty, the taboos against murder?

Not such strong brakes, says her aunt. Not such hard taboos.

True, he had been surrounded by other people involved in these things, people who initiated him into these obscenities. But there is no sign that he was a reluctant participant.

All those officers—lulling themselves with drink, with self-justifying cant.

What do you know about these things? says Drozd, furious.

Not nearly enough, she thinks.

. . .

The bypass surgery is in an hour, and he is awake.

Here, says the nurse, propping him up, handing him a pill in a paper thimble, then a cup of water. A little something to keep you calm, to keep your heart rate down. They'll give you the anaesthetic in the operating room.

The pill makes him unusually talkative, almost chatty—so unlike Gus that it is almost unnerving.

Hospitals. Hospitals, he says, nodding.

You've been in a hospital, he says confidentially. Just a baby. They were over at the house. When your father was still around. She was coming down the stairs with you in her arms.

He yawns.

She tripped—a piece of the carpet. I was in the hall, I saw her. But she didn't grab for the handrail, she kept her body curled around you like a snail. Like a snail. Down she went, banging, crashing, curled around you. She ended up with a concussion, bruises, a broken arm, but you—nothing, you were fine. She made them check you out at the hospital, they kept you overnight.

His eyes are closed again.

The next day she took a picture of you—that camera—a picture of you crawling up the stairs.

He is quiet for a minute. Has he drifted off?

And the other time, he says, suddenly stern.

What other time?

You with your broken leg after the accident. Just a little thing, you were, in that big bed.

Time to go, says the orderly, expertly knocking out the brakes on the bed.

And the fever, mumbles Gus. It wasn't just your leg.

Wait, she says to the orderly. The fever? she says to Gus.

You don't remember? That's why you were in the car. She was up at someone's cottage with you, and you spiked a fever, a high fever. She was taking you to the hospital when she had the accident. Don't you remember?

. . .

I have something for you, says her mother. She holds up a flat paper bag.

What? What is it? says the little girl, hopping up and down.

A colouring book.

She runs to get her box of coloured pencils. They sit down together on the old sofa and she opens the book.

The pages inside are blank. She looks up at her mother, puzzled.

Pick a colour, says her mother.

Green.

She shows her how to scrub it back and forth across the page.

As the page fills in with colour, white lines begin to show up, and then begin joining together. Slowly an image of water reeds, a duck, a frog emerges.

Where does the picture come from? she says, astonished, looking on the back of the page, underneath the book.

Her mother smiles.

. . .

The air wobbles again.

The little girl lies there, stunned, bewildered. She can hear night sounds, the occasional rustle, a squeak, the snapping of bracken. Overhead in the trees, a nasal *heent* sounds twice. The ditch has a rich, sickly smell, the smell of vegetation in stagnant water.

Her throat is dry, burning, she has been crying, calling out for hours, she is exhausted, thirsty. Her mother stubbornly refuses to wake up. The silence is heavy.

With a shock, she realizes that a tall, bedraggled man is standing next to her, his face hidden, so close that one of his arms is almost touching her through the broken window. She freezes with fright. While she sits there stock-still, there is a rustle of wind. The man reaches over with a long arm, and brushes the window with a wet, prickly hand. Her heart bangs in her thin chest, then she sees it is a branch. She begins to wail again.

Now the pain engulfs her again, billowing out the window, into the sky, expanding and shrinking with each breath.

What do we have here? says a gruff, kind voice.

A kid, says another.

Heads bobbing up and down, hands around her, patting, undoing the seat belt. Pulling, lifting gently.

Another burst of pain, and then she is in the arms of a stranger.

TWELVE

No form remains permanently in a substance; a constant change takes place, one form is taken off and another is put on.
MAIMONIDES, *THE GUIDE FOR THE PERPLEXED*

The chauffeur is gone.

This fact drops into the frozen morning, heavy as pig iron.

An enemy of the people. A defeatist agitator.

Who denounced him?

The captain.

A bad sign. The pit of his stomach is icy.

He sees a cluster of three officers, talking in low voices. He skirts them, hoping to overhear something, but they break off when they see him, and he keeps walking.

In the garage, the guard is rattled, even the dog seems tense, prowling around, sniffing at cracks in the wall. Standing on his hind legs, poking his nose at the windowsill, at the pane covered with whorls of frost.

Nothing, says the guard, standing apart from the others. I've heard nothing.

They look at each other, alarm underneath their sealed faces. The chauffeur's running litany of complaints. Who would take them seriously? He was a moaner, a grumbler. But they listened, they were listeners, even if they were not grumblers themselves.

And now they are both thinking the same thing:

Did he name anyone?

Too dangerous to ask.

He watches the officers more closely, though, over the next few days—one man mouthing words, another glancing over a shoulder, a shrug. And he attempts to gauge their reactions to him to a millimetre. Are they looking away from him more quickly? Perhaps. Do they seem a degree cooler? Maybe. But if they are, it will pass, he thinks. Of course they are suspicious, jittery—this was how they were when Plisetsky disappeared as well. They all were.

He had assumed that the men who were not officers—the local recruits—were too unimportant to be arrested. Now he realizes this very fact puts them at risk.

But he is different, he is sure of this, confident that they need him. Look at all the ways they need him: standing in for the officers, enforcing long hours of *stoiki*, writing up confessions. Loading the vans, driving them to the forest. Shooting.

They want everyone who knows about these things to have blood on their hands as well, says Sidorenko. A safety measure.

Even this fact, he thinks, even this shows he is almost an officer. He is sure of it. So close, he can almost feel the serge of the uniform, the weight of the gun belt. Any day now. Not like the chauffeur. He was disposable, he was replaceable.

And if the officers are warier, they are still more desperate to know things, every scrap of information he can glean. Another key to his safety. No, he will be fine. They need him.

The only thing he regrets is that the traffic in the prisoners' clothes and possessions—something that had started up again, very quietly—is abruptly halted once more. Occasionally he inherited items from this flow of goods—a torn greatcoat, an old pair of boots—and he also delivered some of the lots for the officers to resellers or buyers. Another valuable service he had provided. Not anymore, though.

The chauffeur? Unfortunate. Yes, unfortunate. He will almost miss talking to him, almost miss his rants. But he is angry that the man has compromised him, and the fact is that he is no longer here, no longer useful. Although he wonders about his fate. Has he been shot? Sent to a labour camp? Asking about him would be too risky as well.

Still, he is constantly watching, weighing. Calculating every sign, every hint. Is the captain looking at him oddly? Is the *serzhant* drawing away from him? He reads the directives, counts the prisoners, attempts to think of ways to feed the official maw.

Snow has enfolded the city in a soft, cold grasp now, muffling the usual city noises. He comes to work in the dark, a sliver of red on the horizon. He goes home in the dark, the winter sun gone, the air so frozen his clothes are stiff with it. In the early gloom, the lights inside the office give it a hunched down look. And the officers are morose, petulant, snapping at him, at each other. Plisetsky was one thing, an isolated occurrence—the coat in the market, someone had to go. But if this is to become more common, then the map has changed, their own machinery looming over them balefully.

A week later. He is putting a memo on Sidorenko's desk when the man grabs it out of his hand. Then he jerks his head—a tiny movement—towards the door. *Now,* he says silently, urgently, only his lips moving. *Now.*

What? No, this cannot be right. He has misunderstood the man. Go? Run? The idea is laughable. But then what does he mean?

He stands there stupidly.

Sidorenko glances around. *Get out of here, idiot,* he mouths.

That *is* what he means. How is it possible?

Now.

A shot of terror goes through him.

Go slowly, he says to himself. Show nothing.

He tries to walk casually over to the door, to breathe evenly—he makes a detour to collect a tea mug on a desk, to pick up a directive. In the hall, he stops for a second and exhales. Then he starts down the stairs, trying to make as little noise as possible.

The street at last, and now he is running, dodging people, lampposts, carts. Everything he has built up so painstakingly, all his plans—so real, so lifelike, their outlines sharp and clear—gone in a moment, his prospects lying around him in pieces. Now he is running, running until his lungs are searing, until he is gasping for breath. Running until he is dizzy, nauseated, until his legs are aching. Fleeing from his own harsh death, panting closely behind him.

. . .

A stark, desperate trek. On foot, clinging to the roofs of trains, the backs of trucks. Slipping across borders at night, under barbed wire, over fences, around guards. Through Warsaw, Budapest, Trieste, Auvergne, a continent holding its breath. He goes wherever a truck or train is going, heading west, stealing bread, wormy turnips along the way.

Months later, Antwerp. The threat of invasion hangs over the city like mortar gas. A place of watchmakers, brewers, who refuse to believe it will happen, but think about it every hour, every day. *Officially neutral,* they say, over and over, as if this incantation alone will protect them. *Politique d'indépendance*, says the king. It will never happen, they insist in Flemish, as they lay in stores of flour, white sausage, batteries, anything they can get their hands on. Normally a placid, stout-hearted city, pleased with its own orderliness. The gabled houses, the cut-out facades, covered with snow. One eye open, one eye closed.

And something else, a shipping port. A launching point, where he can leave this continent behind, this land strangled by its history. Where he can find a newer, looser country, a country that allows him to crawl through rules, slide around barriers. Where creating the elements of a life is not so viciously hard.

No, says the immigration officer, looking out the window.

No, says the visa agent, almost pushing him out the door.

A Russian? says the customs liaison. Not a chance.

No, says the ship's cook on the *Belgenland*. No more men.

No, says the first mate on the *Zeeland*. A full crew.

He keeps talking, keeps looking, keeps trying until he is exhausted, until there is no one else to ask. Until one thing becomes plainly, grimly clear: he is not getting off this continent, not now at least, not from here.

He turns around and falls backwards into the war.

. . .

Rolling, twisting through a crevice in time, months and years spinning around him, fading into each other. A curve of beach in the dazzling sun where birds pick at a corpse, the tide nagging at it. An old woman hunched on a stool in the street, gnawing at a piece of meat. A jeep of chattering soldiers hitting a land mine, the jeep leaping into the air and falling on its side, men spilling out, their tongues stilled. Ragged children sitting in a half-circle in a bombed-out building, one with a bandage around his head, swaying as an older girl leads them in a song, her hands moving as if she was conducting a choir—*sur le pont d'Avignon, l'on y danse, l'on y danse.* An airplane suddenly sprouting flames, brilliant against the night sky, twisting downward in a long, slow arc. A man lying on a frozen street, one leg torn off, the cobblestones beneath him dark with blood. A can of milk, a can of pears he finds in the rubble, greedily licking the metal, the pear taste blooming on his starved tongue. A dead woman in a raincoat over her lingerie, her body in a grotesque position, her face still wearing a puzzled look. Bombs released from the belly of a German Dornier, black wasps dropping towards the ground. An old man emerging from the damp morning fog, walking slowly, steadily with a bed on his back, the bedclothes tied neatly around the frame. The wind blowing a parachute in a field, dragging a body, the pearly silk inflating and then collapsing, over and over. Immense clouds of smoke billowing out over a strafed factory, grey, white, silver, welling out of each other, graceful citadels of ash and air. The smell of rotting apples, sewage, gunpowder, burnt flesh. A waltz of chaos and destruction that went on and on and on, past reason, past bearing, past belief.

But then it was over.

. . .

The office is cluttered with papers, spilling out of wire baskets, piled on the radiator. Files are stacked on a credenza, alphabet letters taped above each stack. On the wall, a portrait of a borrowed king in epaulettes and medals—a man with a narrow, refined face. On another wall, a calendar, the picture of mountain crags brushed with snow; in a corner, a globe covered with small-print countries.

A glassblower? says the immigration official again, a man in his thirties, a thin white scar along the bottom of his jaw. He has been asking questions from a dog-eared sheet for twenty minutes, back and forth over the same ground, as if the answers might be different from moment to moment. Or to catch him out in a lie. He is brisk, dodging from one area to another.

Yes.

And you worked in a small factory?

Yes.

Drozd has an earache, a throbbing pain, something that makes it hard to concentrate on the questions.

Tell me what you did again.

Bottles. Flasks. Glasses. Vials.

He has picked up pieces of English on the run, and patched them together in broken phrases. And he has rehearsed, anticipating some of these questions, watching his reflection in windows.

Bottles for what?

Wine, cooking oil, anything.

The official—lanky, short-haired—has the face of a man surprised to find he is on another continent, but determined to reassemble himself here. New to the job, barely grasping all the regulations, but filled with fresh authority to move people around the globe. To sift out the rabble, to gather the promising ones, to move them from here to there like pieces on a game board. *You may advance three spaces to the Port of Montreal. You must remain where you are and lose a turn.*

He writes down the answers with a fountain pen, scratching on a pad of foolscap, his arm and hand crooked awkwardly, the writing pinched. The clack of the typewriters, the zing of their carriages comes through from the outer room.

Any other duties?

Driving.

What kind of driving?

Deliveries.

He has been using half an onion wrapped in a cloth as a compress for his ear, but left it behind, so as not to show any sign of weakness or ill-health. Worthless, anyway—it was suggested by a man in a pharmacy, when it became apparent he had no money for any other medicine.

Any security or military activity?

No.

Are you a Communist?

No, he says tentatively. He can see from the man's face this is the right answer. No, he says more firmly. But he has to restrain himself from looking around to see if someone can overhear him, if someone is listening to this heresy.

Any dependants?

No.

Why do you want to emigrate?

To make the new beginning.

The pen scratches on the foolscap.

He looks around while the man writes. A fly dying on the sill, buzzing listlessly. A slatted blind, half rolled up. From the other room, more sounds of activity. Clack, clack, zing.

Are you a member of the Communist Party?

No. *A Party member? If only this had been possible. Although the disappearance rate was high there as well.*

Have you recruited others to Communism?

No. *Why would he? It was all encompassing.*

Did you fight for any country in the war?

No.

Why not?

Night blindness.

Scratch, scratch. Clack, clack.

Do you subscribe to the Soviet system?

No, he says, restraining himself again from looking around.

Are you a Stalinist?

No.

Why did you leave Russia?

Belarus.

To escape Communism, he says in a moment of inspiration.

The man writes down the answer, underlines it, then puts down his pen as if he is suddenly tired of this game. He is satisfied, satisfied enough; if this man does not fit every one of the criteria, he is worthy enough, he will move forward three spaces on the board. He tears the notes off the pad and shuffles the pages together, tapping the bottom edges against the desk.

. . .

A question, she says.

Shredded, says Owen regretfully. I asked about that. Government storage protocols. The only thing left in the file is his landing card.

Then how do you know he lied?

Because the truth would have barred his admission.

. . .

The first year—sleeping on the floor of a basement apartment, taking turns on the sprung bed or piles of blankets with two other men. Displaced persons—a Ukrainian, a Russian, as disoriented as he was. Watching bedbugs crawl across the curling linoleum, the room filled with the smell of the coal stove, the borax soap they use to wash clothes in the sink. Eating *zharkoye* the Russian makes from the cheapest cuts of meat—tongue, liver, shank—combining the stamps from their ration books.

What is this city, this improbable place? This spot where they have landed, like a handful of pebbles flung across the ocean?

Toronto, he says scornfully, rolling the word around his mouth.

But he is largely oblivious to it, this place split by ravines full of red oak, buckthorn, and hickory—a place of reckless storms, eerily lovely dawns. Where icy streets stretch out, dotted with Sweet Caporal signs, milk truck drivers, trolley lines. And below them, below the pavement and dirt, underground creeks run their muddy courses.

A rumbling, muttering place, shaped by factory fires, reigned over by the Lord's Day Act—*it is not lawful to tipple, revel, or use profane language in the open air.* And always the old, deep lake behind it, a swallower of wrecks, of hapless men, of all the debris of the people roosting on its edge—the water rising and sighing, over and over, edging the city in reflected light.

Now he is making the rounds again, factories, stores—a brickworks, a sugar refinery, a hardware store, anywhere that might be hiring. But this is even harder here; at least in Minsk he could speak the language, he understood how people thought. If they looked down on him, it was because of his old clothes, his rough haircut, the holes in his boots. Here, they look at him as if he were something outlandish, as if he had three arms. They seem surprised that he might even want a job at all.

The cold crawls down his back, the wind stings his eyes, his boots make squeaking noises on the snow. Sometimes his ear still hurts, a dim ache, his hearing muted on that side. Two weeks of dishwashing at a nightclub, scouring out pots with steel wool, where he can hear faint strains of music, where he eats the rinds of the smoked hams. A month as a parking lot attendant in a plywood booth, chilblains on his fingers. Two months as a furniture mover with an easygoing supervisor, three weeks washing abattoir trucks.

Then, abruptly, the air turns mild. The ice crusts on the ground hollow out, creating thin ledges over the pavement before breaking into pieces. Bare tree branches drip water, and winter aconite sends up green shoots. Warm winds rustle up the street, traces of spring little more than a rumour, but people—hungry for hope—sniff the air expectantly. It smells only of cinders and mud, but from this they conclude, entirely without reason, that some unnamed good thing is about to happen, that some chance at gladness is about to come their way—if not next week, then the week after that.

These people, he says to the other two men. Fools.

Fools, they agree.

But they are wrong. These people are no fools. Oddly shy, perhaps, but tough, patient, clever-fingered, with a deadpan wit. Above all, practical, convinced they can devise solutions to almost anything—handy, they say—but with a store of tiny, incurable dreams hidden in the crannies of their bodies. They ask questions—insular and kind at the same time—about the war in Europe, his country, his family. He is asked so often about the last that he creates one for their consumption—an ailing mother, a young wife, both killed by Communists, a brother forced into the army.

Oh, say the women dishing out relief food at the church, calmly generous. They say it a little skeptically, but they give him an extra ladle of chili to be on the safe side.

No one wants to hire him, though, for the handful of jobs that come up. They hesitate for a minute, then say: *can't have a Russky here.*

. . .

Early summer, cottonwood seeds floating down, drifting onto his clothes as he dozes in the morning sun on a park bench. The park is covered in the downy fluff, sticking to the grass, the bushes, as if some strange summer blizzard had been through. Black squirrels race around, bounding up tree trunks, and the grackles ruffle their iridescent wings, calling *skreak* from the branches. A small cardinal lands nearby, a flash of red and black.

The air is warm, thick, and a bee is hovering around his face. He slaps at it ineffectually, then rouses himself, a little stupefied from the sun. Sleeping will not get him a job. He will have to begin searching farther away, the factories around the edges of the city, along the river valley.

The first one, a paper mill. A man down with diphtheria, a large order to get out. A temporary job, then, tending the line, watching a river of slurry feed through the rollers and the drying drums. Checking as it wraps onto an enormous roll at the end of the line, another man swinging the roll away at intervals, giving it a pat as if it were the flank of a horse, shifting an empty reel in. Three hundred miles of paper a day, says the man. Three hundred miles? The distance from Minsk to Warsaw, from Prague to Trieste.

In a week, he has learned the different grades of runs, the tricks and twists of the cylinders, he is accustomed to the rotten egg smell, the heat. He still has to look away from the line from time to time to avoid being hypnotized, to avoid falling into a white trance. And then it is over, the sick man is well and back. But the supervisor pulls him aside, tells him he will provide a reference for him, this hard worker, this fast learner. A step forward, small but useful.

A week later.

Potluck, they call it, says the Russian, his tongue awkward. Perhaps other people at the settlement house will have better food, they can trade the *zharkoye* for something more edible. The three of them go with the pot of stew, wrapped in a dishcloth to stay warm.

When they arrive, a group of people are milling around, these dinners grouped by region. This one is for immigrants from eastern Europe, fifteen or twenty countries lumped together, as if sun-spiked Greece and northern Latvia were parts of the same territory. But the food is at least different, briny yellow cheese, spinach pastries, cracked wheat pilaf, walnut custard.

Afterwards, he brings his plate to the kitchen where a small woman is washing dishes—narrow-waisted, her cheekbones flat, a high-bridged nose. Sofija—Lithuanian, but they both speak enough Russian, even enough English to understand each other. She moves sleepily, her heavy-lidded eyes set a little too close together, lips dry, dark hair in a bun on her neck.

A wife. A wife would increase his respectability, would help to separate him from the single men, the drifters. But the right wife—someone who understands the way things should be between a man and a woman.

One night: a lakefront pavilion, the sounds of big band music drifting out from the dance floor. The evening sky is grey-blue, and the light from the windows pools on the ground.

See, she says, showing him some of the dance steps.

Now together.

She keeps the two of them upright in a rough likeness of the dance, but he is too stiff, too wooden, and she gives up.

Another time: they take bread and cheese out on a rocky point on the lake, where they watch the kingfishers diving and fighting over the water. He tells her about getting butter coupons under the table, and slowly, timidly, she talks about her bickering sisters, her dying father in Vilnius. No, no family here.

She is happy to get away from her cramped quarters, a tiny flat with two other women—they take in piecework, sewing collars, basting sleeves, her eyes often aching from the strain. They bully her, he thinks, and stores this thought away.

She allows their hands to touch, but no more than that. If she understands some things only vaguely, if she is meek about many things, she is remarkably clear on how to handle herself as a property.

And then, finally, a job. Something for more than a week or two.

The heat hits him when he opens the door. A flood of recognition—the men feeding the annealers, opening the moulds, cracking the glass off the pipes. The blowers lording it over the workshop floor, swinging their pontils back and forth. The glowing furnaces, the snick and hiss of the hot glass against the damp wood of the shapers. Suddenly, in this city where every possible thing is relentlessly, exhaustingly foreign—the rusty tap water, the taste of the cigarettes, the yowling cats stuck in elms—here is something familiar, something he knows.

He lies about his experience, and they hire him as an apprentice. Glass blowers are scarce, even now. What do they produce? Glass beakers, tubes, vials for laboratories, flasks and bottles for distilleries.

The first day, the warehouse area in the back of the plant. He pauses at the door.

Rows and rows of finished bottles are lined up, regiments of green and amber. Silent, this army, ready for packing. In fact, the whole room is quiet, away from the hubbub on the shop floor. The sound of the furnaces, the shouts of the men are distant, muffled by a heavy wall. The only light here is a shaft of watery sun from the window on one side. Dust particles drift slowly through it, high over the bottles.

So hard, so dense, this glass. Solid now, but shaped by something as fleeting as breath—the form of the air caught forever in these bottles.

Or perhaps not forever. Perhaps only until they are dropped by a careless hand, splintering into shards.

. . .

Let us pass to another curious feature of glass, the fact that it may be made from such a number of different ingredients. One notable example is forest glass or waldglas, *which is constructed of sand together with the ash from burnt bracken and trees. The properties of such glass are markedly inferior to those of other compositions, but it is valued now for its very coarseness.*

. . .

The first time he hits her, the expression on her face is stunned, hurt. She puts her hand to her cheek, and it comes away with a streak of blood, blood from where the cheap wedding ring has grazed her skin. She looks at it uncomprehendingly for a second, and then begins wailing, clutching herself.

This is your fault, he says.

What was her sin? She bought a dress without asking him first. Without his permission. A bleak rage overwhelms him.

He hits her again, and she screams.

But he has calculated how far he can go, measuring her reactions—so far and no further, a gamble on the chances of her leaving. He knows she has no money, no people here. And he has convinced her that staying here, her status in this country, is now dependent on him. Still, he brings her a gift the next day, a small bird he has made out of the ends of glass rods. She is sulky, reproachful, she refuses to take it. Later that evening, though, he sees her looking at the little figure, picking it up, stroking its tail, its green eye.

She will have to learn.

When he does it again, she is less shocked, her wailing lower in pitch. This time, he brings her a fistful of tulips taken from someone's garden. She is cold, scornful, she pushes them away. He puts them in water, puts them on the table on her side of the bed. She moves them away, and he puts them back. Then she lets them stay there.

They all have their faults, says an older woman at the settlement house, shaking her head, pursing her lips. They all have their failings. Some of them drink, some of them cannot hold a job. Some of them hit their wives, this is the way of things. You will get used to it. You must learn how to avoid making him angry. For a woman, it is better to be married. Besides, what would you do if you left, where would you go? Especially now, in your condition.

In her condition.

He is pleased.

This is a good life, he says to her. You are lucky. Look what a lucky woman you are. A flat of our own. An electric stove. Hot water. A bed with pillows, a quilt. In a few years, I will be a journeyman. In a few months, I will buy a car.

Gradually, he sees the little fight that was in her begin to drain away, bit by bit, her face becoming duller. She seems increasingly grateful for any solicitude he shows her, increasingly passive. When he raises his arm, she cowers.

She will have to learn. And there is no shortage of chances to teach her.

But he buys her a ring with paste diamonds, later a washing machine with a wringer on top.

Look what a good husband you have, he says. Say it: *I have a good husband.*

I have a good husband, she says listlessly.

And some days she almost believes it.

. . .

She is showing him a small bundle, wrapped in a blue hospital blanket. Her face is blurred with happiness. The baby has mossy black hair, dark eyes sealed shut. The man looks at the two of them blankly.

You should be proud, she says.

The same thing the men at work say, slapping him on the back when they hear. A boy, they say. Good work, they say. They raise their mugs to him at lunch, even though they are not particularly fond of him.

But now he knows how to get along with them, how to talk with them, to behave the way they behave, to keep his contempt hidden. And he is more like them than before, his English is better, he has a wife, this child. After he becomes a journeyman, he will become the manager—he is forming his plans even now. He has already begun making little comments about the current manager, about a mistake here or there, and he makes a point of flattering the owner whenever he is around. Once he is in charge, he will increase production, he knows the system now, where the snags are. He knows the men, too, the ones who are quick, the ones who are slow, each one's weak point.

At the moment, though, Sofija is showing him the baby's wrinkled hands, a beaded wristband around one of them. The tiny feet, a smear of blood from the birth still on a toe. Proud. Is this what he feels?

No. He feels only empty, hollow. His stomach heaves, and then heaves again, and he vomits into the sink.

. . .

Then:

Another baby on the way, her small body ballooned out again. Now she is a manufacturer of human beings, creating muscles, fat, veins. Her belly sways in front of her, the skin twitching when the child twists and kicks.

The first one is—all at once—a small boy, brown-eyed, long-lashed, the soft skin of a child. Running around, a stick in his hand, chanting something, he bumps into his father. The man swats him, swats him hard, swats him again.

Stop it, says Sofija.

She says this in a strange voice, one that he has never heard before. A voice like concrete, a voice that is completely and utterly final.

Not the child, she says. Not the child.

She picks up the crying boy, kisses him, shoos him towards his room.

The man is still standing there, startled.

. . .

Gradually this existence sinks into him, slowly he begins to accumulate the contents of a life. A small house, the brick darkened with age, the windowsills notched, foundations buried into the gravelly soil. A second-hand car, a Dodge, then after a while a newer car, a grey Nash, with others following. Behind the house, a yard where Sofija grows day lilies, rhubarb, beans, and onions around the grasping roots of a tree. Inside are slip-covered chairs, a bed with a feather comforter, bottles of beer in a refrigerator. Even the thought of these things is deeply satisfying.

I own this bathtub, he thinks, lying back in it. I am surrounded by gallons of hot water that comes out with the twist of a tap. And if I pull out the plug, it will all disappear without any effort.

If he nicks himself with the razor, he inspects the cut, surprised at how localized this pain is, how intact he is otherwise. When he rakes leaves off the lawn, he is gratified by the pointlessness of it, how far he has come that he can afford to do this.

I am cleaning the outside ground, he thinks.

When he noses his car into the small garage, he thinks: even my car has a house.

Little by little, he becomes addicted to this life, to each small piece of it, each small ritual. He craves these things, he navigates between these points to get through his day. While he is swinging his pontil, while he is rolling the glass across the marver, he thinks: I am going home soon where dinner will be ready, a dinner with meat, as much bread as I want, a meal that is cooked for me, that is hot. When he eats his meal, he thinks: later I will go to sleep in my bed with white sheets, a thick mattress.

They are not enough, these things, they are never enough. But they are something.

. . .

And now this faithless country is turning its back on him, has betrayed him. A country hardly worthy of him even at the time, so young, a jumble of people from different places scattered over a massive stretch of land—but the only one that would accept him.

He has made the best of it, though, these thousands of days wrapped around him. Now there is toast and blackberry jam for breakfast, a slow walk in the neighbourhood with the ancient terrier, sour cabbage soup for lunch, cards in the dim cafe in the afternoons. Sofija with her church groups—the choir, the rummage sales. His son, a carpenter, his daughter, empty-headed but married, her fidgety boy and girl.

Naps on the old sofa, the glass of vodka after dinner, his pills, his clothes worn into comfortable bagginess. These routines hold him in place, hold him in their grip. But now they want to cut him away from all of it, sever him from it as if it had never existed, as if the decades of breathing this air, walking these streets were nothing. To send him back to a place he left when he was barely even a man—his life there only a rehearsal of a life, a dry run.

And because of something so old, so natural at the time. He is being punished for doing his best to make his way, for doing his best to stay alive. He had only done the things that must be done, that had to be done. How can he be judged by the ridiculous standards of another time?

Would you do it again? says Leah. Would you do it now?

He says nothing.

There is one tiny satisfaction, though, one small thing. He is being recognized for who he is—who he was—not merely a glassblower, more than a plant manager. Someone who was part of the NKVD, Stalin's fist. After years of being treated as less than who he was, the stinging rebuffs, the contempt for his accent, this country is finally seeing him for the first time. If they want to expel him so badly, they understand who he is, his importance. No, his superiority.

Still, this place is betraying him, going back on its word. A citizen—what does that mean if not something permanent? He had to swear an oath to get his status. Too late, he realizes that there was no oath in return.

Doesn't all that pity of yours extend to me? he says to Leah.

No, she says.

What about my wife? You will destroy her life as well. You will take her away from the grandchildren, the only thing she loves.

Is this the first time you've thought of her?

He says nothing.

She can stay if she wants. No one is deporting her. Maybe she will welcome the chance to get away from you.

She is no different from me.

She never shot anyone, tortured anyone.

I did what I had to do, what was necessary to survive. What anyone would do.

What did you do?

Silence.

I knew you were lying, she says. I knew it.

You knew it, he says mockingly. Then prove it.

THIRTEEN

The world rests on the tip of the tongue.
JEWISH PROVERB

They are here. They are installed in a small hotel, the clerk at the front desk instructed to provide them with any help necessary. The doctor, gruff from the wearying trip, her ankles more swollen than before. The music teacher, tired but inquisitive, intrigued by everything in this new place—taxis, buskers, jackhammers. They are precious goods, these people, human containers of evidence. The possessors of rare facts, of vanishing truths.

The investigator insisted on coming as well, and Louis agreed, with the idea that this would be useful for everyday translation, shuttling the witnesses around. He wants them carefully tended, shepherded and protected. The music teacher is interested in an art museum? Take him there. A concert? Find one for him. The man is in high spirits, delighted to be somewhere new, about this unexpected parole.

The doctor is more subdued—she wants cocoa before bed, ice packs for her feet. But she is willing to be driven around, to see the Flatiron Building, the old university, the cube house—pleased in her own wintry way.

Keep them calm, keep them comfortable, says Leah to the investigator.

Louis has been to see them, to get a feel for their ability to testify, to assess how well—or not—they will withstand cross-examination.

As long as they don't die until after examination-in-chief, he says.

But she can hear the suppressed excitement in his voice, see it in his gestures. The case is attracting attention now, no longer unnoticed, brief clips on the news, opinion pieces, journalists calling for interviews, background material before the day of the hearing. All this seems to have uncovered hidden longing in him, a yearning for some sliver of legal glory. This is his moment, he seems to be thinking, the moment when he vaults to some vague heights, some overdue applause—a moment he had almost given up on, a moment all the sweeter because of that.

In the midst of this, his grudge towards her seems to have almost evaporated. She is relieved, but acutely aware that her future rests on this case, and that the case rests on these witnesses. She drafts questions over and over to prepare them for testifying, hoping to find the perfect way to ask something, the perfect way to evoke the most persuasive—the most damning—answer. She wakes up in the middle of the night, simplifying, untangling, reframing sentences—aware all the while that most of this might be futile.

You know what witnesses are like, says Nate.

Yes.

Unpredictable. Impulsive. Liable to depart from their previous answers without warning. She knows already the sinking feeling when a witness goes off on an unexpected tangent, or reveals something damaging, corkscrewing off into a different story while the case changes shape before her eyes.

What possesses them? she thinks, as if they are actually possessed, in the grip of some malign spirit. Is it that the oath begins to weigh too heavily on them? Is it a form of witness-like panic?

Don't prepare them too much, says Louis. I don't want them to sound rehearsed.

Not much danger of that.

In the office, there is an undercurrent of expectation, the air almost bristling. Even Nate can feel it, but he is torn, she thinks, torn between regret that he let this case go, and summoning up some element of graciousness.

But the deep-sea divers are back, their dark green helmets bobbing.

Another threat. Another search.

Isabel is more fearful as the court date draws closer, treating all incoming mail as if it were enemy fire. *What does a suspicious parcel look like?*

A hoax, says Nate gently. That's what they said.

He is less comforting with Leah, as she waves her pages of questions in front of him.

Litigation, he says, shrugging. Anything can happen.

Her throat closes at the thought. *Anything.* Louis losing himself again, his face wandering, disorganized. Pushing his notes in front of her. *Go on.* No, impossible, this time she knows, she will ask for a recess, an adjournment. She wishes she could talk to Owen, to obtain some assurance in advance that an adjournment is possible, but the last thing she wants to do is remind him of the last time, the moment when his lawyer drifted off and a junior stumbled through the argument instead. It says something for Owen—although she is not sure what—that they are still on the case. But when Louis is good, he is very, very good.

Or perhaps this is only to avoid the cost of briefing other lawyers, perhaps this is the last case they will have from him. Even so, an outstanding performance here, a resounding win might redeem them, might generate more work later on.

But speaking to him is out of the question, she knows this. He will talk to Louis, of course, and she will be fired again, the fastest refiring in legal history. Perhaps she should speak directly to Louis instead. *How are you feeling? Any more of those blank moments?*

No, no, says Nate. He'll be furious. He'll go off like a grenade.

He will. She knows it. A man who sees himself as a small island of intelligence—increasingly beleaguered—in a sea of inanity. Someone who is enchanted by his own intellect, more than that, who thinks of it as the essence of his being. To raise, however delicately, however tactfully, that something might be flawed with his mind would be disastrous.

He must know something is wrong, she says, more to herself than Nate.

Then why say anything? says Nate.

He needs a doctor, she says.

He probably has one. And his wife is likely alert to this. Don't let that effervescence fool you—she can be very perceptive.

Despite everything, she feels a creeping sympathy for Louis. Of all possible afflictions, this is something that goes directly to the core of his being. No wonder he is so busy creating ongoing descriptions of himself, to himself, for himself. Perhaps he is urgently trying to remember who he is. Or discover who he is now, at this minute or the next one. Is it possible he is really looking for bulletins from his own depths?

In fact, perhaps it is this fear that has made him so thin-skinned, so sensitive to any inability to control things. Maybe he has become more rigid as a way of staving off a certain slackness in his mind, a way of grappling with the possibility of disintegration. Clinging to absolutes, to straight lines, unable to stand too much uncertainty. Or anyone not following directions.

A guess, but perhaps a good guess. And a glimmer of understanding.

So no risky questions? says Nate.

Not for now, she says.

. . .

You may have a future here yet.

But the person who needs a future is Gus.

The procedure went as well as could be expected, says the cardiologist. That's all I can say. He's still not in great shape. But I prefer to be cautiously optimistic.

Cautiously optimistic? No, this is not for her. She has decided to be wildly optimistic, madly optimistic. What does this phrase mean, after all? A way of hedging her bets on the possibility of death? She is incapable of measuring degrees of optimism when it comes to Gus, of gauging in small increments his chances of survival. Instead, she has only a sense of hope.

He is home now, staples across his chest, equipped with blood thinners and a handful of other medications. The pain is gradually lessening, although he still moves very cautiously. She sits by his bed, wiggling her feet under the blanket—away from his, no danger of physical contact—and works on her cases, while he skims the sports pages, gardening magazines, his reading glasses making him look smaller, more bookish than he is. Or he watches television, he has become immersed in crime dramas. Hours of people dissecting bits of rotting organs, brain matter, insects, the microscopic details of decay and mortality.

What is it you like about them? she almost says. But this is Gus, so she doesn't.

Perhaps they reduce death to its smallest possible parts, to tiny, knowable fractions.

At the moment, she can hear Rudy walking in the hall downstairs. He is still slightly huffy, as if he had put an early claim on this ailment—a heart attack—for himself. But he is also frightened, she thinks—he needs Gus, Gus is a marker for him, a pin holding the map of his world in place. And the truth is that he is close to him in his own peculiar way—an austere form of affection.

He is irritated as a result, something that has made his cooking deteriorate even further. The trays that he sends up for Gus—reluctantly—are increasingly inedible.

And why he needs to be waited on hand and foot is beyond me, he says.

Malcolm says nothing, for once he has bottled himself up. But she can almost read his thoughts: if anyone deserves this kind of care, it is him, the possessor of swollen knee, a tendency to migraines, bouts of sciatica. For all his peevishness, though, he has his own attachment to Gus—sloppy, self-centred, but real.

When she is not sitting with Gus, she is thinking about sitting there, she is thinking about him, as if this alone could sustain him in some way. But her thoughts are repetitive, an ongoing roiling in her head. *Has he taken his blood thinners? His beta blockers? His nitrates? Is the incision clean? Does he have an infection? Is the bypass—such a simple idea, such an intricate procedure—really working? Is there no way to entirely, completely fix this man?*

She runs her fingers through her hair, pressing on her scalp, as if this will push all this away.

Gus looks up from the bed inquiringly.

Tell me more about this drive from the cottage, she says, seizing on this. My mother. The fever. The trip to the hospital.

I don't know any more, he says.

Unsedated, he is back to being taciturn.

But Rudy and Malcolm have nothing to say about it either. There is a vacuum where the pieces that make up this accident should be. Only the night, the dripping trees, the overwhelming pain in her leg—a half-dream that edges into her days from time to time. But the rest of it is missing.

She is struck by something now, though. This fact, this lost fact—that they were on their way to the hospital—has not yet sunk in. The idea that this fatal outing was not a joyride, the result of some half-drunk impulse, seems suddenly—startlingly—illuminating. There was a reason for this drive, this lethal trip, a spike in a tube of mercury. A reason that reshapes the picture of that night, rearranges it, something that turns it from a child's dark hole—murky, frightening, bewildering—into something almost comprehensible. Almost.

Comfort, a little frayed, begins to spread through her, the easing of an old ache.

But there is still one primitive, childish thought lying there, a long, inconsolable wail that remains.

Where are you come back come back come back.

. . .

I'll stay with him, says Val. Go to work, I'll be here.

Leah is surprised to find she is almost grateful—an unwelcome thought. *Val,* she says to herself, trying to stir up her old indignation, but it seems to have seeped away, overtaken by events. She wants Gus to be under watchful eyes, regardless of whose they are, to be studied hourly for signs of changes, any traces of healing or decline. And Val herself is more restrained—she still slaps his pillows in a proprietorial way, produces vanilla cake, baked pears, lemon loaf—but there is something missing, an element of conviction. She is not fooling anyone, Leah thinks.

Underneath this bustling is a more subdued version of herself, one who has been knocked off course by this change in circumstances. Someone who is beginning to realize that the filmy hopes she created are starting to dissolve. Whether some of them might be salvaged is uncertain, but there is a slight loosening of her attention, a shift in her focus.

He's too stubborn to die, says Malcolm almost regretfully.

For once, Leah wants to agree with him.

But he needs a future. Perhaps she can find one for him, find a better one—or at least a longer one. For example: The stockbrokers who trade in futures, in contracts for coming events. Do any of them cover human futures, life prospects? Perhaps this could be a new form of commodity, listed on the exchange—used to make up any shortfalls in the length of a particular existence.

Another possibility: acquiring a second-hand future, a castoff from someone who died, who was unable to use it. *Like new.* Sad, of course, but there was no point in wasting the suddenly available future. Or perhaps it might be feasible to buy a future at a specialty store, something sold by the ounce. Expensive, naturally, as costly as saffron or a rare perfume. But worth it, worth every penny.

. . .

They play gin rummy each week, a game with an old pack of cards, corners bent, surfaces worn.

Ace is high, says her aunt. So ace, king, queen, jack.

This is a serious business, there is no talking about other things, they are intent, studying their cards. They pick them up with deliberation, discard them with a sigh, as if they regret letting each one go.

Ace, king, queen, jack. The girl studies their faces, the king of spades with his curling moustache, the skeptical queen of diamonds, the jack of hearts so pleased with himself and his yellow hair.

Surprisingly, she is good at this game, she is astonished how good she is. She wins and wins and wins and wins.

Look at that, says her aunt fondly. A genius.

The girl accepts this—who would know better than her aunt? Someday, she and the jack of diamonds—not as vain as the jack of hearts—will go off together, the two of them and her genius. Travelling around, finding roller coasters to ride, eating raspberry pie for breakfast.

Why raspberry? says her aunt.

He likes red things, she says, willing to make this sacrifice for him.

Today the cards are not co-operating, though.

Her aunt deals again.

Nothing, says her aunt, rearranging her hand. Look at that, I've got nothing again. A handful of *nisht*. You must have all my cards.

The game goes on and on, round after round, neither one able to gin.

The girl looks accusingly at her hand, the king of diamonds sitting there smugly, the haughty queen of spades. These double-headed cards, a face at either end. Why are they suddenly such loners, why no friends and relations?

Another round. *Nisht. Nada. Zip.*

I must be losing my touch, says her aunt.

. . .

Later, as she grows older, a whisper of doubt about her card-playing genius begins to surface in the girl's mind. Not a suspicion, too quiet for that, merely a rustle in the back of her mind. Only enough to know this: she should avoid playing cards with anyone else.

. . .

The investigator is circling the two witnesses like an irritable sheepdog. They are sitting in the front row of seats in the courtroom, waiting for the case to start, and he moves restlessly from one to the other. The courtrooms around them have been cleared out, their case the only one listed here. This isolation is one of the security measures; they were given the location only yesterday, the room has been swept with equipment, they were searched and searched again, their briefcases rifled. Additional officers are posted in the halls, in the courtroom itself, a throng of dark blue. But what could they do if there was an explosion? she thinks. Perhaps they are there as a defiant gesture—*we will not allow ourselves to be intimidated*—something to ward off the edginess that has settled over the room, as if it has drifted up out of the air vents. Even the court clerk seems nervous.

Her task for now: ensure that all is in readiness, that all will go as smoothly as possible. She has laid out their materials on the counsel table—the books of authorities, the notes, the tabbed exhibits—with almost geometric precision, the edges of the papers lined up with the edges of the desk. *If only these things are perfectly straight, the case will go well.* The journalists are keeping their distance for now, a group of alert, harassed people, deprived of their coffee cups at the door. Louis has worked out an arrangement with them, they will have interviews with the witnesses after the hearing. And of course, with their lawyer. She can see from his posture, his gestures that he is working hard to conceal his suppressed excitement. He is sharp enough to keep this under control, to keep his wits about him, only a tiny, gleeful leak every now and then.

Raised voices. She glances around. Behind her, in the first row of seats, the doctor is insisting on something with the investigator, a stream of Belarusian. He tries to quiet her, patting the air down with his palms.

What is it? she says to them. What's the problem?

Nothing, says the investigator hastily. Nothing, nothing.

He tell me money, says the doctor in English.

The travel money, says the investigator loudly.

No, not the travel money, the money for to be a witness.

Leah stares at the investigator.

Fifteen hundred rubles, says the doctor.

All rise, says the clerk.

. . .

Opening statements. Louis at his best, painting the outline of the case in long, lean strokes, describing the evidence to come with effortless fluency. He describes the natural—almost inevitable—outcome to this case, how right it is, how preposterous any other result would be—exuding a kind of seductive reason. He sounds as if he is confiding these things to his listeners candidly, letting them in on the real story of the case. But she is barely listening, she is too busy trying to unscramble her thoughts.

The doctor was paid. The music teacher too, likely. *Paid.* Of course, this doesn't mean their evidence is untruthful. Not at all, witnesses are paid for many things—travel, accommodation, meals, even attendance. But most of those things have already been paid for here—this fifteen hundred rubles is merely to testify.

She must talk to Louis about this, he must be told. But Owen is there, and Louis would insist that he be insulated from something like this. If there are any sins to be committed, this is their job.

If there are any sins. No, the witnesses are telling the truth, she is convinced. Their stories are too detailed, they have the grainy feel of fact. And there is something rough, unmistakably genuine underlying them. Then she sees the music teacher's second of hesitancy again, the small sitting room, the investigator nodding at him. What about the identification of Drozd? Was that true as well? But the investigator was only reassuring him, making it clear it was safe for him to talk.

Then why did the investigator lie about it—*only travel money*—when she asked before? Because he knows it might taint their evidence? Or at least that it might be seen that way. A fine line, but still a line.

No, no, say the spiders, groaning. Just this once. Just this once, make sure someone like him gets what he deserves.

But she is so haunted by this case now herself that the idea of it collapsing, of this man eluding any form of reckoning is unthinkable.

Then Louis is coming to the end of his opening, moving into a lower key. A few sentences later, and he is finished. He sits back in his chair while the other lawyer begins lumbering through his own opening, paragraphs of canned words pasted together.

She tears off a scrap of pleadings, writes on the back: *The doctor was paid by the investigator.*

Louis glances at it, crumples it up.

Obviously he needs time to think about it, how to handle it. Undoubtedly he will ask for a break. He will wait until the other lawyer is finished, he will request a brief recess. He will get to the root of this, he will sort it out—what it means, what effect it has.

As the other lawyer drones on, though, Louis does nothing, unperturbed.

Eventually the man comes to a halt and Louis is still not moving.

Call your evidence, says the judge.

Another note. More urgent. *Fifteen hundred rubles. About eight hundred dollars.*

He looks at her warningly, and crumples this one up as well.

The doctor, the court interpreter—a man with an acerbic face and a deep voice—are sworn in. *The evidence given by you touching on the matters in question.*

The doctor begins her testimony, speaking tensely but steadily, as if she is walking along a narrow ridge of facts. She is wearing a dark green jersey dress with a cowl neck today, her grey-streaked hair tied in a bun. A sobering presence, a spare dignity of her own. The resonant voice of the court interpreter becomes her voice, carrying them along—even the journalists are engrossed.

The mushrooms. The shots, her mother. The barbed wire. A foot sticking out of the sand.

Her words seem to expand, become taller, fuller. The room is unnaturally quiet and still. There is no coughing, no rustling, no creaking. Even the noises from outside are muffled, all that matters is in this room, her voice. No sounds of movement, no murmuring, no clearing of throats. They are all listening, transfixed.

This moment, thinks Leah. A moment without any warning. When fragments of leftover history spill into the present. When a living story falls out of the past, redrawing the lines of understanding. A moment that alters the bargain with time.

The other lawyer shambles up to the lectern, robes flapping around his legs, and begins his cross-examination. He is surprisingly capable at this, darting into the corners of the doctor's story, sniffing out uncertainty, collecting whatever he can find. He may not be much of an orator, but he is clever enough. And he harps on the doctor's age, her memory, how long ago it was. She is giving up very little, though, she is determined to deliver her evidence, determined to have it believed. Her black eyes become even darker, they seem to absorb the questions into their depths and then reflect the answers back. He slogs away for an hour, doing what he can to fluster her.

As he nears the end, Leah starts to relax slightly, to unclench her jaw. Is it possible the doctor, her testimony will make it through without too much damage? She straightens out the papers on the table in front of her, aligning their edges again.

He has almost finished now, scratching the back of his head with one hand while he leafs through his notes one last time.

You're a long way from home, he says finally.

She nods.

Have you received any inducement to testify, has anyone promised you anything?

Objection, says Louis instantly, almost before the end of the question. A witness is entitled to be paid a reasonable allowance.

Overruled, says the judge. Save it for argument.

Go ahead and answer, says the other lawyer.

Only the witness money, she says.

How much was that?

Fifteen hundred rubles.

And that's that, says the lawyer, closing his binder.

. . .

A reasonable allowance?

Look how far she had to come, says Louis. Look how old she is. Look how many days she had to spend here.

. . .

A break for lunch. The bomb threat, momentarily forgotten, looms up again. More security, more searches. A swift meal of paninis and espresso in a cafe, the doctor visibly relieved, the music teacher swivelling his head most of the time, intrigued by the meal, the place. And then back to the courtroom and their next witness, the music teacher. After him, two researchers who work in the War Crimes Section will testify.

And may I say that you've made them very happy, says Owen.

The investigator, she says. He was the one who found them.

The music teacher is nervous, twisting in his seat, rubbing the backs of his knobby hands. What is he so worried about? She has gone through the questions with him several times now. But his testimony is coming out in streams, he is almost gabbling, and the court interpreter is having difficulty keeping up.

A weakling, says Drozd scornfully. A Jew.

A weakling? A man who survived what he has survived? No, this is a hardy man, a tenacious man—an enduring man.

But she knows he might be more vulnerable here, out of his element, that he might become tied in knots more easily than the doctor. Or that he might become belligerent, flaring out at a questioner. And she can see that Louis is having difficulty keeping him on track; he is deliberately slowing down his questions, trying to set a pace for the man.

He pauses now, to allow a small break in the current of words.

But this pause is suddenly too long. She looks up at him sharply, dismay flooding her. There it is again. The empty look in his eyes, the lack of recognition, as if he has been cut loose from himself, as if even the chairs, the desks were unfamiliar things, unknown objects. He shakes his head, as if he has water in his ears.

She tries to collect herself, leans over to Owen. An adjournment? she whispers, indicating Louis with her head.

No, he says quickly. No adjournments. We need to get this case over, over and done.

A recess? she says desperately.

No, you pick it up, you go ahead.

Go ahead? After the last time? Could he have forgotten how badly it went?

Go ahead, he says.

She stands up stiffly, moves to the lectern. The journalists, sensing something, lift their heads. She feels her throat starting to close, her tongue starting to swell.

And then all at once her breath comes back to her in a gasp. She realizes that she has gone over and over these questions, that she knows them inside out, that she knows this witness better than Louis. She gathers the remnants of her confidence, pulls them up around her. *At least try. Take a crack at it. Be bold.*

She smiles at the witness, as if it were just the two of them, as if this were just another preparation session. He looks at her, puzzled, and then smiles back, his creased face lighting up. For a moment, he seems almost mischievous, as if this were a game that only the two of them were playing.

Then she begins going back over what he has said, slowing him down, breaking the questions into smaller parts. She feels oddly calm, her panic is muffled, remote. She can hear it circling the edges of her being, but it stays there, going no further. And she is too intent on what she is doing, too busy to be surprised at herself.

The man is less nervous now, listening carefully to the questions as he unwinds his story.

The arrest. The prayer shawls, the books, the sheet music. The packed cell, the smell. The interrogation, the beatings, the broken fingers. The pits, the shooting, the dirt.

This is good? he says through the investigator at the mid-afternoon break, before his cross-examination.

Good, good, she says, a little too heartily. But we're not allowed to talk to you about it at this point in the case.

He looks disappointed.

More rules. A thicket of constraints, designed to keep evidence as pristine as possible. How pristine is that? Memory—so wily, so brittle. So corruptible. But what else is there?

She smiles at the music teacher in what she hopes is a reassuring way. Then Louis is there beside her, restored now, entirely normal. More than normal, he is bantering with Owen, chatting with the witnesses, skilfully keeping several balls in the air. As if nothing had happened, as if his dazed moment was nothing more than a bout of absent-mindedness.

You really have to do something about this, she says to him silently.

About what? he says.

. . .

The music teacher is more loquacious in cross-examination, running the other lawyer over with words.

Just answer the question, says the lawyer in a petulant tone.

I *am* answering the question, the teacher says indignantly. It requires a big answer.

She is tempted to laugh at the lawyer's predicament, the way the witness is swamping him. This small man, this elderly man, shrunk with age and circumstance, but getting the better of the lawyer on his own ground. *Bravo.*

Although this spate of words is dangerous for them, too—the man might blurt something that could undermine his story. What could that be? Anything. Lying, deception, duplicity, these get all the attention—the glib fakers, the masters of deceit are the ones usually in the spotlight. Ignored are all the people who tell the truth badly, who can make a fact, solid as a truck, disappear simply by talking about it. The wrong intonation, too much hesitation, a hurried sentence or two, a shifty look for no reason. Some people are born with question marks in their throats, she thinks.

But this man—voluble as he is—is not one of them. No, his downfall might be to drop an innocent fact into the wrong place, some unlucky spot that gives it a damaging meaning, some shadow. She notices that even Louis is gripping his pen more tightly than usual.

Another hour is gone, though, before the lawyer surrenders.

One last question:

And were you paid to testify as well?

Objection, says Louis.

We've done this, says the judge.

. . .

Still no bomb, no explosion.

. . .

The next day, Louis takes the two researchers through their documents, the admission of one record after another. They are skilful witnesses, expert, tidy. One—a purist—manages to get snarled up in cross-examination briefly, but he recovers after a minute or two.

And then they are done.

Counsel? says the judge, turning to the other lawyer.

No evidence, says the lawyer.

No evidence? Drozd is not testifying?

After all his outrage, his fury, he is not willing to swear to his story under oath? To expose it to cross-examination?

You coward, she says to him. You odious coward.

What did you think? he says. That I would serve myself up to you like a piece of meat on a plate?

. . .

Final arguments. Louis, in superb form, casting out lines of thought, opening them up, then reeling them in. He is agile, sure-footed, he knows his way around these arguments, knows their twists and curves. And he lures the judge down one pathway and onto another, weaving the words around him. *Hold him responsible... the fabric of justice... right the balance... the ethical imperative... escape the consequences... the suffering of his victims... meaning... terrible acts made up of small parts.*

On he goes, eloquent, his voice climbing and falling, gripping and then releasing. He speaks so easily, so unselfconsciously that his sentences have a natural elegance to them. He talks about *justice* and *morality*—these unwieldy ideas—as if they are everyday thoughts, as if they can be taught to sit and stay.

Is that an unfamiliar note in his voice, something new? Yes, there *is* something else, something beyond his usual verbal skill. His voice sounds throatier, thicker. He does fall for his cases, but not like this, this is different. This case must matter to him, must matter in some indefinable manner.

Or perhaps not so indefinable. *So many of them Jewish.*

But then he is finished and the other lawyer begins.

A low-paid clerk, a proxy... a stand-in for the crimes of NKVD officers... political purposes... satisfy the demands for prosecution... witnesses unreliable... too long ago... paid to remember things that never happened... his youth, his circumstances... shaky evidence... a blameless life... send an old man back to a country he has not seen in decades... cut off from his wife, children, grandchildren.

He is reading his notes again, but with more emphasis than usual—even he has been roused by the case. But finally he, too, is coming to a close.

A brief reply by Louis, a last flourish.

Reserved, says the judge.

...

She is exultant. They did it. Louis did it. She did it, her part. Did you see that? she says to Nate. Did you see that? she says to Gus. She wants everyone to know, Isabel, the police officers, the people outside on the street. She wants to whoop, to jump. Of course, she feels badly that Louis had another of his lost moments, that he misplaced himself again. But she is still jubilant—she wants to spin around in the middle of the floor, spin and spin until the room is a blur, trailing drops of law from her fingertips.

. . .

No bomb.

Isabel is suddenly relaxed again, restored to her tart self.

Nothing, she says, marveling. Nothing.

Nothing, says Leah.

Are you surprised? says Nate.

Yes and no, she says.

She feels the bomb threat slowly pulling its claws out of her, beginning to disappear.

. . .

One more time. One more time, and she will speak to him.

Have you seen a doctor? Do you know what it is? You really must do something.

No, says Nate.

Yes. What if these are tiny seizures? What if he doesn't remember them? What if he is ignoring them, hoping they will go away?

One more time.

. . .

The doctrine of wilful blindness. A jockey, a horse trainer, and another man were playing cards in a private room at an inn. The innkeeper was charged with suffering gambling to be carried on in her licensed premises. She claimed that she was not aware of the card playing and that they did not have the cards of her, but was convicted on the basis that she had taken pains not to know what her guests were doing. I cannot say whether or not I should have drawn the same conclusion myself, said Lord Blackburn.

. . .

The cells of the eyes replace themselves, his son said once, self-important from school. Some of them. And blood cells, liver cells, the cells of the stomach lining are the same, constantly turning over, new cells generated. After a while, almost an entirely new body.

If this is true, Drozd thinks now, then he is made of this country, has been made of this country many times over. His skin, his fingernails, his bones built from food grown in this soil, rainwater from these lakes, oxygen from this air.

I belong here, he thinks.

They are hounding me, he says.

Persecution, says his lawyer.

I have done nothing but mind my own business here. This country has nothing against me. Even in the old country, I did what I had to do. And I was a child. I did what I had to do, we all did during the war.

Of course, says his lawyer.

These people who think they can get through a war with clean hands are dreaming. They have no idea what war is like.

True, says the lawyer.

It is impossible that they will win this case. Impossible that they would deport someone like me.

If we lose, we'll appeal, says his lawyer. It has to go up the ladder anyway, and then we can get a court to review it. We can probably spin this out for years.

How much will that cost?

How much do you want to stay here?

. . .

A child? she says. Sixteen is not a child.

I've worked like a madman for everything I have, he says. I've earned it. Why would I let some stupid bitch like you take it away?

. . .

We do the job, says the doctor. Now you pay us the money.

She is turning her rings around on her blue-veined fingers.

The music teacher nods emphatically, bobbing his head.

They are at the office, wrapping up, a few minutes of talk about how well the case went before they go back to the hotel. Louis has left after summarizing the case for them—or for himself—in the best possible light, buffing up the high points, glossing over the low ones. She watches as he turns the case into something finer, more impressive, although perhaps a little hard to recognize. Then he shakes their hands, tells them he has to go, he has other cases, other clients.

But this is not what he will be doing, she thinks. No, he will feel he has earned a rest, he will be immersing himself in his books, sinking into them with a sigh. Allowing them to carry him along, drifting through their well-worn pages.

Now she is sitting with the witnesses, waiting until the taxi comes for them.

We do the job. What does that mean? What *exactly* does that mean?

She turns towards the investigator.

But before she has time to ask, to say anything, Nate is there, at her elbow, his face tightly set.

What? she says, half-annoyed, half-alarmed.

Come here, he says, pulling her up and into the hallway.

He puts his hands on the sides of her face, then on her shoulders.

Gus.

FOURTEEN

Into the darkness they go, the wise and the lovely.
EDNA ST. VINCENT MILLAY, "DIRGE WITHOUT MUSIC"

The rain, fitful, hesitant all day, has stopped now. A bruised-looking cloud is stretching across the horizon, darkening the bottom half of the sky. Above it a band of sun is visible, giving off an unsettling evening light. It slants across the grass, a misshapen willow tree, the gravestones, a small bird sitting on a branch. The bird hops sideways, jerks a black-and-white head, and ruffles its feathers, sending out a chipped, piercing call.

Underfoot, the grass is still wet, leaving a dark rim on her shoes. She stares at an ant crawling across one of them, watching it move from one side to the other. She should lift up her foot, shake the ant onto the grass, but she feels locked in position, as if every part of her body has become too heavy to move. Even her thoughts seem to be coming from a great distance, like weak radio signals. Faint and slow, drifting into her head, then out again.

All these people. From his bowling team, from the pub, neighbours. This left-handed, silent man. How did someone so guarded, so close-mouthed acquire so many friends? Perhaps they were people like her, people who had detected the dusty kindness he seemed to exude through his skin. Or perhaps he had given them a hand at some point—repaired a rotten floorboard, a drafty window. What will she do now with his shelf full of hammers and screwdrivers, his jars of washers and nails? These things were so much part of him, she is surprised that they are still there, that they have not disappeared as well.

She keeps stumbling across this fact, the fact that he is dead, forgetting about it for minutes at a time—it seems so ludicrous, so impossible—and then coming across it again with an agonizing jolt. How could this man, this living being, so full of personhood—decades of experiences, thoughts, memories lodged in him—be utterly, entirely extinguished, from one minute to the next?

Take this all away, she wants to say now. Rub it all out—the grass, this clump of people, the green tarpaulin on the ground. Take away the bird, take away the pile of dirt, the granite slabs. Pull the inky-purple cloud out of the sky, fill in the dark rectangle in the ground. Erase this picture, this is all terribly, hideously wrong.

But she has no say in it, in anything, she has wandered into a foreign territory, into the chilly landscape of grief. Desolate, a blasted-out area, a scattering of rocks, nothing living here.

Val, in a black blouse and skirt, looking paler than ever. She is reciting something in her small voice, something torn out from a magazine. *They do not leave, they are not gone.*

Standing beside her, Rudy seems crumpled, his fly-away hair forming a nimbus in the damp air.

Don't faint, she says to him. Don't faint.

Has she said it out loud?

He puts his hand out to steady himself, but there is nothing to grab, and the hand stays there, trembling a little, hanging in the air.

Next to him, Malcolm seems bewildered, his cockiness has deserted him. She looks for the third one, and then remembers again. In spite of her attempts to hold on to them, her efforts to keep them from vanishing, one of them has slipped through her careless hands. A naïve idea, anyway, keeping them safe, the idea of a six-year-old. A six-year-old who knew too little about death. And too much.

One of them has always been missing, though, lost even before she had begun to count. Was that her fault as well, her father, another person who dropped out of sight? Perhaps while she was busy thinking about something else, some childish thought. *What do fish drink? Why are there stones?*

This rumour of a father, this threadbare myth. A faint memory, and then hearsay. A tale of a tale. Now, a muddy, short-tempered man, knotted up in himself. If that was him.

This is your last chance, she says to him. Your very last chance. The prodigal brother. The prodigal father. What kind of un-ordinary life have you had? *Chasing it like a distracted dog.* Did you find what you were desperate to find? Was it worth it?

The blue-black cloud is spreading out, creeping farther across the horizon, the band of dreary light growing thinner.

Perhaps it had been worth it to her, though. She realizes this with a flicker of surprise, something that cuts through her wretchedness for a second. If he had stayed, would she have had Gus? Her aunt? Rudy. Even Malcolm.

His absence, then—an accidental legacy. A gap, with one person after another falling into it, becoming hers. Only on loan, these people, as it turns out. But hers for a while.

The wind rustles through the trees, a dull patter of raindrops from the branches. The air smells like the clay earth piled on the tarpaulin, the sodden grass. The bird gives another high cry, then abruptly flits away.

She shivers in her thin shirt—once again the weather has fooled her.

Someone from the bowling team is talking now, a man in a yellow and black windbreaker, looking uncomfortable.

He was a good man. A good bowler. He had a hook shot you could take to the bank.

A gravestone nearby, white marble, grey seams running through it. *Morrison,* it says. Who is this Morrison, this imposter, to be lying here next to Gus?

He will have a raised marker—a pillow stone, they call it. Val proposed it, and they all agreed quickly, so that there would be no more talking about it. A pillow stone, as if it were soft and feathery, instead of a lump of granite. So many details to this business of death, this grim love affair with the unknown.

She swallows a sob in her throat.

The bowler has finished talking now. She knows she should say something, should talk about Gus. But when she opens her mouth, it seems to be full of nothingness, a nothingness so thick that it stifles everything else.

Don't go, she thinks, as they lower the coffin into the ground. Don't go, she thinks, as they shovel in dirt.

The sky splinters into pieces, fragments sliding away.

. . .

She is immensely tired. She is so exhausted she can barely breathe, pushing her lungs in and out. Face down on her bed, staring blankly at a seam unravelling in the coverlet, she wonders if she will ever have the energy again to move an arm, a leg. In her head, a low keening, a dirge. She has lost some crucial instructions for operation, for functioning. Perhaps if she lies there for long enough, she will remember them, perhaps they will come back to her in a rush.

In the meantime, she has a question.

What kind of lawyer are you? she says.

Rabbi Yitzchok turns his head.

My daughter, he says kindly.

What kind of a lawyer are you?

I do what all lawyers do. I argue. I plead, he says calmly. But I am not in charge here.

He holds out his hands, as if to touch her lightly.

Who *is* in charge? This crazy, tragic circus. *Who?*

The knife edge of grief is making her bones ache.

. . .

She pushes herself off the bed, forces herself into motion. Now she feels like a marionette, as if someone is working her limbs for her, making her walk, moving her arms, even her mouth when she talks.

Take some more time off, says Nate.

Take some more time off, says Louis.

Her stricken presence must be unnerving, must be making them uncomfortable. All that raw grief. They treat her gently, warily, but with a vague sense of self-righteousness, as if they are putting up with some breach of etiquette on her part. Look what a mess your sorrow is making, slopping all over the floor like that.

But she would rather be here than at home. Malcolm has been going to the racetrack, where he is spending money he doesn't have in elaborate bets—exactas, trifectas, pick threes. Each time, he comes home in a temper, cursing the horses, the track conditions, the drivers, chain-smoking, littering the kitchen with rye and Scotch bottles—every so often, a moment of desolation in his eyes.

Rudy is worse, though—he sits in a chair, looking out the window, as if he is expecting Gus to arrive at any moment, as if he waits long enough, patiently enough, the world will somersault again, will turn back into something recognizable.

He should be working, he has a new commission, a reference book for eye, ear, nose, and throat specialists. He should be creating illustrations—a fawn-coloured retina, traced with delicate veins, a cutaway of a larynx, a cochlea curled behind a pale blue eardrum. But instead he sits there, looking out the window, the golden retriever lying mournfully at his feet.

At least at work she can think about other things.

We should speak to the witnesses directly, she says to Louis. We should ask them outright. We can do it over a video call.

The witnesses, the investigator are back in Minsk.

No, he says.

We can have Polina interpret, so that the investigator isn't coaching them. Or at least coaching them at that very moment.

No, he says.

But we need to know. We could be suborning perjury.

No, he says.

She is too tired to say anything more.

. . .

Whereas the wicked, pernicious and abominable Crimes of Perjury and Subornation of Perjury have of late Time been so much practised, to the Subversion of common Truth and Justice that it is necessary, for the more effectual preventing of such enormous Offences, to inflect a more exemplary Punishment on such Offenders than by the Laws of this Realm can now be done.

But we don't know, she thinks. We don't know if it's perjury.

You never know, says her aunt.

. . .

Turning lead into gold is quite possible, says Nate. Entirely possible. The problem is that the cost of the ingredients and the process is more than the value of the gold.

. . .

Drozd, awake. Staring up at the dark ceiling. He dislikes this part of the night, his head full of raging thoughts, his body feels as if he has grit under his skin. He knows that there will be no real sleep now for the rest of the night, he will only doze on and off.

These people. These vicious, stupid people. All their weaselly talk. How is it possible they can do this to him? How can such scum have so much power over his life?

But they will not stop. He can see that. And this judge—what does he think? He seems restless when his lawyer is speaking. Although, if the government wins, he will appeal. But if he wins, they will appeal. He is an old man, how much time does he have left? Is this what his old age will be?

By the way, his lawyer said casually. Was it you that phoned in the bomb threat?

No, he said, as convincingly as he could.

He has a glimpse of a bleak future—whatever there might be of it—filled with endless proceedings, the threat of deportation constantly hanging over his head. Watching his money dribble away, watching his life become poorer and more cramped. And the possibility that he may lose in the end, that he will be exiled to some place he barely knows now, some place where he has nothing, is nothing. Severed from everything he has, all the possessions he has built up, these trappings of his life.

This house, for one thing—solid, sturdy. These walls stuffed with insulation, pink glass wool. The floors of polished ash wood, the furnace rumbling away in the basement, a comforting sound. Above him, the black roofing tiles, the rain gutters, cleaned only last week of leaves and mud.

And the house is only the beginning. Inside, the house is filled with things, a collection he had never imagined, could not possibly have imagined. Lamps, cast iron pans, wool blankets, china plates, cushions, pictures on the walls. The oak chest of drawers in the bedroom, the white stove in the kitchen. The cupboards filled with jars and cans, sardines in mustard, currant jelly, oxtail soup. And in the garage, his car—dark green enamel, the leather-like seats. The thought of losing all this makes him feel airless.

He looks over at Sofija, sleeping heavily, her grey hair loose, some strands across the side of her face. She makes small purring noises in her sleep, not quite snoring. If he has to leave, it seems unthinkable that she would stay without him—that she could even exist without him. Without him, she is nothing, a shadow of a person. And he needs her, to cook his pork roasts, to wash and iron his shirts, to sweep and mop. She is a habit, his habit—the way she nods her head to herself, the almond smell of her soap, the way she fingers her thin silver necklace with the crucifix. But he is suspicious, too—he sees the way she looks at him sometimes, her face closed, hiding her thoughts. Does she think about the possibility of another life, away from him? Foolishly devoted to those grandchildren—she spends too much time making nut cookies for them, listening to them read to her, admiring their schoolwork.

Something he hadn't realized, hadn't understood with his own children—that they would grow up, establish other anchors for her. That she would no longer be so isolated, that the walls he had built around her would shrink. Too late, he understands that some shift has occurred, that his hold has been eroded. And he has been lax over the years—letting her join the church groups, the choir. He realizes now there is no end to her possible disloyalties. Would she take this chance to leave him? No, impossible. Impossible. *Look what a good husband you have.*

So dark in this room, even darker than before. Dark as a tunnel, a cavernous tunnel. He is standing in it, dirty water at his feet, a foul smell in the air. The other end is dim but lighter, he can see a figure, shrouded in grey mist, carrying something. A pail of ice water.

Stand up, shouts the man, the sound bouncing down the tunnel.

Who are you? he says.

Stand up, shouts the man again.

I am standing up.

Stand up. Stand up. Stand up.

Then the tunnel is empty, echoing with hollowness, a hollowness that bounces off the walls, that engulfs him, engulfs everything.

He is awake again, in a sweat, heart pounding.

Why has he been singled out for this—this humiliation, this punishment? Why are they pursuing him? There must be other people with worse to their names. This country. This preachy country, its ignorant, windy ideas of justice. Egged on by the Jewish groups.

So much self-pity, says the woman coming towards him, out of the grey mist. The lawyer. Do you have even a grain of compassion for the people you tortured, the people you killed?

He stands up, reaches towards her.

Sliucha. Whore.

. . .

The cellist's bow is fraying, a few hairs swinging from the end as it moves back and forth. They shimmer faintly in the light on the small stage, the stage itself a glowing pocket in the dark evening air. Neither he nor the violinist seem to notice the hairs, although surely this is impossible, at least for the cellist.

The sun is gone, but in the distance, the sky over the lake is still not entirely black, still tinged with dark blue, traces of yellow. The air is warm, almost downy.

A distraction, Nate says.

He has been tender, carefully picking his way through her despair. But he is convinced that she needs to have her head filled with other thoughts, that new things will rouse her, stir her, will wake her from this numbness.

You need taking out of yourself, says her aunt.

Taking out of yourself. Is that possible, can one existence be pulled out of another?

She can see that Nate is becoming impatient with her grief, with its balkiness, its persistence. *Yes, yes, this is sad,* he seems to be saying, in his posture, his gestures, *but dwelling on it is pointless.*

So far they have hiked in a ravine, seen a sculpture exhibit—blue tentacles descending from the ceiling—gone to a greenhouse with a collection of bamboo and papyrus. Now an open air concert.

She goes along with all this because she is too listless to object, and because he may be right. And even if he is wrong, this is what he wants, and what he wants means something more to her now. She is hungry for the feel of his skin against hers, lying against him in a way that brings the surface areas of their bodies into the most contact. Applying him to herself like a balm. Or sometimes her hands stray across his body, lost in a silent dialogue of their own. She inhales his clean breath—is it more powerful, more sustaining than hers? She is now entirely persuaded by his physical being, by how legible he has become.

At the moment, though, she is transfixed by the hairs on the cello bow, by the possibility that the hairs might fray through completely. One last stroke, a snicking sound, and the bittersweet, melancholy notes would come to an end. How likely is this? She doesn't know. But if some of the hairs can break, why not all?

As she sits there listening, though, it is the notes that begin to fall apart, scattering over the grass, rolling towards her. They become distorted, jarring, the flow lost. She wonders if there is something she should be doing. Holding out her hands to catch them. Picking them up. Rolling them back.

She shakes her head hard, and the notes fall back into line.

The program is almost over, this piece Glière's "Berceuse," the haunting sound of the violin over the dusky cello. The music glides and soars and falls, drawing exquisite patterns in the night air. But she is fixed on the bow again, barely noticing the surroundings.

This park, where they are sitting, where the concert is taking place. Built to embody a piece of music itself, a Bach suite given physical shape, winding trails of greenery and boulders. Rolling, waving, the paths are in motion, filled with old rhythms—*prelude, allemande*. Beside the paths are tall grasses spilling over in waterfalls, long drifts of blue sage, the scent of lavender in the dark.

She has an odd, restless feeling in her chest, something that has been growing slowly—very slowly—all evening. What is it? Something elusive, just out of reach.

And then the piece is over. The cellist holds the bow up, suspended in the air for a second or two, the hairs swaying as the sound fades away.

Let's walk, says Nate.

They wander through the park, along the spiralling paths—the dance movements in the suite. *Courante, sarabande.* Tall plumes float in the dark, their stems invisible, white phlox loom up suddenly and then disappear. The air is mild and fragrant now—earthy, coppery.

Nate is talking about a case, holding forth about the witless client, the judge's crustiness.

He sounds like Louis, she thinks. Is this what we're going to become?

She should be saying something, laughing at his descriptions, scoffing along with him, reassuring him. But summoning up thoughts, words is too hard—her brain is flat. He keeps on, though, working hard to carry both sides of the conversation.

A bed of irises, their petal tongues hanging down in the dark, as if they had just finished talking. The dizzying scent of the lilies. The paths curl and uncurl in their formal patterns—*minuet, gigue*. For a moment, she can almost see shadowy dancers in their satin dresses—ivory, pale grey—winding under the trees, pacing out the steps, their transparent bodies turning and bowing.

The feeling in her chest seems to be rising, expanding, hardening. What is it? A decision, she realizes with surprise. A decision she has made without knowing she was even considering it, the various parts of it gathering together silently. A decision so clear that there is no arguing with it.

She turns to Nate.

Have you lost your mind? he says a minute later, interrupting her. You have to let this go.

You have to let this go, says her aunt.

The case is in, finished, he says. Credibility is up to the judge.

I need to know, she says.

Now his voice is rough with irritation, with something else. Louis will be furious.

A man brushes by them on the path.

Louis will know nothing about it unless I get the wrong answers. And if I get the wrong answers, he should know.

How can you possibly think he would agree with that? says Nate, his mouth tense. Look, your perspective is off right now.

You're not seeing things clearly. At least take more time to think about it.

No, she says. I'll lose my nerve.

Please, he says in a lower voice, looking at her strangely. Don't do this. You'll ruin things for both of us.

She turns, a half-question on her face. Isn't that a little excessive?

I don't want this to end, he says.

He looks miserable, crossing his heavy arms tightly in front of his chest.

This? Could he possibly mean their soft, drunken sprawl of a relationship, this thing that envelops her, absorbs her? He would do that? She searches his eyes for something, something that isn't there.

She is speechless, impaled on his words. Then she is angry. And then she is furious, the blood rushing into her head, her head tight.

I think I see things clearly now, she says.

. . .

She is lying on the bed, holding the pillow in her arms. Gus, the smell of his shaving soap, old sweat. The antiseptic for his incision. Cigarette smoke, even though he had stopped smoking for the operation. Shc inhales deeply. Perhaps the smoke had embedded itself in his fingers, his hair, over so many years. Something else he has left behind.

There must be other things—skin flakes, oils, microbes, hairs on towels, sheets, clothes. His DNA, his genetic essence, on his glass on the bedside table, on door handles, light switches. Forensic evidence of his own, of his existence. But slowly this will disappear too, the sheets will be washed, the handles wiped, his imprint gradually erased. Some residue might stay for longer—on the things he touched, the things he handled that are personal, that are only his—reading glasses, belts, shoes.

The things he touched.

A massive sob erupts deep inside her chest, and then a spate of other sobs come bursting out of it, primitive sounds buried inside her body. She clutches the pillow convulsively, unable to bear this torrent of despair, but unable to stop it, her body shaking. She sobs wildly, harshly. On and on it goes, until her lungs are aching, her body exhausted, her throat hoarse.

An eon later. The spasms are weaker, further apart, and her clenched hands begin to loosen. And then a narrow opening, an old understanding, an understanding that begins spreading through her. The very last thing she wants to know, a brutal, queasy truth. That there is no life she can live that will not be pierced with agonizing losses, that these losses are not avoidable, not negotiable. That she will not be able to prevent them by keeping her head down, by asking for too little, by clinging to the rules. By summoning up enough fears in advance to ward them off.

And running through this, another truth: that her only chance is to go out to meet these losses, these casualties. To go out to them unarmed, crooning hopeless songs to them to save herself from despair. Only this will allow her to throw herself into her own life, into the chaos of living, to wrestle with its risks, its scarred beauty. Only this will allow her to summon up the perverse courage necessary for existence, for living with the ruthless edge of happenstance.

She is unable to move for a second or two, unable to think. But then she is overwhelmed by a sense of coherence, a growing symmetry, something that holds the possibility of other ways of being.

In a single sideways moment, she realizes that if she, too, has a damaged, obstinate heart, she might still survive it.

. . .

The future becomes a snake, straightening itself out from a cramped position.

. . .

Come in, come in, she says to them. What a night, so much rain, although at least the thunder has subsided. Let me give you a drink. Go ahead, dry yourselves off by the fire. How are you? Look, the candles are on the mantel. See, the barley porridge, the honey, the eggs are on the table. Sit down, take a break from your shadowy labours. I'm curious about them, I admit, but this is your night. A night to settle down, to be at rest, if only for a while, to sit here in quiet company. Near, but not too near, close enough to feel the touch of hazy fingers, to hear the rustle of limbs, to feel the sighing of sweet dead breath. Close enough that we can even hum a scrap of a song together, a few bars of something low.

But take your time, there is no urgency, no rush. Linger as much as you like, take all the solace as you can find here, let yourself be soothed by this rare truce between the living and the dead. Take all the time you want, all the time you need. Take all the time in the world.

. . .

The music teacher first. There he is, on the screen, his creased face, his mischievous smile, pulling at one of his ears, scratching his neck. Polina is beside him, her dark hair shorter, a sleek, angular cut against her white skin. They seem delighted to be in each other's company again, although they are still soundless at the moment.

Fifteen hundred rubles.

Polina is fiddling with one of the microphones, her bitten fingernails painted dark blue. She is working on the sound problem, going through the settings, checking the signal, the connection. Sorry, she mouths to the screen.

Leah waits as patiently as she can, willing herself to be calm, to ignore her heart beating rapidly, one small thud threatening to overrun the next.

It's not too late, says Nate. You don't have to do this.

He is leaning against the side of the door with deliberate casualness, his hands in his pockets, head freshly shaven.

Yes, I do, she says.

For a moment, his face changes, the casualness slips, she can see the expression underneath—angry, forlorn. Then it is back, fixed firmly in place.

Now they are both watching Polina try one thing and then another, looking puzzled. Still no sound, nothing.

Why are you still here? she says to Nate.

No answer.

Finally, Polina holds up the unplugged end of the microphone cable and laughs, a soundless laugh, and then the music teacher laughs, bobbing his head, still scratching his neck.

And then, surprisingly, a small laugh erupts in her own throat—rusty, a little painful, almost unrecognizable.

We're starting, she says to Nate. Time for you to go.

Not yet, he says. He takes his hands out of his pockets. Not yet.

The sound comes on abruptly. Polina's cool, clear voice fills the office.

Ready? she says.

ACKNOWLEDGEMENTS

In my last book, I described my partner, Peter Dorfman, as extraordinarily smart, kind, daring, and funny. He hasn't changed. In fact, he has only become more so—living with him is an exhilarating experience, and his comments on the manuscript were invaluable. Other people I cherish include Daniel McCormack, Julia Dorfman, Ben Ferdinand, Elijah Ferdinand, Sacha Ferdinand, and Naomi McCormack—people who admittedly had nothing to do with the book directly, but who are so dear that they enrich my life and hence my writing immeasurably. I have also been inspired by the Jewish side of my family, especially my grandfather, Jules Herman, a tailor who came from Belarus.

Of the people who did have something to do with the book directly, I want to thank first the experts who read and provided crucial observations on the manuscript: Professor Lynne Viola, whose book *Stalinist Perpetrators on Trial* was the source of much of my information about the Stalinist purges and the NKVD, including the "physical measures of persuasion"; and Max Wolpert, former counsel to the Crimes Against Humanity and War

Crimes Section of the Department of Justice. Other experts who were extremely helpful were immigration and refugee lawyer Barbara Jackman, criminal lawyer Donald Bayne, and (then) PhD student Aleksandra Pomiecko. It goes almost without saying that any errors and liberties taken are my own.

More specifically, the doctor's evidence is inspired by the testimony of Volha Barouskaya, parts of the bookkeeper's affidavit were informed by Professor Viola's series on the Oxford University Press blog *Academic Insights for the Thinking World* and the quotes in regard to hearsay were taken from a turn-of-the-century article by John Wigmore in the *Harvard Law Review*. One of the quotes about glass is from *Curiosities of Industry*, an 1858 volume by George Dodd, and, of course, the allusion to hope and feathers is from Emily Dickinson.

Kurapaty is a real mass grave where NKVD officers killed between 30,000 and 250,000 people between 1937 and 1941. All the doctrines and statutes are also genuine, as are the quotes from cases, although most have been edited.

And speaking of editing, I am very grateful to Dinah Forbes as well for her superlative literary services, not the least of which was connecting me to my excellent agent, Marilyn Biderman, one of the most heartening people I have ever met. I am also indebted to Dan Wells, my publisher, for his patience, editing, and counsel, as well as Vanessa Stauffer, John Sweet, Ingrid Paulson, Michaela Stephen, and the rest of the Biblioasis crew.

To all my friends: thank you for your encouragement, your support, and your distractions. I am deeply lucky to know you. And thanks to Brent Knazan as well, who let me attach his reading habits to a person wholly unlike him.

Finally, I must thank John Metcalf again and again—for his astute and inspired editing, for his help at pivotal moments, and for other kindnesses.